THE NIGHT MAULER

AN ALICE BERGMAN NOVEL
BOOK TWO

DREZHN

PUBLISHING

THE NIGHT MAULER

Edited by Drezhn Publishing LLC

Published by Drezhn Publishing LLC
PO BOX 67458
Albuquerque, NM 87193-7458

Print Edition - June 2023
Version 1.6

Cover design by Dan Van Oss, CoverMint

HARDBACK (DUST JACKET) ISBN: 978-1-947328-34-1
HARDBACK (CASE LAMINATE) ISBN: 978-1-947328-80-8
PAPERBACK ISBN: 978-1-947328-35-8

BOOKS BY DANIEL KUHNLEY

SUPERNATURAL SERIAL KILLER

Alice Bergman Novels
*Birth Of A Killer (novella)
*The Braille Killer
*The Night Mauler
*The Chrono Slasher

EPIC DRAGON FANTASY

The Dark Heart Chronicles
*† The Dragon's Stone
*Reborn
*Rended Souls
True Heir

Scourge (novella)

CHRISTIAN YA SCI-FI/FANTASY
(As Daniel Luke Kuhnley)

VR Academy
Kiara Kole And The Key Of Truth

* - Also available as an audiobook
† - Previously released as Dark Lament

Visit Daniel's website to find these books and more!
danielkuhnley.com

READ *BIRTH OF A KILLER* FOR FREE

Curious how Alice gained her sight as a teen?
Want to read about the attack that started it all?

danielkuhnley.com/become-a-conqueror

Sign up and read *Birth Of A Killer*, An Alice Bergman Novella. Be the **FIRST** to get sneak peaks at my upcoming novels and the chance to win **FREE** stuff, like signed books.

A paranormal serial killer thriller that'll keep you turning the pages.

Be careful what you dream when murder is on your mind.

My name is Alice, and I'm a sixteen-year-old ghost. No, I'm not actually dead, but I was born blind. The sad thing is the world's more blind to me than I am to it.

That is, until the day he noticed me. A bully. He ruined my life and turned my dreams into nightmares, so what could I do? The same thing any girl my age would do—I wished he'd die.

Then… he turns up dead. Naturally, I freaked out. Am I to blame? Did my nightmare kill him? Would anyone believe me if I confessed?

It's absurd. I know it. Nightmares don't come true… do they?

Birth of a Killer is the suspenseful prequel novella to *The Braille Killer*. If you like unique sleuths, origin stories, and a hint of the supernatural, you'll love Daniel Kuhnley's nail-biting tale.

Buy *Birth of a Killer* today to see how Alice's story began!

THE NIGHT MAULER

DANIEL KUHNLEY

CHAPTER ONE

THE ROAD SIGN FOR Desert Springs Nature Preserve says it's half a mile ahead on the right. Most Mondays, there is little to no traffic in the area, but this Monday is an exception. The place is a zoo, and Seth and I haven't even reached the parking lot entrance yet.

Multiple TV crews line the main road, each broadcasting live on the situation still unfolding in the woods. As with most reporting these days, it's likely five percent news and ninety-five percent speculation and opinion. They'll say and do just about anything to get viewers to tune in, truth be damned.

Vultures.

Officer Mike Brex stands in front of his cruiser, blocking most of the entrance to the dirt-and-gravel parking lot when we pull off the main road. The man's built like a tank, solid muscle from his thick neck down to his massive calves, and he's always ready to engage. Sunlight glints off his freshly shaved head, distorted by plumes of steam rising from his scalp. It's a bitter cold morning, especially for Desert Springs. He dips his head toward us and waves us into the parking lot.

The lot stretches a good quarter mile across the front of the preserve, able to accommodate more than a hundred vehicles during peak seasons and hours. At present, there are a half-dozen police vehicles spread across the lot, including the DSPD CSI van that Charlie drives. Only two other parking spaces are occupied.

Two uniformed officers huddle together with Detective Terry Roland next to one of the patrol cars close to the main trailhead entrances. A young woman sits on the rear bumper of the car. Bloodshot eyes and trembling hands tell her story. She's the one who must've discovered the body and called it in.

Head to toe, the woman's dressed in pink running attire, save an oversized brown jacket draped over her shoulders. Raven locks are pulled tight against her scalp and drawn into a braided ponytail that lies over the front of her right shoulder. A small, pink bow hangs from the end of the braid. High cheekbones and a narrow jawline frame her bronze face. A beautiful woman lurks beneath those swollen eyes and tear-stained cheeks.

The woman is likely around the same age as me. Maybe a year or two older. To be honest, I've yet to master the art of predicting one's age. I blame my sixteen years of blindness, but it might just be one of the many things I'm not good at.

Detective Roland rubs his bare arms nonchalantly, clearly the donor of the jacket the woman huddles beneath. Kindness isn't something Terry lacks, especially when a beautiful young woman is involved. Unless that woman happens to be me. He glances my direction as Seth and I walk past the four of them. His smile fades, and he says nothing to me, but the contempt in his eyes speaks volumes.

Guess I'm still a sore spot.

The light reprimand and short suspension I received after closing the case on the Braille Killer didn't sit well with Terry. He'd expected me to be fired. In a way, I don't blame him. The information I withheld during those several weeks we hunted the Braille Killer was inexcusable, and my actions reprehensible. I've yet to forgive myself for it. If I ever do, it won't be before I locate and bring down the Shadow Priests. I owe Sarah Johnson and Cara Strum that much.

More than that.

Loose gravel and freshly fallen leaves crunch beneath our boots as Seth and I enter the starting point of Trailhead 4A on the 50-square-mile preserve just northeast of town. The sound echoes in my ears. Grates my nerves. Conjures images in my mind of cracking bones; prey caught within the constricting grasp of a boa. The thought is fleeting, but the chill it produces latches to my skin and sticks with me as we head toward our destination.

Toward death.

My feet move at twice the pace of Seth's just to keep up with him. He's nowhere near running, but his pace has urgency. Everyone knows the dead never rise and walk away—except in the zombie apocalypse—, but convincing Seth of such facts proves fruitless time and again. He's as stubborn as they come. A mule at times. Then again, so am I. Perhaps more so than him.

"If I'd known we'd be going for a jog, I would've worn my running shoes." The words half-stutter from my lips, broken between gasps of air.

Seth's gaze stays locked on the trail as his left hand arcs downward toward his thigh, slicing the air between us. "Can we not do this right now?" The sternness in his voice warns me to back off more than his words do. Crime scenes always bring out his angry side. I'm still waiting for his skin to turn green and his seams to burst.

Maybe one day.

The beauty of the fall leaves, a rainbow of reds, oranges, yellows, and some fading greens, takes my mind away from Seth's foul mood and the cool morning air. The tension in my shoulders and neck melts away as I take it all in, but the tranquil sensation is short-lived.

Strung across the path ahead of us is the notorious black-and-yellow crime scene tape. The hairs on my arms stand on end underneath my jacket sleeves as we approach. This is the point where things become real.

Officer Frank Bartoli stands just beyond the tape, a clipboard clutched in his left hand and a pen in his right. He nods curtly. "Mornin'." The pen scratches against paper as he adds our names to the crime scene entry log.

Seth returns Officer Bartoli's nod and skirts underneath the tape, hardly missing a step as he continues marching down the path. I stop short and take a deep breath, steeling my nerves against what lies ahead. Officer Bartoli lifts the tape high enough for me to walk beneath it without the need to stoop. For his effort, he receives a nod and a small smile as I proceed underneath it.

"Good morning, Frank," I say.

The tape thrums low when Officer Bartoli releases it. "Gotta warn ya—" He glances back over his shoulder in the direction Seth went and sighs heavily as he crosses himself. "—it's a bloodbath up ahead."

Dread seeps into my bones as I nibble on a piece of loose skin on my lower lip. "Aren't they always?"

"Guess so, but nothing like this one." Frank scratches the side of his neck with the corner of the clipboard. Three red streaks bloom on his tanned skin. Several white scars mark his temples and cheeks, and several black stitches surrounded by puffy purplish-red skin run parallel beneath his right eye, evidence of his ongoing battle with melanoma. "Just watch your step."

Frank and I go back more than a decade, far more years than what I've shared with Seth. My first memory of Frank rises to the front of my mind and takes me back to 2006. It was a breezy spring Sunday as we stood on the church steps after service. Frank had been attending just a few weeks, always alone, so Mother invited him over for lunch. The offer lit his brown eyes, and he accepted without a moment's thought.

To say the least, he and Mother didn't hit it off romantically—for the record, I never thought they would—, but it sure stirred up a hornet's nest at church. If only I could've witnessed the priceless look of disdain Father Benito Rogallo must've worn when he found out about the lunch date. He tore into Mother that next Sunday, his jealousy over the trivial affair obvious. Somehow, Mother didn't catch on to the fact that Father Rogallo had feelings toward her; I beg the gods daily that she never does.

The past fades as my mind returns to the present and Frank's grim expression. "Watch my step. Noted." The trail stretches north twenty paces before bending eastward. "See ya later," I say and head up the trail.

Rounding a sharp bend in the trail, I spot Seth a dozen paces farther ahead. He's crouched down, his back to me and his head cocked to the side. Seth's body position blocks a good portion of the trail from my view, but the part that isn't blocked captures my attention.

The morning light shimmers on the surfaces of several crimson-brown puddles. The effect mesmerizes and sickens me. Stills my beating heart, if only for a moment as my breath catches in the back of my throat. Then my pulse races.

A nearly severed head lies on the blood-soaked gravel. Brown eyes, wide and glassy, stare in my direction, but they'll never see again in this lifetime. Closely cropped hair and a shaggy, brown beard several inches in length cover much of the victim's face, along with bits of gravel and dried blood. The man's mouth is agape and shifted to one side, perhaps from a broken jaw. From what I can see, a good section of his throat is torn away, exposing bone and ligament and leaving his head twisted unnaturally.

As I draw nearer and kneel next to Seth, the full scene comes into view. Deep lacerations mar the victim's hands, wrists, and forearms, and the front of his black jacket is torn to shreds, along with his blood-soaked shirt. Eight gashes crisscross his chest, from pectorals to external obliques. The skin is ripped like paper around them, and blackish-red blood is congealed within them.

My stomach gurgles, churning the French toast sticks with syrup and the single cup of coffee I downed on the way over. It threatens to push it all back up my esophagus, but I've seen far worse. Nothing compares to child victims, especially when they've been violated. Suddenly, my hands feel tacky, and not from sweat. I don't need to look at them to see their crimson hue, yet my gaze falls to them. It's all in my head. Every last drop. But I'll never forget.

Sarah and Cara.

Each time it happens, I'm thrust into their memories once again. A whirlwind of emotions I cannot seem to control. Hands balled at my sides, fingernails biting into the flesh of my palms, I ride it out. For once, I manage to hold back the tears. It's a small victory, and I hold on to it with all my strength.

Eyes closed, I breathe deep to settle my nerves and calm my beating heart. Given the location and frigid air, the smell isn't entirely unpleasant. Earthy, with a hint of decay, but not from the body. The victim must've showered in Axe Dark Phoenix body spray before coming out here. I know the scent well, thanks to several male students at Desert Springs College. In a few hours, when the heat of the day reaches its peak, the smell will become unbearable.

Other than Seth's shallow breathing and the sound of Charlie Jones, a member of our CSI team, snapping photographs, the forest is quiet. No birds chirp. No leaves rustle. No chipmunks chatter.

Death silences them.

Opening my eyes, I take in the full scene, cataloging every last detail with my nearly photographic memory. Dried blood spatters and smears the foliage and gravel in a good dozen-foot diameter around the body. Several yellow, tented markers sit throughout the scene, bringing attention to details that might otherwise be lost in photographs, sketches, and video: a chunk of flesh submerged in a pool of blood, a broken watch drenched in blood and covered with leaves, and a satchel, still hanging from the victim's right shoulder, ripped open and its contents strewn about. A few pens, a box of Wintergreen Tic Tac mints, a pair of handcuffs, a folded switchblade, and a blank, shredded notepad smeared with blood.

Several feet from the victim's left hand lies a Colt Government pistol, still cocked and locked. From what I can tell, the serial number's been filed off. There's only one reason someone would do that, and it's not because they intend to use the weapon lawfully.

A stepping-stone path constructed from clear, anti-contamination stepping plates circles halfway around the body. Charlie kneels across two of them as he takes several closeup photographs of the body, the blood spatter pattern and radius, and the various items of interest designated by the tented markers. He's thorough, and one of the best at what he does.

My knees pop in protest when I stand. From a higher angle, I see nothing else of interest. Other than a few oddities, the scene screams animal attack. I fail to understand why we're here.

Seth looks up at me. "It's an animal attack."

Thanks, Captain Obvious.

The source of the deadly wounds would be apparent to a child. Heat rises in my cheeks, but as I stare into Seth's grayish-blue eyes, my anger quells, so I nod. "That's what I gathered."

Charlie pulls himself to his feet and lowers his mask below his chin. "And you should both be concerned by it."

Seth slowly rises. Concern distorts his features. Wrinkles his brow. "More so than usual?"

Charlie nods as he looks between Seth and me. "For certain. There are several reasons, but the main ones are the viciousness of the attack and the fact that the animal didn't feast on its kill."

Seth interjects, "Maybe something or someone scared it off before it had a chance."

"Perhaps, but not likely." Charlie rubs his nose with the back of his latex-gloved hand. "An animal that kills for food, especially a human, would likely defend its kill."

Now my brow wrinkles. "What are you saying, Charlie? You think this animal was hunting for sport?" The notion sets my pulse racing.

"Precisely," confirms Charlie.

Seth rubs the back of his neck. "Ugh. If that's the case, we could have a real problem on our hands."

"More kills…" My shoulders jerk as I cringe.

"Exactly." Charlie looks around and nods to himself. "The more information we can gather about this beast, the more likely it will be that the men and women over at Game and Fish can track it down."

A light breeze rustles what remains of the leaves in the trees and tousles my hair, leaving several strands dangling across my face. Seth reaches over and tucks them back behind my ears. The simple gesture wrecks my train of thought and takes me back to a time before everything got derailed between us.

Perhaps we'll find that path again.

The tender moment is lost when Seth resumes the conversation, his tone grim. "No one in Desert Springs will be safe at night until the beast responsible for this is captured or killed."

My mind conjures images of a beast the size of a grizzly bear, but with claws as sharp as razor blades. "The Night Mauler."

Charlie's face scrunches up as he surveys the scene once more. "Well, this was most definitely a mauling."

Seth stares at me for a moment and then shakes his head. He can't quite hide his smile. "Not sure you need to start naming this thing just yet. I don't think a beast with a single kill is worthy of having a name. Besides, the news media will go nuts if they catch wind of this *Night Mauler* of yours." He emphasizes Night Mauler with air quotes.

I shrug, fully aware of the fact that he digs the name. "Fine. I'll keep the name to myself. For now."

"Good." Seth turns to Charlie. "Anything you can tell us about the victim?"

Charlie crouches back down and pulls his mask back up. It muffles his voice a little when he talks. "From what I can tell, the victim was surprised by the attack." He points to the Colt Government pistol. "As you can see, he didn't get a shot off."

"Saw that," I confirm.

"Most likely, he raised his arms to defend his face and throat." He points at the victim's ravaged hands and arms. "That's where he got these wounds. The ones on his chest came next, likely after he was knocked to the ground."

"And his throat?" My hand rises and massages my own.

Deep trenches stretch across Charlie's brow. "That's where things become a bit strange."

Strange? The hairs on my nape stand on end.

Seth crouches again and meets Charlie's gaze. "Strange how?"

"Postmortem strange." Charlie shakes his head. "I've never seen an animal kill its prey and then return later to inflict further damage. At least not one that isn't feeding off the carcass—or cadaver in this instance."

"Then perhaps something *did* scare it off." The three of us turn our heads toward Detective Roland as he approaches.

Eying the victim again, I just can't get the facts to add up. "What could scare off an animal that'd just taken down a six-foot-four, 260-pound man?"

Detective Roland shrugs. "Maybe the victim wasn't alone or was meeting someone here. Could explain the gun."

"Yes, but why would an animal return later and rip out the victim's throat?" questions Charlie. "As I said, the wound happened postmortem."

"Or it just snacked on the victim's throat and decided that it didn't like the taste," mused Seth.

"I'm fairly certain that the animal consumed none of it." Charlie points toward the trees behind him, south of the trail. "There's a pile of discharged tissue just over there."

"Discharged tissue?" The mental image nearly triggers my gag reflex.

"Gross, right?" says Seth, swallowing hard and rubbing his throat.

Detective Roland scowls, his nose wrinkled on one side. "Without a doubt."

Charlie continues, "Once Deborah and I get samples back to the lab, I'll be able to determine if those tissues were spit out or thrown up. Again, my initial thought is that they were simply spit out."

"Why?" asks Detective Roland. His scowl deepens.

Charlie looks up at Detective Roland. "If you're asking why I believe the tissues to be spit out, it's because they didn't look to be chewed. However, if you're asking why an animal would do something like that, then I've got no rational explanation for you. It just doesn't happen in nature."

The more details that Charlie piles up, the more uneasy I become. A picture of this beast forms in my mind once again, but this time it's more human-like than bear-like. The hairs on my nape rise. "What kind of animal could be so cunning and vindictive?"

"What kind, indeed?" asks Charlie, as much to himself as to me. He cocks his head and frowns. "Not a one comes to mind. Unless of course you include humans in that category. We can certainly be animals."

"Don't put too much thought into it," says Detective Roland. "We don't possess the kind of strength required to inflict such damage without a weapon." He looks to Charlie and changes the subject. "Any ID on the victim?"

Charlie reaches across the victim and carefully extracts a wallet from the victim's back pocket. A long, silver chain attaches it to a front belt loop. He retrieves an ID from the wallet and holds it toward the light. "Ernesto Vasquez." Cocking his head, he peers between the ID and the victim's face. "Looks to be the right man."

Seth pulls on a latex glove and takes the ID from Charlie. After a few seconds and several glances, Seth confirms the victim's identification. "It is Ernesto Vasquez. Born May 28th in 1961. Six-foot-five and 256 pounds. Pretty good guess, Bergman." He hands the ID back to Charlie and stares at the victim. "So what the hell were you doing out here in the middle of the night, Mr. Vasquez?"

One touch, and I could have an answer.

"Perhaps answering that question will be easier than you think," says Detective Roland. The three of us look at him and he continues, "There are several webcams located throughout the preserve to monitor animal activity, plus there are cameras stationed at both the entrances and exits of all seventeen trailheads. We've already requested footage from all cameras and webcams be delivered to the station."

"Good." Seth stands. "And what about the woman who discovered the body? Did you get anything out of her?"

"Besides her number," I add with immediate regret. Sometimes I just can't keep my mouth shut. "Sorry."

Detective Roland glares at me as he answers Seth's question. "Samantha George. She's run these trails every morning for several years and never encountered any animals beyond the usual fare: birds, rabbits, chipmunks, squirrels, snakes, lizards, and the occasional deer. Never once could she recall feeling threatened or uneasy here, but this morning she couldn't shake the notion of being watched. *Before* she discovered the body."

"Watched or hunted?" I ask. "There's a difference."

"Watched." Detective Roland looks to each of us in turn and then continues, "She removed her earbuds and stopped several times along the trail so she could listen for any sort of movement, but she never heard anything out of the ordinary. However, she swore she saw the same yellow eyes staring at her through the brush and trees each time she stopped. It totally spooked her.

"A few minutes after her last stop, she came upon the body. Had her senses not been heightened already, she might've stumbled right over it, given the gloom of the morning. As it was, she had to use the light on her cellphone to confirm what she knew to be there.

"She immediately called 911 and headed back the way she'd come, toward the trailhead exit. Officer Bartoli met her there fifteen minutes later and took control of the scene until I arrived ten minutes after that."

My eyes scan the packed gravel and decaying foliage. Clues could easily be missed in such an environment, especially with the way the trees filter the sunlight. Shadows distort everything. One thing I don't recall seeing raises alarm bells in my mind. Charlie stands and cocks his head when I look to him.

"Something's brewing in that head of yours, isn't it?" says Charlie.

"Did you find any footprints or paw prints in the blood surrounding the body?" I ask. "Perhaps under one of the stepping plates?"

Charlie smiles and shakes a finger at me. "You've got a good eye for detail, Detective. I didn't find a one. But there are several places where the blood is smeared." He bends down and points out a few of them.

The taste of maple syrup blooms on my tongue as I nibble the end of one of my fingernails. It's a gross habit, but there are worse things I could be doing. "I'd noticed that. Any guesses as to what caused the smearing?"

"I do, but it's quite silly, given the circumstances of this situation," says Charlie.

"Spit it out," says Seth.

A tinge of red blossoms on Charlie's cheeks as he briefly glances skyward. "Were the attacker human, I'd be inclined to say they were covering their tracks."

Covering their tracks?

My eyes widen as I kneel and stare at the ground with fresh vision. The places Charlie had pointed out certainly looked suspicious, and I can't think of another reason as to why they'd all be smeared. A few during the attack, for certain, but all of them?

Mathematically impossible.

Detective Roland scoffs, "That's not just silly, it's absurd."

Charlie shrugs and nods. "I agree, but that's the only explanation I have for it." He stares at me for several seconds when I rise back up, and then he smiles. "Quite curious, isn't it?"

"Disturbing, more like." I take a deep breath and exhale slowly. "I'll be interested to know what the forensics and cameras reveal."

"Same here," says Seth.

Detective Roland clears his throat. "We already know the answer, and the evidence will support it. The only question in my mind that needs answered is what kind of animal did this. A wolf? Bear? Mountain lion?"

Fingernails bite into my palms once again as heat burns in my neck and cheeks. *How can he just dismiss everything?*

Seth crosses his arms. "Obviously something strong."

I huff. *Seth can't see it either.*

"There's no doubt about that fact," confirms Charlie.

He glances at me again for only a moment, but in that moment, I sense we share the same concern. A concern that springs up from my gut and constricts my chest. I swallow down a growing lump in my throat.

Something isn't right.

Detective Roland looks around and then checks his watch. "I think we're close to wrapping up here." He eyes Seth, avoiding my glare. "I'll keep you informed of the progress."

In all this time, it hadn't occurred to me that Detective Roland would take the lead on this case even though he'd arrived on scene first. There's no denying that Terry's good at his job, perhaps almost as good as Seth and me, but his apparent failure to see that something's amiss concerns me. It's obvious that he's already written the case off as an animal attack, and it ticks me off. There are several details that potentially contradict the animal attack narrative he thinks to be true, but he's not going to give them a second thought.

The side of my nose twitches and lifts the corner of my mouth. I'm about to say something to Terry, but Seth glances over at me and interrupts.

"Please do, Terry." Seth's eyes tell me exactly what he's thinking, and I don't like it one bit. "Let's go, Bergman."

In my mind, I know stepping back is the right thing to do, but my heart aches for me to push Terry on this. Perhaps I can persuade him to hand the case over to us.

Or force him to.

Seth gently takes my arm and pulls me around, obviously sensing that I'm about to say something I'll likely regret. He has some sort of sixth sense when it comes to me. It's both endearing and annoying. He whispers, "We can talk about this in the car."

"Fine," I say through gritted teeth as I push Seth's hand away and slowly inch my way back toward Officer Bartoli and the crime scene tape stretched across the trail.

I glance back just before rounding the bend in the trail. Detective Roland stares at me, his arms crossed over his chest and a smug grin on his face. It takes everything I've got to keep from flipping him the bird. Jaw tense and teeth gritted, I turn back and march on down the trail, Seth in tow.

This isn't over, Terry Roland. Not by a long shot.

CHAPTER TWO

SETH STARES AT THE road ahead as we head back toward the police station. "Look, Alice, I'm not saying you're wrong about this case, but taking it up with Lieut. Frost might not be the wisest decision for you. You're on a short leash as it is."

Seth's right, but my mind was made up to petition Lieut. Frost for the case the moment Detective Roland postulated that the facts led to a foregone conclusion of a textbook mauling case. In truth, I have zero evidence to say otherwise, but I've learned to trust my instincts over the years, and something just doesn't add up.

But what is it?

The rubber floor mat thwacks underneath my foot when I stomp it. "I can't let this go," I growl, sounding stubborn even to myself.

"Fine, but don't say I didn't warn you when your conversation with Lieut. Frost doesn't go according to plan." His hand grips the steering wheel tighter, his knuckles turning white as the blood drains away. The car lurches forward ever faster.

The lead-foot master.

We spend the last ten minutes of the drive in silence. Probably not the best option given my current state of mind, but there's nothing Seth could've added to the conversation to ease the tension or change my mind. In fact, another word would've set me off. He must've sensed it.

The car hasn't even rolled to a stop in the parking space before I fling my seatbelt off and throw the car door open. My mind locked on the office upstairs, I nearly rip my arm off as I eject myself from the car, failing to notice it's still hooked through the seatbelt. The stupid thing jerks me sideways and throws me off balance.

My right ear erupts with pulsing pain before I realize I've smacked my head against the doorframe. A string of four-letter words spews from my lips, a faucet of filth that would take the breath from Mother's lungs and make a seasoned sailor blush, and I'm just getting started.

I turn my heat ray vision toward Seth when he exits the car, ready to blast a hole through his thick skull, but he doesn't even glance my direction as he walks away. His quick thinking has granted him a second lease on life.

Well played, Seth. Well played.

My arm untangled and my ear sufficiently rubbed, I slam the door shut and follow Seth inside. Seconds later, I'm standing outside the door to Lieut. Frost's office on the second floor. My chest heaves and my pulse thunders in my ears, but I don't recall the moments prior. Given my current state, I must've run up the stairs. I close my eyes for a moment and draw a deep breath. I'll need my wits about me to have any chance of convincing Lieut. Frost to give me the case.

Lieut. Frost's door is closed. It never is unless someone's in there with him, so I must wait. As I do, I start forming pieces of conversation in my head. No matter where I start, it sounds all wrong. How will I convince him to see things my way when I can't even explain it to myself where it makes sense?

I sigh. *Maybe Seth's right and I should just drop it.*

The office door opens and Officer Amy Janis steps into the corridor. A cloud of familiar stank trails her. Lieut. Frost's skunk-butt cologne. My gag reflex triggers as tears form in my stinging eyes. Makes me think of what new recruits might be subjected to during basic training camp in the US Army. Somehow, Amy seems oblivious to it. Perhaps she's lost her sense of smell or never had one to start with. Either way, I envy her.

"Alice!" Her eyes light up and her cheeks glow, exuding genuine joy. It's doubtful she has a mean bone in her. The only time I've ever seen her out of sorts was the day Tommy Todd died, but that can't be counted against her. His death took the joy from the entire department.

Amy latches onto my hand and gives it a tight squeeze. "It's good to see you back. We've all missed you around here."

She's referring to my two-and-a-half-month suspension. Squeezing her hand back and then pulling away, I say, "It's good to be back."

Amy gestures backward with her thumb out and whispers, "Got a bit of a lion in there today. Might wanna watch your step." She winks and then heads down the corridor, quickly disappearing as she descends the stairs.

As I continue to second guess myself, the all-too-familiar gruff of Lieut. Frost shakes my eardrums. "Bergman. Either you get your happy ass in here and state your business or you move on. My doorway isn't a break room."

What am I getting myself into?

"Yes, sir." My skin crawls on my bones as I step through the doorway and into the lion's den.

Every muscle in my body tenses as my heart screams at me to run away. But my mind is a steel fortress. Impenetrable. Unchangeable. It cannot be reasoned with and will not back down, no matter how desperately my heart pleads with it.

"Well don't just stand there," the lion growls. "Shut the damned door and take a seat."

The thought of being trapped in an airtight room with the man and his cologne just about sends me over the edge, but my traitorous hand complies with his request, and my turncoat legs carry me the three steps over to the wooden chair facing the front of his overbearing desk. My butt parked firmly on the chair, I stare into his cold, calculating brown eyes.

Lieut. Frost leans over his desk on forearms the size of my thighs, his white, long-sleeved shirt rolled above his elbows. A purple tie with gold stripes hangs from his thick neck, the tie too thin for his massive frame. His heated glare nearly melts through the thick plastic of his wire-framed glasses as he adjusts them on his nose with a single finger. It's no coincidence he uses his middle one.

Air bubbles gurgle in the back of my throat as I search for the right words to break the silence between us. Right now, I'm hating Seth. Had he kept his mouth shut, I wouldn't be second-guessing myself and hesitating to broach the subject.

"You've got two choices, Bergman." He raises two meaty fingers. "Either you can spill whatever you came here to say, or you can drop your gun and badge on the desk and never look back. Your choice. I'm good either way."

Fire stirs in my belly. "I'm not here to turn in my badge, sir."

"Well that's a pity." His hand slaps the top of the desk with a thunderous clap, sending the spoon sticking out of an empty mug rattling around. My legs tense and my eyes widen, but I remain still in the chair.

He shakes his head. "I harbored high hopes that you were leaning toward the second option."

"Well I'm sorry to disappoint you, sir." I lean forward in the chair and raise my head to match his glare. "I'm here because I want the case from earlier this morning."

His brow wrinkles, and his gaze hardens further. "The animal attack at the preserve?"

I nod. "That's the one."

He blows air through his nostrils and leans back in his chair. "Spoke with Detective Roland not fifteen minutes ago. Said the case was a textbook mauling."

"Figures—"

"Also said you'd likely be in here chewing on my ear about it."

"Sir, I respect Terry."

Lieut. Frost laughs aloud. "No sense in lying out the side of your mouth, Bergman. Respect is the last thing either of you have for one another."

"Look, we might not get along, but I'll be one of the first to admit that he's a brilliant detective. Normally, I'd trust his assessment of a case, but he's wrong about this one. There's far more to it than what's on the surface."

A lopsided frown twists his lips. "And what makes you think that?"

At this point, I'm all in. Do or die. "There are too many anomalies to ignore."

He crosses his arms over his chest, veins bulging along his forearms like he just worked them out. "Enlighten me."

"For instance, there were no footprints or paw prints found at the scene. Given the excessive amount of blood at the scene, it's mathematically impossible for an animal to have avoided stepping all through it. Not just that, but some of the blood was smeared as though the attacker attempted to cover up evidence. What kind of animal does that?" Somehow, I've managed to leave my seat. Now, I'm halfway across the desk shaking a finger in Lieut. Frost's face. Heat burns in my cheeks as I return my butt to the chair. "Sorry, sir."

Lieut. Frost strokes his bulldog chin. "I'll admit that there are some anomalies, as you say."

"Thank you." After a few moments, I drive the final nail into Detective Roland's coffin. "But there's more. What kind of animal leaves its kill and returns later to rip the throat out?"

He shrugs. "A hungry one, I'd guess."

"Yes, if the animal actually ate it. But that's not the case here." My butt rises off the chair once again, and my voice follows suit, jumping several octaves. "It was thrown up or spit out a dozen paces from the body."

Lieut. Frost removes his glasses and sticks one of the earpieces between his teeth. He does it often when he's thinking. I'm not sure he's even aware of the habit.

Returning to my chair once again, I lean back and await his response, satisfied I've made my case. In my mind, I retrace every last detail of the crime scene. I'm not sure what I'm hoping to discover or where this case will lead, but excitement tightens my chest. My left foot *tap-tap-taps* the floor.

When he lays his glasses on the desk, I know he's come to a decision. All decisions are final. I sit up straight and prepare myself for his response as I search his face for a clue as to what he's about to say. But there are no secrets to be had. His poker face is among the best I've seen.

"I'll admit, Bergman, just when I think you've got less of a chance of survival in this business than a snowball has in hell, you surprise me. You might just make a name for yourself yet, and maybe even in a positive way."

My stomach gurgles with excitement.

The case is mine.

He continues, "I'll assign you to the case."

"Thank you, sir." Excitement pulls me to my feet. "I won't let—"

"I'm not finished, and you don't seem to be listening."

"Sir?" His words play back in my mind, and it hits me. He used the word "to." I slump back down on the chair, deflated.

"Good. You understand. Detective Roland will continue to lead the investigation, and you will *assist* him. It'll do both of you some good to work together. Who knows, you might even grow to tolerate each other."

Working *with* Detective Roland would've been torture enough, but working *for* him? I suddenly find myself on the verge of vomiting. Never have I been so stunned. Yet, in a way, Lieut. Frost gave me exactly what I asked for.

The next thing I know, I'm walking into the office I share with Seth. He's at his desk, hammering away on his keyboard. Not really hammering it as much as two-finger pecking it. The concerned look on his face when he sees me tells me everything I need to know about the expression I must be wearing.

The pecking ceases. "What happened?" he asks.

Having turned over a new leaf where Seth is concerned, I sit down and tell him everything. And, if I'm being honest, it feels good.

Seth leans back and rests his head against his weaved fingers. He stares up at the drop-tile ceiling for so long that I begin to wonder if he's fallen asleep with his eyes open or if he's counting all the holes in the acoustic tiles. Either way, his silence irks me and sends me teetering back and forth between meltdown and breakdown. More often than not, I choose meltdown and can feel it coming on.

I'm about to go off when Seth finally speaks. "Look, Terry's a good guy. As you know, I worked with him quite a bit during your two suspensions. He has a good head on his shoulders and works like a dog to see a case to its end, no matter the outcome. Just tread lightly around him, give him a reason to trust you, and for God's sake, don't do anything crazy."

Fingernails dig into the meaty flesh of my palms. Pulse rises. Eyes narrow. One more misstep on his part, and there will be another homicide to investigate. "What the hell's that supposed to mean?" I growl.

Seth nearly falls out of his chair trying to sit up and get his arms raised in submission. "Whoa! Step back, Homicide Mary. All I'm saying is you might not want to go around touching bodies and sharing your experiences with him. It won't win you any favors and could get you kicked off the force. Anything you present to him must be hard facts. Nothing more. Understood?"

In a flash, every last ounce of anger dissipates. Laughter rumbles in my chest and manifests in a concussive bout of snorts and coughs. When I regain my composure, I ask him the obvious question. "Where did you come up with 'Homicide Mary?'"

He rises from his chair and rubs the top of his head, a smirk on his lips. "A case I worked a few years before your time. This nun named Mary snaps and goes on a rampage one evening during confession, killing several people with a crucifix she'd sharpened to a deadly point. Turns out she didn't like everyone saying hail Mary. Partially deaf, she thought they were wishing her a pleasant trip to hell and finally got fed up with it."

I cross my arms and frown. "Seriously?"

Seth waves me off. "Look it up if you don't believe me. Happened over at Our Lady of the Good Shepherd on 22nd St. When we brought her in, she just kept repeating 'Homicide Mary' between sobs." He shrugs. "The name stuck."

"You know, now that I think about it, I might be in the market for a good crucifix." I poke Seth in the stomach with a finger but hit solid abs. My finger crumples. "Ouch!"

He drums his stomach. "Like a rock, babe."

"Sorry Seth, but Dwayne Johnson's my only Rock."

"Ugh." He grabs his gut and exhales loudly. "Punching hard today."

"Just getting—"

"Bergman, let's go." Detective Roland stands at the door, a sour expression on his face.

"Where we headed?" I ask.

"You, not we." He points at the floor. "Media room in the basement. You've got dozens of hours of webcam and security camera footage to scour through."

Seth chuckles. "Nice." I throw him a death glare, but it doesn't wipe the smile from his face. Instead, he mouths, "You asked for it," and then winks.

Detective Roland continues, "Glad you volunteered for the job, Bergman. Saves me the trouble of doing it myself."

"Happy to be of assistance, Terry." I shoot Seth a dirty look and then squeeze past Detective Roland and into the corridor. Halfway to the stairs, Terry calls for me. "Yes?"

"Do me a favor and never call me by my first name again. It's Detective Roland."

"Got it, *boss*." He definitely deserves a middle-finger salute, but I consider myself above such behavior, so I give him a thumbs-up instead. He shakes his head and then walks the other way. Somehow, the bird escapes. I quickly cage it, but not before Seth sticks his head outside our office door and catches me.

"Behave," he mouths.

The bird rears its ugly head once again, this time accompanied with a devious smile. Seth rolls his eyes and retreats back inside the office. Satisfied with myself, I turn and head down to the media room.

Upon arrival, I find myself alone in the room, so I sit down at one of the closest terminals to the door. After logging into the system, I open the folder named 13-7505, the case number given to the Night Mauler. The sheer number of files it contains overwhelms me. "Two hundred and four," I mutter. "Two hundred and four stupid files."

According to my cellphone, it's 15:40. There's no chance I'll be able to meet up with Veronica later, so I shoot her a quick text and a sad face emoji. When I look up, there's a fresh-faced kid staring down at me. He's got a goofy smile plastered on his mug, his lips spread wide on the left side of his mouth and nearly closed on the right.

I sit back in the chair. "Can I help you?"

"Kenny Parker." He proffers a hand. Long, skinny fingers with fingernails too long and unkempt. Skin dark as night, scabbed and rough around the knuckles. Many thoughts skitter through my mind as our hands meet. Cold as ice, I find myself shaking the bony hand of Death himself.

"Detective Bergman." Hand retracted, the warmth begins to return to my fingers.

"Yeah." His goofy smile widens. Much wider, and his mouth might consume his entire face. "Heard you were back."

I never forget a face or a voice, and neither is familiar. "Yeah. Just so. Is there something I can do for you?"

Kenny looks around twice and then leans close. "Bribed Detective Roland to assign me to you." He winks with such exaggeration that he couldn't possibly be serious, yet I know he is.

"And why would you do that?"

He pulls up a chair next to mine and sits down. His legs are so long that his knees don't fit underneath the table. "You're the reason I took this job, Alice."

The way my name hangs on his lips and rolls off his tongue catches me off guard, but the implication can't be mistaken. My heart and mind wage war with one another as a team of horses gallop within my chest. Thunderous hooves. The sound rages in my ears. Fills my head. My gut twists with certainty as to whom this young man is, but why is he here when I still have my vision?

They've sent another Shadow Priest after me!

CHAPTER THREE

DRAWING A GUN IS an art form. Everything I learned about guns came first from watching old westerns after gaining my sight. As stupid as it sounds, it taught me to be steady and quick when drawing. Trust me when I say that I'm far quicker than anyone I know. Kenny has no time to react before my gun is aimed at the center of his forehead. This first part of my plan works flawlessly.

With a scream akin to a six-year-old girl's, Kenny falls from his chair and lands on his back with a thud. Hands over his face, he whimpers and begs me to back off. I didn't anticipate such a move. Throws me off. If I continue with the second part of my plan, I'm certain he'll ripen the room with the scent of urine. I'm not willing to take that chance.

"Don't you dare move," I hiss.

Kenny nods vigorously. Backing away from him, I holster my gun and stick my head outside the media room door. No one is around. Few people ever venture into the basement anymore. Satisfied we're alone and that no one is on their way to investigate the girlish screams, I push the door shut behind my back, cutting off any chance of Kenny escaping without him going through me.

"Get up and sit back down on the chair," I growl.

Kenny obeys without hesitation. His eyes are wide with fear and glassy with tears. There's no doubt in my mind that he's no killer.

So who the hell is this kid?

Perplexed, I grab a chair and take a seat several feet from him. "Explain yourself, Kenny. How do you know who I am, and why did you request to work with me?"

His gaze falls to his lap. Stares at trembling hands. His voice stutters for the first time. "I ad-m-m-m-mire you."

Admire me? Guilt thrashes in my stomach. *What in God's name have I done to this poor kid?*

Situations in my life always escalate quickly, and I can't seem to keep it from happening. In my mind, a monster lurks behind the eyes of everyone I meet, waiting for the right moment to attack. Suspicion rules my world and keeps me at arm's length from almost everyone in my life. Russell and Denise made me this way, but I no longer blame them. I control my actions and reactions, not some monsters buried six feet under. Responsibility rests on my shoulders alone.

Risking an adverse reaction, I move my chair closer to Kenny. On the table to my left is a box of tissues. I grab one and hand it to him. "I'm sorry I frightened you. I thought you were someone or something I now know you never could've been." I place my hand on his bony knee. "Take a deep breath and start again."

Kenny blows his nose into the tissue and then takes a deep breath. With each subsequent breath, his breathing evens out and his hands stop shaking. When he rubs them together, I expect the sound of bone scraping bone to fill my ears, but it never does. A foolish thought.

I stare into his eyes. Pools of milk chocolate. Seeing him for who he is and not the monster I expected, I realize the depths of my madness run deeper than I ever imagined. I'm far more broken than I ever thought possible.

I am *the monster at the end of the book.*

Fighting back tears of my own, I ask him the only question that matters. "Why do you admire me?"

How could anyone?

There's no hesitation in his response. "You fought back."

His answer, so simple and to the point, pulls the breath from my lungs. *You. Fought. Back.* Those three words echo in my mind, an anthem that sums up my twenty-six years, yet I'd somehow forgotten the words.

You. Fought. Back.

I'm a fighter. I've always known that, but to hear those words from the lips of someone who knows so little about me overflows my heart with elation. For a few moments, my dark world brightens as joy tugs at the corners of my mouth.

You. Fought. Back.

How can I follow up a statement like that? No words come to mind, so we sit in silence for what feels like several minutes.

When Kenny speaks again, his eyes fill with tears and cling to his lashes, pearls of light against the drabness of the basement we sit in. "For years I lived with an abusive mother, too afraid to lift a finger to defend myself or my little sister, Kellie."

Several tears streak down his face, so I hand him another tissue.

"Thank you." He wipes his face and draws another deep breath. "Kellie isn't quite what some people would call whole. She's severely autistic, and my mother can't stand it. Every outburst or reaction from Kellie is met with a severe beating. When I try and step in, she beats us both. To make matters worse, I think Kellie's lost the ability to smile, and it breaks my heart."

His hand moves to his ribs, and I'm certain he still has lingering bruises. My heart aches with sorrow for what I just put him through. "What can I do to help?"

"Listen." He smiles through tears. "I heard your story on the news. Heard how you gained your sight after being blind for sixteen years and then became the youngest detective in DSPD's history. As extraordinary as that is, it's not what gave me the courage to change my life."

I lean closer. Take one of his precious hands I'd thought so vile not ten minutes before. "Then what was it? What gave you the courage?"

Kenny eyes our joined hands and smiles. I'm a pale vampire contrasted to his beautiful, dark skin. "After you took down the Braille Killer and rescued that little girl, I dug into your past."

"Why?" I ask.

He looks around cautiously even though we're the only ones in the small room and the door is closed. "I needed to know everything about you."

My stomach is in knots. Cramps the way it does when it's that time of the month, but it isn't. "And what did you find?"

Kenny leans forward. His lips are so close to my ear that I can feel the warmth of his breath. Smell the maple syrup lingering on his tongue. Reminds me of my breakfast and the fact I skipped lunch. My stomach rumbles.

"I know what that man and that girl did to you. How they tortured you. The look in her eyes disgusted me." Anger burns in his tone.

If the tension in my chest increased any further, it'd crush my heart. I pull my hand away from his and lean back in the chair, stunned. Breathless.

How did this kid discover my darkest secret?

He grabs both my hands. Shakes them. "But you fought back!"

Those three words again. Powerful words. They bring me back to life as I gasp for air.

Kenny smiles big again. "After getting to the truth, I knew I couldn't sit back and allow my mother to abuse Kellie and me anymore. That very day I took steps to change our situation. Today, my mother serves time for child neglect and abuse, and Kellie and I live with my aunt. Once I've put myself through college and get a good job, I'll be able to take care of her. Seeing Kellie smile again is the only thing I want. That's why I'm interning here. That's why I know who you are and why I want to work with you. As I said, I admire you."

Standing up, I pull Kenny to his feet and wrap my arms around his bony frame. I'm unworthy of his admiration and praise. A wretched soul with a black heart. Crimson stained hands. He clings to me for several moments before finally letting go.

His eyes search mine. "Your secret is safe with me. I promise." Mind reading must be one of his superpowers.

"I believe you—" Really, I do. "—but how did you find out? That information is only in my personnel file. Restricted access."

Kenny shrugs, that goofy grin back on his face. "Let's just say I'm good with computers."

Now I'm the one looking about and hoping no one's eavesdropping on our conversation. "You hacked into the police department?" I whisper-yell. "That's at least a class B misdemeanor."

"If I were to get caught." He picks at a scab on one of his knuckles and smiles wryly.

"Don't be foolish. Everyone gets caught eventually. Trust me, I know." I pull my hair back and tuck it behind my ears. "Think about Kellie the next time you want to hack into some computer system."

His smile fades. "You're right, but I had no hope of escaping my mother before I did it. I promise I won't do that again... without good cause."

"Good." Turning to the computer monitor, I log back into the system and stare at the list of 204 video files. Based on the file names, there are fifty-one cameras in total. Each camera has four videos that span a twenty-four-hour period, each video six hours in length. Using the file timestamps, I surmise that the earliest video footage begins roughly seventeen hours before the mauling and the last ones end about seven hours after the mauling.

Twelve hundred and twenty-four hours of video. Numbers fly through my head. Even at 10x speed and dividing the work with Kenny, we'll need a good six days to get through it all.

A deep, long, exaggerated sigh rumbles from my lips. "How about I watch the videos of the first thirty-four cameras, and you take the last seventeen?"

Kenny pulls a thumb drive out of his pants pocket and wags it between his thumb and finger. "I've got a better idea. Move over."

I push his hand and the thumb drive away. "You can't just stick that into the computer. It must be department owned, virus scanned, and encrypted.

Not only that, but only authorized software can be installed on the system."

"Trust me, Alice." He glances over at the door. "This will save us a lot of time, and no one will ever know."

"*I'll* know," I say, poking my own chest. It's strange being the voice of reason. "Again, you must do everything with Kellie in mind."

He shoves the drive back in his pocket and sighs. "Fine. We'll do it the hard way. Just thought you'd want to save *days* of your time. And mine."

He's caught my attention. "Days?" My voice drips with skepticism. "What the hell do you have on that drive?"

Kenny shrugs. "Like I said, I'm good with computers. One of my science fair projects in middle school involved writing software that could parse out commercials from recorded television shows to cut down on disk drive storage. It won me an honorable mention. Over the last few years, I've improved it quite a bit. It's something that could get me a full-ride scholarship to MIT now."

"We're not looking to cut commercials, Kenny. We're looking for clues as to what happened last night at Desert Springs Nature Preserve."

"Exactly." He retrieves the flash drive again and shoves it into the USB port. I didn't even try to stop him this time. "My program will scour the video footage and save off any anomalies in the footage so that we can watch it back without having to search through the video for it."

A small command window comes up with a prompt on the computer screen. The window title catches my attention. "Project Artemis?"

"Homage to one of the greatest guide dogs to have ever lived." Kenny grins. "Like I said, I've read everything I could find about you."

Grabbing the keyboard, his fingers set to work. I've never witnessed anyone type so fast. Several windows pop up and disappear every few seconds for a solid minute before one final window fills the screen. An empty progress bar stretches across the screen. Underneath it is an estimated finish time of five hours and six minutes.

Pointing at the screen, I ask, "Is that an estimate per video or per camera?"

Kenny leans back and chuckles. "That's for everything. All twelve hundred and twenty-four hours of video."

My mind explodes, unable to process what he's just told me. "How?"

"Simple. Project Artemis can scan an hour of video every thirty seconds. That means it will scan through all the videos in 306 minutes. I.e. five hours and six minutes. Bam!" He claps his hands together, his eyes beaming with pride.

"But aren't we going to get back a lot of false positive video? Wind rustling through the trees and whatnot?"

Kenny shakes his head and pushes air through his nostrils. "You'd think so, but that's the beauty of Project Artemis. I've built AI into it that allows a variance threshold in the video footage for those very reasons."

The more this kid talks, the more I like him. "Smart, but what about birds and other small animals? Won't they skew the results too?"

"Not a chance." He pops his thumbs. "I've set the threshold so that the variance must be at least the size of a medium-sized dog before it copies the video footage."

"Then we just sit back and wait for it to finish running?"

"I'll sit here and wait. You can go grab us an escargot and mushroom pizza. And a six-pack of pop. Your choice on the pop."

"Ew! I don't care how brilliant you are. There's no way in hell I'm ordering snails on a pizza." My gut wrenches at the thought of squishy, blubbery, gritty snail guts bursting between my teeth and sliding down the back of my tongue and into my throat. "Sorry, but it's pepperoni and pineapple or nothing. With a side of cinnamon breadsticks and Mountain Dew."

He proffers his hand and chuckles. "Deal."

Five hours and three slices of pizza later, Project Artemis finishes its run. A new folder named "results" sits inside the file folder with the case number. The folder contains fifty-three video files: three from the parking lot and fifty from various webcams throughout the preserve. A total of forty-nine minutes and seventeen seconds.

Almost forty minutes of the copied footage is from the parking lot, most of it the ensuing police activity captured after the body was discovered by Samantha George. However, there are two notable segments.

At 01:37, Ernesto Vasquez, the victim, arrives in a red Mercedes-Benz SLK 350. He looks nervous as he steps out of his car, scanning the parking lot. Twice, he verifies his gun is loaded before leaving the side of his car. Cocked and locked, he holds it inside his jacket pocket. He scans the parking lot one last time just before entering the northern end of Trailhead 4A and moving out of range of the camera.

Samantha George arrives at 05:49 in a blue Toyota FJ Cruiser. She parks at the far end of the parking lot, close to the southern end of Trailhead 4A. She's out of her car and out of camera range in less than thirty seconds. It's obvious she comes to the preserve every morning.

"Well, we've got our victim and our body discoverer. Let's see if those webcams picked up anything useful."

As the footage rolls by from the webcams, we're privy to a plethora of deer and other small woodland creatures foraging, plus a sighting of a full-grown bobcat. It's got a rabbit clutched in its jaws. Then, at 06:28, Samantha George comes jogging into the far side of the webcam frame. She nearly passes out of the frame before halting. She backtracks a few steps and removes her earbuds, just as she'd told Detective Roland she'd done.

A lump rises in my throat as Kenny and I lean closer to the monitor. Looking to her right—away from the webcam—, Samantha freezes for seven full seconds and then moves on. It's the second to last of the footage captured. Seven minutes later, at 06:36, she'd discover the body. At 06:41, she runs back through the webcam frame, her cellphone pressed against the side of her head.

Kenny sighs. "Wish those webcams had audio as well."

"Agreed, but Samantha George told Detective Roland that she didn't hear anything."

I chew on my fingernail, lodging the tomato sauce deeper underneath it. *So why did you stop for so long?*

"Roll it again, Kenny. But this time frame-by-frame at the point where she stops. Something drew her attention."

The frames progress like watching through one of those old View-Master toys. Samantha's head begins turning away. Click-click-click. Anticipation pulls me closer to the monitor. A few more inches and my nose will leave a smudge mark on it.

"Stop!"

Kenny freezes the video, but whatever I thought I saw is gone. "Back it up two frames." When he does, my breath catches.

I look at him and he nods slowly, his gaze transfixed on the monitor. We see the same thing. Two yellow dots glow in the darkness. They seem as though they're peering around the trunk of a tree.

Kenny resumes the video and the eyes disappear a frame later. The entire time Samantha stares at that tree—a good 200 frames of video—those yellow dots never reappear.

Until she turns away.

Kenny grabs my arm and squeezes it. "They're back!"

My heart hammers against my ribcage as those yellow dots seem to follow Samantha out of the frame before disappearing again. "Pull up the original video. Maybe we'll get lucky and find something more definitive."

"On it." Kenny brings up the original webcam video.

We scour the footage for a solid hour but find nothing else. The only thing we have is about four seconds—ninety-nine frames in total—of two yellow dots, and the video quality is poor at best. To complicate matters further, the shadows beneath the canopy of trees where the dots appear are inkwells. Voids.

Leaning back in my chair, I stare at the ceiling. "There isn't enough evidence here to convince Detective Roland of anything. Hell, I'm not even convinced we have something notable."

But I can sense it. We're so close to breaking this case open, yet I feel it slipping from my grasp. "Got any tools on that drive to enhance the image?"

"Yeah, I can manipulate the image a bit."

Kenny pulls up a program called GIMP and sets to work adjusting levels, saturations, highlights, and shadows on a single frame of video. Due to the video's low quality, only so much manipulation can be done to it before the effort starts having the opposite effect and becomes a distorted mess.

Thank God Kenny's doing this and not me.

With each pass of the renderer, the shadows slowly fade and the background separates from those eyes.

My finger presses into the LED display just above and to the left of the left yellow dot. "Right here. This looks like a pointed ear to me."

Kenny's head tilts as he leans forward. "Whoa… something *was* watching her."

"Yeah, but this still isn't enough evidence. We've spotted an animal in the preserve that is alerted by human presence. What kind of animal wouldn't be? That's what Detective Roland would ask."

"Maybe not enough yet, but you've convinced me that there's something strange going on. For instance, look at the placement of those eyes…" Kenny bites the end of his tongue and frowns at the screen. "Give me a sec."

A command window opens, and Kenny starts typing away. My eyes can't keep up with what he's doing, but the end result is obvious when it comes up on the screen: he's calculated the distance from the ground to the eyes. Seventy inches.

It's six feet tall…

Kenny and I lock eyes. His wide eyes echo my wonder. "My God… what have we found?"

CHAPTER FOUR

THE NEXT MORNING, I arrive at the police station earlier than usual, knowing that Detective Roland is an early riser. He sits at the desk in his office, his back facing the open door. I knock on the door as I enter, my single shred of evidence in the Night Mauler case clutched firmly in my left hand.

"Got something for you, Detective Roland."

He turns and faces me. "Already?"

I hand him a printout of the frame Kenny enhanced from the Desert Springs Nature Preserve video footage. "Tell me that's not intriguing."

His eyebrows furrow as he stares at it. "Not sure I can tell you anything." He looks up at me. "What am I supposed to be looking at?"

Rounding the desk, I stoop down and begin pointing out the handful of significant features in the image. The eyes, the outline of an ear, and the distance of the eyes from the ground. "I believe this thing is what Samantha George felt watching her. Those eyes closed when she looked in its direction and followed her as she walked away."

"I'll admit that there's some sort of animal in the trees, and perhaps it is watching Ms. George, but we already know the victim was mauled to death by an animal." He tosses the printout onto his desk. "That image won't do anything to help Game and Fish identify the animal, so what exactly is this supposed to do for the case?"

Groaning, I point at the image. "Look at it again. Those eyes are almost six feet off the ground. What kind of animal stands up on its hind legs other than a bear?"

"I don't have an answer for you on that, but, as usual, you're not asking the right questions. This is always the problem you have, Bergman. You set your mind on some sort of crazy conspiracy idea and let it run rampant. Get a grip on yourself and see the facts for what they are. This case is a mauling and nothing more. End of story."

Three steps from his desk, I turn around and storm back, finger wagging. "You think you're smarter than me, don't you? Is it because I'm a woman? Is that why you can't stand me?"

He grabs his head and groans. "Listen to yourself, Bergman. This has nothing to do with intellect or what you do or don't have between your legs. You're irrational and impossible to work with."

My hand smacks the paper on the desk. If only it were his face. "Since I'm irrational and can't seem to ask the right questions, explain the eyes to me."

He folds his arms across his chest. "I can come up with several other explanations besides a six-foot-tall animal that stands on two legs. Perhaps the animal is hanging onto the tree trunk with its arms or claws. Or maybe it's sitting on a stump or branch that isn't visible. Or hanging from a branch by its tail. Good enough for you?"

Why didn't I think of those things?

The wind in my sails dies a horrible death, leaving me stranded in the middle of an ocean of shame. "You're right, Roland." My legs tremble as I park my butt in the chair facing the side of his desk. "Sometimes I just get this feeling about a case, and I've yet to be wrong."

"Until now," he quips.

"Maybe I am this time. No one is perfect."

"Then we're finally on the same page." His desk phone rings, and he leans over to see who's calling. "It's the forensics lab. Might as well stay and listen in." He presses the speaker button. "This is Detective Roland."

"Good morning, Detective. This is Dr. Deborah Dages from the forensics lab. I've got some preliminary results for you, but I don't think you're going to like them."

Detective Roland eyes me. "Go ahead, Dr. Dages."

"Yes, of course. We collected several samples from the crime scene at the preserve, including blood and tissue samples, hair follicles, and other fluids. Unfortunately, most of our samples are contaminated."

"Contaminated?" Detective Roland frowns. "With what?"

"Human DNA."

"Hi, Deborah. This is Detective Bergman. What do you mean the samples are contaminated with human DNA? Which samples?"

"We swabbed the bite wounds on the victim's neck for saliva and ran tests against it. We removed the victim's DNA markers from the results, but what we had left is a bit confusing. There are markers left in it from both human and non-human DNA. Because of that, we also filtered out DNA markers of everyone involved in the collection of the samples. Oddly enough, we haven't been able to identify the non-human part of it.

"What's stranger still is the fact that the two sets of DNAs seem to go together. As for the discarded tissue, it had the same DNA markers as the saliva and had no evidence of being thrown up. The last thing we ran was an analysis of the red hairs we found embedded in the chest and arm wounds. The makeup of the hairs is quite unique. They are extremely thick and porous. Almost wolf-like in color and feel, but like nothing we've ever encountered before."

Detective Roland and I stare at each other for several moments. There's no way he can deny that something is off with this case now.

"What about the DNA from the woman who discovered the body?" I ask. "Samantha George."

"We didn't collect a DNA sample from her," admits Deborah. "Perhaps it would be a good idea to get a sample from her so that we can rule her out."

Detective Roland glares at me. "Thank you, Dr. Dages. We'll get that sample for you as soon as possible." He hangs up the phone. "You and I both know Ms. George had nothing to do with the mauling."

"Maybe not, but it'll give you an excuse to go see her." He doesn't deny it.

He picks up a pen and taps it against the edge of his desk. "Other than this animal having red fur and yellow eyes, it looks like Game and Fish are on their own tracking it down."

My lower jaw drops, nearly unhinged. "Seriously? That's what you got out of that call? Game and Fish are on their own?"

"Admit it, Bergman. We're at the end of this." He tosses the pen down and stands. "There's nothing to suggest foul play, we have no evidence of anything but a mauling, and the evidence we did collect is clearly contaminated. Consider this case closed."

The hell it is.

My blood boils so hot that I can hardly see. I need to step away and get some air before I say something that can't be retracted. Detective Roland doesn't even blink when I jerk myself up and out of the chair and storm away. I'm certain he's glad to see my backside exit his office.

Outside, the cool October air feels refreshing. Clarity returns to my thoughts. To the victim. There's at least one more thing that can be done.

I need to touch the body.

* * * * *

The last thing I thought I'd find myself doing today was going back into Terry Roland's office to bargain with him, but he holds all the cards where this Night Mauler case is concerned, so I knock on his door once again and enter.

"Thought we were finished," he says, not bothering to look up from his computer.

The chair creaks when I sit down. "Do me one small favor and I'll leave it alone."

He glances over at me for half a second. "I don't owe you any favors,

Bergman."

"Right, but if you give me access to the body, then I'd owe you a favor."

"And just what do you think you're going to find by inspecting the body yourself?"

I shrug and shake my head. "I don't know. Maybe nothing, but what harm will it do? I swear it'll get me off your back on this."

"Fine, but I'm coming with you." He locks his computer and stands up. "We'll go late this afternoon."

Dammit.

There's no way I can touch the body with him around. He'd have my badge on Lieut. Frost's desk within the hour. My mind races to formulate a plan to rid myself of his escort. As always, everything will hinge on enlisting Seth's help.

I rise and meet Terry's gaze. "Thank you, Terry. I'll meet you at the City Morgue at 15:30."

"Perfect." He shoots me a glare as he walks out of the office. "And it's Detective Roland to you, Bergman."

Bite me.

Five seconds later, I've got Seth on the phone. "Where you at?"

"Following up a lead across town." He sounds tired.

I chew off a hangnail and spit it into Detective Roland's trashcan. "Got time to meet me for a quick bite?"

"I know that tone. What's up?"

"Got a play going down and need some interference. You in?"

He sighs. "We can talk about it over coffee. The usual in twenty?"

"Yup." I love Wired Coffee.

Twenty-three minutes later, Seth walks through the doors of Wired Coffee. "You're late," I say when he settles down on the chair across from me.

"After my morning, you're lucky I'm here at all."

"Wanna talk about it?" My fingers are mentally crossed that he doesn't.

"Nope."

Good.

Verna, our usual waitress, comes over to the table. "What'll it be, folks?"

She always asks even though we order the same thing every time we come in. One day I'm gonna order something different and throw her for a loop. "One black and one loaded."

Verna taps her right temple. "Comin' up." She walks away.

There are fifteen tables in the cafe, but only three of them are occupied besides our own. One man huddles over his laptop in the far corner, a pair of blue Beats headphones wrapped over the top of his head and cupped over his ears, oblivious to everything going on around him. I've seen him before, but he's not a regular.

An older woman sits two tables beyond ours, carrying on a conversation with herself. Like us, she's a regular patron. Until about a year ago, she'd always come in with her husband. According to Verna, the man died of prostate cancer. The woman still orders hot tea and pound cake for both of them. I dread the day I become her.

A young girl, perhaps seventeen, sits across the aisle from us, her focus locked on a steaming cup of tea sitting in front of her. Fire-red hair covers her head and waterfalls down her face and shoulders in wild curls, hiding most of her freckled face. Her long, dark-green trench coat seems an unusual choice for a girl her age, but what do I know?

As much as Seth and I frequent this place, I don't recall seeing her in here before. Then again, I'm usually absorbed in my own thoughts or engaged in hushed conversation with Seth when we're here. Discussing a case. Same as today.

The TV's on in the corner. Late morning news. The screen flashes with an update alert about the mauling early yesterday morning and a woman comes on screen, the nature preserve in the background. "We've just received new information about the animal attack at Desert Springs Nature Preserve yesterday morning. The identity of the victim has been confirmed to be local businessman Ernesto Vasquez, 57 years old."

Glass shatters. Startles me and Seth both. The young girl's tea has become a pond in the middle of the floor, the cup shattered into a thousand pieces.

Our eyes meet for the briefest of moments just before she leaps from her chair and sprints for the exit. She narrowly misses knocking a tray of coffee from Verna's hands.

Verna sets the tray down on the nearest table and heads back into the kitchen, her head shaking on her shoulders. A few seconds later, a thought occurs to me. The girl had the most unusual eyes. Almost a shade of yellow.

Like those of the animal in the video.

I'm on my feet and slip-sliding across the cafe on a sea of tea and broken glass before realizing what a dangerous endeavor it is. Thankfully, I reach the door without incident and head outside, but the girl has vanished.

Seth meets me at the door as I reenter the cafe. "What the hell was that about?"

Honestly, I don't have an answer. "Not sure."

"You could've broken your neck bolting after that girl the way you did," says Verna. "It's just an old cup and some spilled tea. No big whoop."

"Still, she should've paid before she ran out," I say, knowing full well my reaction had nothing to do with the girl running out on a check or damaging property.

"She's never been a problem before," says Verna. "She's a bit skittish around people and loud noises. Probably scared the wits out of her is all."

Seth and I return to the table with our coffees, and Verna starts cleaning up the mess. The other two patrons didn't even react to any of the commotion, each lost in their own little world.

"So what's this scheme of yours?" asks Seth. He takes a sip of his coffee. How he drinks the stuff black is beyond me.

Sewer sludge.

I take a sip of my own before answering. The blend of cream and sugar with a hint of coffee is perfection on my tongue. "I'm meeting Roland at the morgue at 15:30. You're coming along as well so that you can keep him occupied while I do my thing with the corpse."

He shudders. "You realize how morbid and disgusting that sounds, right?"

I cock my head and smile. "Is that a yes?"

"What do you think you're going to see by doing that? If it even works."

Three fingers rise from my extended hand. "That's how many times it has worked, Seth. Three times. Stop pretending you don't believe me."

"But why this one? The guy was mauled to death. Do you really want to experience that? Live through that experience, as you say you do?"

I retrieve the printout from yesterday from my back pocket and toss it across the table. "Tell me what you see."

Seth unfolds the paper and studies it for a good four seconds. "A dark, pixelated image."

"At least pretend to give it an effort, genius boy. I'm sitting right here."

He smooths it out on the table and looks at it again. "What am I supposed to see?"

"Look at the area where Samantha George's head is turning toward." I tap the area on the printout when he shrugs. "Right here."

He leans closer. "Those... those are the yellow eyes?"

"Exactly. Whatever that thing is, it watched Samantha intently. She claimed that she felt watched the entire time she was out running."

"And what did Detective Roland say about this? Or did you not show it to him?"

"Oh, he saw it. And sloughed it off." Another sip of perfect coffee lightens my mood.

"But you think this thing with yellow eyes is what mauled the man to death, right?"

"You get me unsupervised access to the body, and I'll be certain one way or the other."

Seth licks his lips. "And what's in it for me if I agree to this asinine scheme of yours?"

"You've got it all backwards, my love. You should know how the game works by now. You need to think about what you're willing to live without if you don't do this for me."

"You think you hold all the cards, don't you?"

"Are you saying I don't?"

He takes a long swig of his coffee, his gaze locked with mine, before answering. "All I'm saying is that I'd appreciate a reward now and again."

"This isn't little league, Seth. No participation awards will be handed out. You've gotta earn your keep."

"Oh, that's real funny." The sides of his mouth curl into a grin. "One of these days I'm going to turn the table on you and hold out."

I laugh aloud. "The day you can do that is the day you fully earn my respect."

Seth shakes his head. "What else you got? This picture can't be everything."

"It's not," I assure him.

After filling Seth in on every last detail from the phone call Detective Roland and I had with Deborah from CSI, he's fully on board. Or at least intrigued enough to lend a helping hand. Either way, it's good enough for me.

"Let's go get that corpse to talk," he says, a devious glint in his eye.

"And you think I'm the creepy one?"

Seth smiles and lays twenty bucks on the table as he stands up. "We're a pair of creeps."

"I'll get your change," says Verna, sweeping the money off the table as she walks by.

"No change," says Seth.

Verna turns back, her hands on her hips. "I won't take a seventeen dollar tip for three dollars' worth of coffee, especially from you."

"Of course not. I'd never dream of tipping so much," he jests. "The rest is to cover the broken cup and the girl's tea."

Verna opens her mouth, clearly about to argue her way out of the money, so I jump in. "It's non-negotiable, Verna. You can give us a cup on the house next time we're in."

The woman sighs. "Very well. But don't you dare think I'll forget."

"The thought never crossed my mind." Grabbing the printout off the table, I fold it up and shove it back in my pocket.

Seth pecks my cheek when I rise from the chair. "See you at the morgue in a couple of hours."

I grab his hand as he turns to walk away and pull him back around. "It's a date."

"Like old times." He chuckles, gives me a proper kiss on the forehead, and then walks out of the cafe, leaving me standing there with a head full of thoughts about intelligent animal-human hybrids created in a lab and trained to kill.

A few years ago, I would've written off such ludicrous ideas, but now I know it's not far from the truth. The world is full of mad scientists bent on destroying it or at least turning it into something it was never meant to be. So the question remains: what are we hunting?

Assassin werewolves.

I can't hold back a snort as I walk out of the cafe. As absurd as it is, it's the only rational answer I can think of right now. Divulging this truth to Seth and Detective Roland and seeing their reactions to it would likely be the highlight of my day. It might end my career as well.

Like Agent Fox Mulder from the *X-Files*, I know the truth is out there.

I just need to find it.

Seth and Detective Roland are waiting outside the morgue when I arrive at 15:27. It's surprising that Seth's here before me considering I'm three minutes early. He's never on time for anything, especially work. It saves me the usual trouble of having to call him to see where he's at, though.

The two of them are chatting it up like old pals and laughing about something I can guarantee is inappropriate. My jaw tightens. *Probably me.*

Once I get my hands on the body, the joke will be on them. That's what I keep telling myself as I exit the car and walk over to them. "Let's get this over with."

Sasha, one of the morgue attendants, greets us at the door as we enter the building. "Good afternoon, Detectives Roland, Ryan, and… Bergman, yes?" Her Russian accent is thick, and I love the way she says my name.

My eyes meet her gaze. "That is correct."

"Good." She turns to Detective Roland. "I suspect you've come to see the body of Mr. Ernesto Vasquez, yes?"

"Indeed," he replies. "We will only take a few minutes of your time."

She nods. "Follow me."

Sasha ushers us down a long hallway, toward the positive temperature cold chamber room. The temperature drops significantly as we enter the room, and I'm hugging myself within moments. One day I'll remember to bring an extra jacket or sweater with me when coming here.

Tannish-brown, four-inch rectangular tiles cover the floor, and slate-gray tiles of the same size cover three of the four walls. The fourth wall comprises a dozen flush-mounted, galvanized steel doors, six uppers and six lowers. She leads us over to one of the lower doors designated by a number four on its top-right corner. Nodding to herself after checking the tag, she pulls the door open. The galvanized steel roller drawer slides out with ease, but the problem is immediately apparent.

"Where the hell is Ernesto Vasquez's body?" asks Seth.

My thoughts exactly.

* * * * *

Three hours later, the morgue is a madhouse. It's rare that Lieut. Frost leaves the police station, but he's personally leading the investigation into the missing body. According to him, this kind of crime or mistake, whichever it may turn out to be, falls and reflects directly on him.

A handful of us huddle around a raised metal table inside exam room one where Lieut. Frost has set up his command station. We all listen as he goes over every detail we know so far.

"Sasha and Mr. Massey, the two morgue attendants on duty, were questioned first. It's their responsibility to keep track of every single body in the morgue and document when and where they are moved, whether it's to an examination room for autopsy or if the body has been released to family or a funeral home.

"According to the documentation, Mr. Vasquez's body was returned to the cold chamber at 10:17 this morning, after Dr. Deborah Dages finished her examination of the body. The transfer of the body was signed off by Mr. Massey. Video footage from within the cold chamber room proves that Mr. Massey had indeed returned the body to chamber 4 at that time.

"Video footage also shows that no one else entered or exited the cold chamber room between that time and when Sasha led Detectives Roland, Ryan, and Bergman in there at 15:35. Also, according to the visitor's log, no one else had been in or out of the building all morning other than Dr. Deborah Dages and Charlie Jones, who both work in the forensics lab upstairs."

Becky Cummins, a female uniformed officer, enters exam room one and addresses Lieut. Frost. "Sir, Officer Jaramillo found an anomaly in the video feeds for the morgue and the parking lot."

"What kind of anomaly?" asks Lieut. Frost. Concern wrinkles his brow.

Cummins continues, "Jaramillo first noticed that the clock on the wall in the lobby stopped keeping time at 12:14. Then, seventeen minutes later, the clock starts running again and displays the correct time. Once he noticed this, he was able to run the other feeds through some software that verified his hunch. They'd all been hacked and put on some sort of feed loop."

"And why the hell would anyone go to all that trouble to steal a body?" questions Seth.

"He was a prominent drug dealer," says Roland.

Lieut. Frost rubs the back of his neck. "But who knew he was dead, let alone here?"

"Everyone, sir," I say. "They released his name on the news earlier today."

Lieut. Frost turns to Detective Roland. "You released his name to those vultures?"

Detective Roland swallows hard before answering. "Yes, sir. In my mind, the case was closed. Still is, isn't it?"

Dr. Deborah Dages walks into the room. All eyes turn to her. "I thought so at first, too, but now I'm not so sure. Not only did they take the body, but they took all the samples and notes from the lab as well. Why would anyone do that unless they're trying to cover something up?"

Butterflies flutter in my stomach. I really want to scream I told you so in Terry Roland's face, but it's not the appropriate time or place for it. Not that there *is* an appropriate time and place for it. But it would feel really good to do so.

Lieut. Frost glares daggers at Detective Roland. "Looks like this case is far from over, Detective Roland. I expect you and Bergman to find and recover the body and get to the bottom of this."

A smile cracks my lips. Can't help it.

Lieut. Frost notices and turns his glare on me. "Is there something you want to add, Bergman?"

Holding his gaze proves impossible, so I look to Seth for strength and a reprieve. "No, sir."

"Good. Get it done, and quickly." With that, Lieut. Frost walks out of the room.

Seth crosses his arms. "Don't want to step on any toes, but I'm more than willing to pitch in on this one."

Detective Roland nods. "Good. Stay here and get this thing wrapped up."

"I can handle that," says Seth.

"Make sure every surface in this building is checked for fingerprints," says Detective Roland. "It's unlikely we'll get a break, but we've got nothing else to go on at the moment."

"You got it. If there's evidence to be found in this building, Deborah and Charlie will find it." Seth squeezes my shoulder and walks off, barking orders to several people as he moves out of earshot.

"Where does that leave us?" I ask.

Detective Roland rubs his chin for a moment. "I've got a friend in city planning and engineering that owes me a favor. I'll get in touch with him and have him check traffic cameras around the area between noon and 13:00. Maybe we'll get lucky and get a hit on a vehicle."

"And what about me?"

"Just stay out of my way. I'll get the body back." He pushes past me.

I grab Detective Roland's shoulder and yank him back around. "Enough with this brooding, tough guy crap. Say what you gotta say to me and let's move on. Give me a chance, and you'll see that I can be an asset."

"You're an ass hat, not an asset."

"I accept that, but no one's being a bigger ass hat right now than you. Just ask Seth how helpful I can be."

"His opinion of you became worthless the moment the two of you started sleeping together."

The dig is deep, but I slough it off. "Maybe so, but ask yourself why Lieut. Frost kept me around after everything that happened."

He shrugs. "For all I know, you're sleeping with him, too."

Thwack!

My fist connects with his jaw, sending bone-jarring waves racing up my arm.

Detective Roland stutters back a few steps, stunned. Blood trickles down from the corner of his mouth. He massages his jaw where I socked him. "Damn, that hurt." He sticks his thumb in his mouth and then pulls it back out. Crimson saliva covers it. "You made me bite my tongue."

"Say something like that again, and it won't be your tongue that's bleeding."

He nods. "Guess I deserved that. Sorry."

"Good." My knuckles are throbbing, but there's no way in hell I'm going to rub them in front of him.

"Where did you learn to pack such a punch?"

"Ninjutsu. I'll be taking my black belt exam soon."

His eyebrows rise and his eyes widen. "Seriously? I've been studying BJJ for a few years now."

"Brazilian Jujitsu? Nice. Never would've pegged you for it."

Detective Roland's features soften. It's the first time he hasn't looked at me with contempt in months. "Maybe we can spar sometime. Blow off some steam."

Those were the last words I thought I'd ever hear him utter. Maybe we're finally making some progress, but I won't hold my breath. "Sure. I'll go easy on you."

Kenny appears out of nowhere. "Heard the chatter. The body went missing?"

"It did." I frown at him. "Why are you here?"

Kenny looks around, but we're alone in the hallway. "Thought we might go check out the trail," he whispers. "See if we can find something."

"Fine—" My phone buzzes in my pocket. The display reads St. Thomas Psychiatric Center when I check it. My pulse soars. "I've got to take this call—hello?"

"Is this Alice Bergman?" asks the woman on the line.

"Yes." I cover my other ear with my hand.

"You're listed as the only emergency contact for a patient we have here. An Isaiah Mallard. Is that correct?"

Suddenly, I'm short of breath. "He's my father. What's happened?" My chest tightens.

Seth meets me in the hallway and interrupts my call. "Just got a call. We've got a dead body at St. Thomas Psychiatric Center."

The phone slips from my hand and smacks against the floor. Pieces of it scatter in every direction.

Seth catches me by the arm. Takes my weight onto his shoulder. "What's wrong?"

Deep within, my soul cries out, but tears will not come for a man I hardly know.

"It's my father."

CHAPTER FIVE

SETH AND I RUSH inside St. Thomas Psychiatric Center and head straight through the lobby. Seth mashes down the call button next to the main entrance into the ward.

"I'm going in there alone," he says. "If it's your father lying on the floor of that room, I won't allow you inside."

"It must be." The lobby spins around me. "I can feel it." Weakened legs barely keep me upright. I grab onto the counter. "Why would they have called me otherwise?"

Seth bangs on the glass when no one arrives at the window. "I don't know. Perhaps it was a coincidence. Or maybe he's a witness. Until we know what's going on, there's no point in speculating."

Several deep breaths calm the maelstrom I stand within. "Fine, you can go in first and check it out, but I'm going in no matter what the outcome. He might be my biological father, but I hardly know the man."

He grabs my arm and stabilizes me. "You're already a mess, Alice. You care about him more than you think."

"Sorry to keep you waiting," says a male voice through the speaker on the wall. I don't recognize the man's ashen face through the glass window, but his voice is unmistakable. "Unfortunately, the ward is closed—"

We hold our badges up to the glass window.

"Oh, thank God you're here." The man disappears, and then both sets of double doors swing open into the psychiatric ward. He meets us on the other side. "I'm Nurse Vance. I take it you've been informed of the situation?"

"We have," Seth confirms.

"I'm a nurse, for God's sake. I worked in the ER for several years but never saw so much blood." Nurse Vance's voice shakes almost as much as his hands.

"You don't need to come with us, Vance," says Seth. "Just tell us where we're headed."

Nurse Vance points across the expansive common area toward the three resident halls. "Central hallway. Room B15."

B15.

In that instant, every last thought gets thrown out the window. "Father!" I scream and dash across the common area like a madwoman.

* * * * *

As I run toward my father's room, the only thing I can think about is how much I need him to be alive. We have no past, but our relationship has just begun, and my future depends on him.

Rounding the corner into the central corridor, I see a security guard standing watch in front of room B15. His eyes widen as I barrel toward him. He reaches for the mic hanging from his shoulder.

I rip my credentials out of my back pocket as I surge forward. "DSPD. Step aside!"

My badge flies from my hand and skids across the floor, stopping just beyond the security guard. He bends down, scoops up my badge, and checks it. By the time he hands me back my credentials and steps away from the door, Seth's caught up to me.

Seth nearly tackles me to the floor, wrapping his arms around mine and pulling me back from the door. But it's too late. I've already unlatched the door. Caught a glimpse of what lies beyond it.

Seth and I freeze in the hallway, both of us panting like dogs as the door swings wide open.

Crimson floors. Crimson streaked walls. Everywhere my eyes look, there's more blood.

Once-white, blood-stained sheets cover a form on the floor.

"Don't go in there," Seth whispers, releasing my arms.

My legs give out, and I crash to the floor before Seth can catch me. Knees collide with vinyl tiles. Jarring. Painful. But not as painful as staring at the form underneath the sheet. Yet I cannot look away, mesmerized and horrified.

Seth kneels next to me, his hand on my shoulder. "You alright?"

I nod, but I'm not. Far from it. My insides feel as though they've been turned inside-out. A low hum fills my ears and quickly grows with intensity.

Seth's voice calls to me from a great distance, almost an echo from the past. A fading memory. Then the humming dissipates, and silence engulfs me. Swallows me whole. Nothing exists but me and the form beneath the sheet.

Father…

The man I never knew draws tears from my eyes. I wipe them away, but more replace them. I can't keep up with them as they cover my entire face. Drip from my chin. Soak my gray shirt.

Seth steps past me and into the room. Blocks my view of the form underneath the sheet. Then the door closes. Lock engages with a soft *click*. He's shut me out, but I no longer want in.

No, Father…

How could he leave me alone again? Why would he do this to me? My soul cries out for answers, but none come. Anguished, I fold myself over and weep for the father I never knew.

But then laughter rings in my ears. Echoes in my head. Boxing my ears only makes it worse.

I'll never forget the source of that laugh, no matter how hard I try. His face rises from the darkness and fills my mind. Deep scars. Yellow teeth. Lips hug a lit cigarette.

"You'll never stop me now," he says.

With all my strength, I push Russell from my mind and focus on the handful of conversations I've had with my father. I can count them on a single hand, and the thought plunges the knife of despair deep into my heart.

I'm sorry, Father.

Then the door to B15 swings open wide. Seth kneels before me. His lips move, but he seems to have lost his voice. I beg him to speak louder. But that's when I see the blood. Gushing from the wound across his throat. Gurgling. Coughing. Choking.

"I can't lose both of you," I cry.

"Alice!" Seth's voice shocks my ears. Daggers through my eardrums.

Black rose petals of darkness fall from my eyes. Seth does kneel before me, but his throat no longer gushes with blood.

"Take a deep breath," he says. "It's not your father."

It takes a few moments for the words to register. "Not my father?"

"No," Seth confirms. "As far as I can tell, it's one of the female nurses."

"Then where's my father?" I ask. He's my only concern right now.

"That's a good question." Seth rises and turns to the security guard hovering a short distance down the corridor. "Are you the one who discovered the body?"

"No, sir. Mackenzie did." He narrows the distance and proffers his hand to Seth who takes it. "Zach Tritt."

"Detective Ryan." Seth releases Zach's hand and glances down at me. "This is Detective Bergman."

Zach dips his head toward me. "Pleasure."

"How did what's in that room happen?" asks Seth. "The struggle must've been loud."

"In truth, no one heard or saw anything until it was over. These rooms are designed for maximum sound resistance, utilizing soundproofing materials and thick, insulated walls, floors, and ceilings. Helps keep the other residents calm when one of them is having a bad day or night."

Seth crosses his arms. "No security cameras in the rooms?"

"Yeah, but we have a lot of rooms to monitor." Zach rubs his hands together. "And, from what I understand, everything happened right as Mackenzie took a bathroom break. What are the odds of that?"

Bad odds.

I wipe my eyes and nose and pull myself to my feet. "And where have they taken Isaiah Mallard? Was he injured? Detained for questioning?"

"I'm sorry, but I just came on shift about twenty minutes ago, and now you know everything I do." He looks to Seth. "I'm guessing you'll be around for some time?"

Seth gazes at the door to room B15. "Through the night from the looks of it."

Zach nods. "Let me go fetch Mackenzie. He'll be able to fill you in on more of the details. Give me about an hour. Things around here are still a bit chaotic." He turns and quickly walks away.

"I'm gonna go find Nurse Vance," I say. "I'll be back."

Seth smiles wearily. "I'm not going anywhere."

It takes several minutes for me to track down Nurse Vance. When I do, I find him consoling an elderly woman in a room in the next corridor over. Apparently, the entire ward is in disarray over what has happened. But I don't care.

"Where's Isaiah Mallard?" I demand.

Nurse Vance looks up at me. His head cocks to the left, and then recognition flashes in his eyes. "You're... the blind woman." He frowns. "Aren't you?"

"No. Well, yes. Ugh!" My hands ball into fists at my sides. "It doesn't matter. Where's my father?"

His eyes widen, and he gasps. "Didn't they call you?"

"Yes, but the phone call got interrupted. Tell me what happened."

"We found Mr. Mallard in his room about an hour ago. He'd lost a lot of blood from several deep lacerations and was almost dead when we discovered him. Thank God we're located right next to the hospital. Any farther and he might not have made it in for surgery." Tears begin to fall from Nurse Vance's eyes. Bloom in dark circles on his scrubs. "Nurse Samantha wasn't as lucky."

"And what do they think his chances of survival are?" I ask, my voice catching in the back of my throat.

Nurse Vance looks away. Fuels my rage. I don't have time for games. "Answer the damn question."

He slowly shakes his head, his gaze refusing to meet mine. "His chances are low. Very low."

Stunned, I stagger back toward room B15. My mind tumbles down the rabbit hole once again as my nightmares rise from the dead. Seth's kneeling next to the uncovered body when I get back to the room.

"What are you doing?" I ask, confused. "Why aren't you waiting for CSI?"

"The integrity of this scene was lost the moment they came in to rescue your father. Figured I might as well have a look. Plus, they covered the victim, further deprecating the evidence."

"Degrading…" My gaze settles on the woman.

The woman's blonde hair is short on the sides and back, almost a butch cut. She looks to be in her mid-fifties, crow's feet stretched from the corners of her eyes to her temples and deep rows of wrinkles across her brow. All the crevices are caked with congealed or dried blood. She wears pink scrubs, stained several shades darker across most of her body. Her throat and the sheet wrapped around it are bathed in blood.

Was she the primary target of the attack, or was it Isaiah? My gut says Isaiah, and it's rarely wrong.

"What did you find out about your father?" asks Seth.

"He's in surgery. Might not make it." My voice cracks. The truth sounds worse from my own lips.

"He's a fighter," says Seth.

In all honesty, I don't know who Isaiah is or how strong he might be, but

Nurse Vance's words hang in my mind, swinging from the end of a noose.

His chances are low…

Shoulder against the doorframe, I lean into the room. "Can I borrow your cellphone? I need to call Mother and let her know. She claims to hate the man, but I don't believe her."

"I don't believe her, either." He stands and walks over to me, his arms raised. "It's in my left jacket pocket."

I fish the phone from his pocket. "Thanks. I'm going to go check on my father's status as well. I'll be back once Mother shows up."

He nods. "Not going anywhere."

Deborah and Charlie from CSI exit a second elevator just as the doors of my elevator close. I don't have time to even wave. The elevator jolts and climbs upward as the phone connects.

Mother picks up on the third ring. "Seth? It's nearly nine o'clock. Is everything okay with Alice?"

"It's me, Mother." I'm barely holding it together enough to talk.

"Alice? Why are you calling me from Seth's phone? Are you okay?" Concern strains her voice and tugs at me through the phone. Makes me feel worse than I already do.

I'm a terrible daughter.

"I'm fine." Nothing could be farther from the truth, at least mentally. "I broke my phone, but that doesn't matter right now. I just wanted you to know that Isaiah's been attacked."

"My Lord in heaven!" she exclaims. "Is he okay?"

"No." I bite my lower lip and choke back a stream of tears. It takes several moments to recover enough to continue. "He's lost a lot of blood and is in surgery right now." My voice falls to a whisper, and I barely manage to say, "His chances of pulling through aren't good."

Several moments of silence pass between us, and then something unexpected happens. Mother curses. Clear as day. It's the first time in my life I've ever heard her do so. A four-letter word I didn't know she knew.

"I'm on my way," she says.

The line goes dead just as the elevator doors slide open on the third floor. My gaze rises and meets that of a man who stands on the other side of the doors. He's a menacing hulk, his thick, bald head circled with a crown of thorns tattoo.

I dare not look away as my hand slips over my gun. Tightens around the grip as tension crawls into my neck and shoulders.

The man steps to the side and gestures toward the elevator lobby with an arm. "After you, ma'am."

"Thank you." I side-step around him with caution, giving myself as wide a birth as possible.

His big smile seems genuine, but that's how they always draw you in. Demons dressed as saints.

"You're welcome," he says before entering the elevator car. He presses one of the buttons with a meaty finger and stands there without as much as a sideways glance.

A sigh of relief escapes from my lips when the doors close, and the tension in my jaw and shoulders dwindles away. This day has had the better of me for the length of it, and I'm ready for it to end.

As usual, Eddie's manning the information desk in the main lobby of the hospital. He's chatting up a woman with jet-black hair and waves at me when he spots me. The woman turns around. Even though I met her when I was partially blind, I'd never forget her face. She kept me calm and Seth alive in the ambulance when he was shot several months back.

Angela.

Angela's face lights up. "Wonderland!"

I wave weakly as I approach the desk. "Hey, Angie. One of these days we'll have to meet on better terms."

Eddie's smile fades. "What's going on?" he asks, his voice laced with concern.

"My father was attacked and is in surgery right now."

Angela meets me before I reach the desk and snakes her arm around my shoulders. "Oh, I'm sorry to hear that." She squeezes me and leads me the last few steps to the desk.

Eddie stands and leans over the desk. His arm's just long enough to reach my hand. "Me too."

Sometimes it's strange where you meet and make friends. Angela and Eddie will both be on my Christmas card list if I ever send one out. "It's okay. I'm headed over to the ER to see if I can find out what's happening."

"Keep your chin up, Wonderland." Angela squeezes my shoulder again before releasing me. "I'm certain everything will work itself out."

"Thanks, Angie. See you guys around."

When I reach the nurses station in the ER, no one has a clue as to what's going on with my father. The only information they give me is an estimate of how long he'll likely remain in surgery—at least another six hours. Perhaps longer if they run into complications. Basically, I'm on my own until Mother arrives.

Time slowly ticktocks away as I stare at the analog wall clock hanging on the tan wall across the empty waiting room. The second hand stutters and pauses with each passing moment, shallow, painful breaths of time that taunt me. Which of them will signal my father's last breath?

Don't think like that.

Alone and left to my own twisted thoughts, the recent past buds with life anew. It follows me everywhere I go, relentlessly haunting me. The hospital walls tremble, quake, and begin encroaching upon me. Invading my personal space.

I thought I'd moved past this. Crucified this demon in the chapel beneath the asylum. Clearly, I was wrong.

Wrapping my arms around my sides, I hug myself tight and squeeze my eyes shut. "This isn't real." The words repeat both from my lips and within my mind, but they're lifeless and hollow.

Like me.

Offering me no comfort, my pulse rises. Spikes. Dread and despair follow close behind, a brushfire rushing through my veins, burning and consuming me from within. Once started, there is no escape from these moments.

Clutching myself tighter, I brace for what comes next. This isn't new. I know how it ends.

The darkness builds around me. Latches onto my ankles and pulls me down into the depths of despair. Within the darkness, I sense his presence once again. Smell his reeking skin.

Garlic. Pickles. Ash.

A glowing, red, cycloptic eye burns in the distance, and Russell's all-too-familiar voice fills my head. Laughs at me. Taunts me.

"Your Father's blood is on your hands."

* * * * *

"Alice."

Mother's voice. A melodic beacon of light guiding me out of the darkness. Her hand squeezes my shoulder and pulls me free from Russell's snare. But I know he'll be back.

The fluorescent lights in the ER waiting room sting my eyes when I finally force my eyes open. I don't need a mirror to see that I'm a mess. A cold, sticky tendril of drool hangs from the right side of my chin, anchoring my head to my shoulder. Lake Michigan sits atop my shoulder and dribbles down the front of my shirt. Wet and crusty-white around the edges.

According to the wall clock—a blurry mess through a crusted layer of eye boogers—nearly twenty minutes have slipped past me since I sat down. It's no wonder the right side of my neck throbs with pain when I straighten my head, but how did I make such a mess of myself?

"According to the woman at the desk, Isaiah's still in surgery. She assured me that one of the nurses will be out in a few hours to give us an update on his condition." Mother hands me a tissue. "Clean yourself up."

The tissue helps with my neck and face, but an entire box wouldn't be sufficient to soak up the salty shoulder lake. Dabbing at it only widens its shores, and the nasty, sticky sound it makes when I do so triggers my gag reflex. It's a lost cause, so I aim at the wastebasket nestled between the chairs across from me and fling the tissue toward it. The tissue, wet with drool, clings to my fingers longer than expected and falls a foot short of its target, tumbling to a stop a good four inches from the wastebasket.

Mother's out of her chair and picking up after me before I give it a moment's thought. To her, I'm still the helpless little blind girl from a decade past. The one she still longs to care for and secretly mourns over. I don't hold it against her, but I was never helpless.

Except that single time she left me home alone.

I shake it off, along with every thought not pertaining to the present situation. "How long have you been here?" Digging my thumb into the side of my neck produces both relief and pain from the hulking knot, and it leaves me wincing and short of breath.

Mother returns to the chair next to mine and settles with a grunt. "About ten minutes. You looked as peaceful as Christ himself, sitting there with your head lolled to the side."

Christ? The only peaceful image my mind conjures is one of him hanging lifelessly on a cross. The thought pulls me back into the hell of Russell's world. Down into the asylum. Fingernails dig into my palms, and my teeth grind together as tension builds in my jaw.

Seth hangs upside-down on the cross. Blood pools beneath his head. His beautiful eyes stare at nothing. Cold and lifeless.

Hate-filled laughter fills my head. Rings in my ears. *The Braille Killer.* Even now I smell him. Pungent. Nauseating. Causes my skin to crawl. A pulsing, undulating pile of maggots on my bones.

Will he never stop haunting me?

Pulling myself to my feet takes more effort than it should. My legs quake beneath me. Two unsteady stacks of misaligned rocks. One false move will send me crashing to the floor. But I can't stand here forever.

A deep breath brings with it some stability. Enough that I'm confident I'll keep on my feet. "I need to get back to Seth. Call his number if you need me."

Mother nods. "I will." She reaches into her large purse and retrieves a set of crochet needles and a large skein of purple-and-blue yarn. "I'll let you know as soon as I hear something."

Those needles, while in Mother's hands, produce beautiful works of art, but they're not imbued with some sort of otherworldly magic. Trust me, I know. The only thing I'm capable of conjuring with them is something akin to a hairball coughed up by an oversized cat. Mother's artistic gene failed to fuse itself into my genome, but, unlike her, I'm a ninja.

As fate or karma would have it, the end chair catches me right in the shin when I take the corner too sharp. Several four-letter words rumble under my breath and manifest as deep growls, a habit I formed early in life when around Mother. I stop for a few moments and rub the pain from my shin. Perhaps my ninja skills are a bit rusty.

Seth's phone buzzes in my pocket just as I exit from the ER. The display reads St. Thomas Psychiatric Center when I check it. I answer the call. "This is Detective Bergman."

"Any word on your father?" It's Seth.

"Nothing yet. Perhaps in a few hours we'll get an update."

"Okay, I just wanted to check in. I…" Seth hesitates.

"What is it?" I demand.

"It's nothing." He clears his throat. "I don't want to pull you away from your father."

"There's nothing for me to do right now—" I'm already halfway to the elevators that lead over to the psychiatric center building. "—and you know I can't handle just sitting around."

"Yeah, I know, but I'm sure Mother needs you." Seth's called her Mother ever since we started dating, and she'd have it no other way.

"She's fine, Seth. Spill it. What've you got for me?"

"The entire conflict between your father and this nurse was caught on video, but I haven't had a chance to watch it yet."

Thunder rumbles in my chest. "Did you say *between* them?"

"Yeah. Turns out this dead woman *isn't* Nurse Samantha after all."

My stomach leaps into my throat. "I'm on my way over. Don't you dare view it without me." I hang up and shove the phone in my pocket.

Eddie calls to me from the information desk as I sprint through the hospital lobby, but I ignore him and the security guard who urges me to slow down. A single thought bombards me with every step.

She must be a Shadow Priest.

CHAPTER SIX

BANKS OF MONITORS FILL the security office at St. Thomas Psychiatric Center, each displaying live footage of various rooms throughout the ward and within each of the myriad of private rooms. The room is cold, given the dozen racks of servers whirring away as they record every moment of the various lives contained within the brick and mortar walls of the center.

Stan Wright, the head of security at St. Thomas Psychiatric Center, pulls up the black and white video footage from Isaiah's room and starts playback of it on a large, central monitor. Most of Isaiah's room is captured in the wide angle, including his bed and the door leading into the room. The overhead lights are dim, casting shadows everywhere.

But a blind man needs no light.

The audio hisses with static as Isaiah sits back on his bed, propped up with several pillows. His gaze focuses on the wall straight ahead as his fingers glide across the page of an open book. He's reading braille, and I'm curious to know what book it is that has him so captivated.

A thriller, perhaps?

The door latch disengages with a faint *click*, disrupting the static lull. My breath catches as Isaiah's fingers pause on the page. His other hand grasps a length of sheet. The door opens just wide enough for the nurse to squeeze through the opening before securing the door behind herself. She brandishes a scalpel in her right hand, its blade gleaming in the dim light.

Fury races through my veins like wildfire, stirring up hatred in my heart. I'd kill the bitch if she wasn't already dead.

Isaiah calmly closes the book on his lap. Clutches it by its spine. Even in the deep shadows and poor lighting, I can see that its cover reads *Holy Bible*. Stuns me a bit, to be honest. Never pictured my father as a man of God. Not that I know anything about him at all.

"I knew this day would come," he says, his voice far calmer than it should be.

The woman's words slither from her mouth, *"You didn't think you could hide from us forever, did you?"*

"Huh. Never dreamed they'd send another woman." Isaiah's head rises from the pillow as he sniffs the air. His nose wrinkles. *"Wait… I know that perfume."* His head turns toward the woman. *"Dashna? But you're supposed to be dead."*

"Dashna was my sister." She stalks closer to the bed, the blade twirling between her fingers. *"I can still see her body floating in the water."*

"You were there?"

"Not soon enough." She hesitates. *"You don't think I can kill you?"*

"Your twisted sister tried once before. Look where that got her."

"Dashna's death will be avenged." She switches hands with the scalpel. *"I've had much more practice than she ever did. I assure you, it will be your life that's taken this time."*

A Shadow Priest? My pulse rises.

"Oh, I'm certain you'll give it your best shot. Might even succeed. None of it matters. I am curious as to what took you so long to find me again."

"Some things fall through the cracks, so to speak, but they're never completely lost," she sneers. *"Trust me when I say your daughter's time is limited as well."*

Isaiah's glare upon the woman gives me pause as to how blind he really is. *"You dare threaten my daughter's life? It's the last thing you'll ever do."*

"I am one of legions," she hisses. *"You are few, and soon your kind will cease to exist in our world. That includes your wretched daughter, even if it's not by my*

hand." The woman lunges toward Isaiah, scalpel first.

For a blind man, Isaiah's timing is impeccable. He smacks the woman across the face with his Bible. She grunts, but the blow doesn't prevent her from carving up his left arm with her scalpel. His face contorts with pain, but he doesn't scream.

From that moment forward the violence escalates, each landing blow after bloody blow. They tumble to the ground, and Isaiah wraps the sheet around the woman's neck. Pulls it tight and knots its ends.

All the while, she's stabbing and slashing at him, never once attempting to remove the sheet. Even in black and white, the copious amount of blood is evident. The two of them slip and slide around, neither seemingly capable of getting the upper hand. But then Isaiah grabs the woman's hand and drives it and the scalpel into the side of her throat. Her hand falls away as blood gushes from the wound and out of her gaping mouth.

Isaiah yanks the scalpel out as tremors shake his hand violently. The sheet around her neck blooms with darkness ever faster. She convulses, coughs, and then stills beneath him. The scalpel drops from his hand, and he grows still atop her.

A growing pool of dark liquid covers the floor as minutes tick by. Neither Isaiah nor the woman move at all. Ten minutes later, the door swings open.

Stan stops the video, and the entire room falls into a deep silence. I don't need to look around to confirm we're all stunned by what we just watched. Every stab, slice, and jab Isaiah suffered plays back through my mind and leaves me with a single question.

How the hell did he survive?

* * * * *

Seth and I walk back toward room B15 after viewing the security footage several more times. I still can't wrap my head around the fact that Isaiah survived the assault. Nor can I understand why the Shadow Priests chose this moment to come after him.

Back in the room, Deborah and Charlie are still sorting through the bloody mess. I'm certain there's little evidence left uncontaminated. Other than discovering the woman's identity, I'm not sure it matters.

"So where's the missing nurse?" I ask.

"Nurse Samantha?" asks Seth. "That's a good question. No one's sure. She left for lunch and this woman came back in her place. I hate to say it, but I'm pretty sure it'll be her body that turns up."

"Feels right," I agree. "Sorry, that sounds bad."

"I know what you meant." Seth checks his watch. "You think you could grab us some coffee? I'm about to hit the floor and crack my head wide open."

"Sure. It's just about time for the nurse over in the ER to give an update on Isaiah."

Seth touches my shoulder and gives me a half smile. "It's okay. You can call him Father if you want. It's what he is to you, right?"

Seth's right, but I'll never admit it. "He's gonna have to survive and earn that title. Until then, he's Isaiah."

"Fair enough." His gaze returns to B15 and the body. "She threatened your life. What do you make of it?"

"She's a Shadow Priest, just like Russell was."

Seth scratches the back of his neck, leaving three red lines. "I'm still not buying into the whole cult thing. What would they have against you and your father? I mean, do you really think they hate blind people that much?"

"It's more than that, Seth, and you know it."

He shrugs. "Perhaps, but you can call me doubting Thomas. Without physical proof, how can I dare believe something so... I don't know. Superficial."

"Supernatural?"

"Yeah." He turns around and eyes me. "I one hundred percent believe you do what you say you do, but I just can't wrap my brain around it."

"And yet you're a man of faith?"

"I know. I'm ridiculous. Certifiable."

"That wasn't what I was implying."

"Maybe not, but I struggle with my faith daily. Especially after seeing evil displayed so openly. It sickens me."

"You and me both." I rise on my tippy toes and kiss his cheek. "I'll be back in a little while with a piping hot cup of sludge."

"Sounds perfect, just like you."

I walk away, refusing to acknowledge his last words. I'm anything but perfect.

Retracing my steps back to the ER waiting room, I just get settled in the chair next to Mother when a male nurse comes out of the ER and calls my name. Tension gels the air and creates a formidable resistance against me as I fight to rise from the chair. The struggle is real, but victory is mine.

Mother pulls herself up and locks her arm through mine. She pulls us forward, toward the nurse. Without her fortitude and resolve, I'd still be moored to the floor next to my chair or lost in a thick fog without a lighthouse to guide me. Even with vision, sometimes I still need her by my side to guide me down the right path and steer me away from danger. The latter I'm prone to attract.

The male nurse's nametag reads Jonas. He stands before us and towers over us, a hulking mass of muscle and brawn underneath blue scrubs and a seafoam green cap. Reminds me of the man at the elevators earlier. Samson would've been a more fitting name, but how could his mother have known he'd grow into a colossus?

Mother's arm tenses. Pulls me closer to her. "Is Isaiah going to make it?" she asks.

Jonas's gray eyes lower to meet Mother's gaze. Intense, yet kind. A white mask clings to his neck underneath his squared jaw. He hugs a clear clipboard to his chest, forearms pumped and veined as though he just finished his morning workout moments before bursting through the ER doors. Makes me wonder what kind of duties he has in the ER.

Lines crease his brow, and he sighs before speaking. "We've never seen anyone come into the ER still alive after losing as much blood as Mr. Mallard had." His tenor voice carries with it a note of reverence and a twinge of astonishment. "By all accounts, he should've been DOA."

"Yes, we understand that, but is he still alive?" asks Mother. Her impatience rivals mine, but my jaws are locked with a growing dread bubbling up from the depths of my churning stomach.

I'm not ready for an answer, but Jonas nevertheless provides us with one. "Mr. Mallard is still in surgery. Both lungs were punctured, and his heart pierced. I still don't understand how he survived. Doctors Joshi and Prabhakaran have stabilized him and repaired his heart, but the lungs are proving difficult. From what I gleaned, he should be out of surgery within the next two hours."

Mother nods. "Thank you, Jonas."

"You're welcome. I'll let you know once Mr. Mallard is out of surgery." He turns about and reenters the ER.

"So we wait," says Mother.

"I promised Seth I'd find some coffee for him."

She nods knowingly and pats the top of my hand. "You take care of that man. He's good for you. Jesus knows you need a good man in your life."

Jesus knows everything, or so I've been told. If it's true, I'm certain he's no fan of mine. My soul is a black hole deeper than the depths of space.

I lead Mother back over to her chair. "Call me when you hear more."

"I will." She picks up a half-knitted afghan of purples, blues, and greens and sets to work again, her crochet needles twisting and pulling purplish-blue yarn from its skein with fury.

My search for coffee begins, and not a moment too soon as my head begins throbbing with vengeance. From past experience, I can tell it's likely brought on by the lack-of-caffeine gods. They hate me.

As I bury myself farther into the formidable hospital labyrinth, I find my throat drier and rawer. I swear I must've swallowed every last grain of sand in Death Valley while I slept on that chair with my mouth gaping. It matters not, for relief will come soon.

Now, I'm a warrior on a quest. Or perhaps a thief. Goes better with my ninja skills.

Definitely a thief.

Signs abound, hanging from the walls like ugly decorations on a dilapidated Christmas tree. Makes me think of Charlie Brown and brings a smile to my cracked lips. However, none of the signs mention anything about a cafe or vending machines, so my quest continues.

Corridor after corridor lead me nowhere. Into oblivion. Or the minotaur's lair. I can't be sure. But then I see a sign above the door to my left.

"Hospital Chapel," I scoff.

Most days, it's the last place I'd ever willingly go, yet for some unexplained reason I'm drawn toward the room, so I push the door open and step inside. Thankfully, it's empty. Five wooden pews, stained dark brown and showing their age with nicks, gashes, and pockmarks, stretch across the narrow room and face a large, wooden cross mounted to the wall to the right of the door. The crucified body of Christ doesn't hang from its white cross members. Had he been there, I would've bolted immediately.

With reluctance and a deep sigh, I sit down on the front edge of the back pew. Run my finger across the top of the pew in front of me, expecting a wad of dust to build in front of it but find none. Nor is there a streak left in its wake. The chapel must be part of the hospital cleaning schedule.

I scooch back on the pew and allow its concave seat to cradle me. It's surprisingly comfortable. More so than the wretched benches that line the sanctuary at Mother's church. Those ones should've been replaced decades ago, their surfaces dry and cracked. One false move on them leaves splinters in your jeans or through your shirt. Sometimes both.

For several moments, I just close my eyes and breathe. Push back the stress of the day and relax. My hand reaches up to clutch my trusty cross-pendant necklace, but it's not there. Panic constricts my throat and burns in my lungs as my eyes shoot open, but the sensation lasts only a few moments.

Remembrance of the necklace's fate and its location calms my mind and settles my nerves. Well, not its exact location. It lies somewhere beneath the rubble of overturned pews in the asylum chapel. That solitary place where I chose to take a man's life. Where I chose to reject Mother's God and seal my fate.

A groan slips through my parted lips. That stupid necklace means nothing to me, so why do I feel so naked and unprotected without it? It's irrational. Absurd. A contradiction to who I am and what I believe. Or rather, what I don't believe.

Yet my gaze is drawn to the cross on the wall. Two pieces of white-washed wood. It beckons me. Invites me to lay my burdens upon it. It will give me rest. Bring me peace.

Words bark from my hoarse throat. "Save my father."

It surprises me. Enrages me. Tension pulls my hands closed. Balls them into fists at my sides. It's a lie. Every last word the cross speaks to me. There's no peace in life.

At least not for me.

God had a chance to change my life but chose to sit on the sidelines and watch instead. A spectator. Not that he actually exists. Only a fool would believe such an obvious lie. And if only fools believe, then that makes Mother one of the biggest fools I know.

But she's not.

Misled perhaps, but she's certainly no fool. In reality, I'm the fool for coming into this room to begin with. I blame my lapse in judgment on a lack of caffeine and sleep. And my father's attack. We all make mistakes. I'll do my best not to repeat this one.

What I don't understand is the sense of relief that lifts my spirits as I exit the room. It's irrational and without merit or warrant, yet I'm certain my father will make it through the surgery. I know very little about him, but what I do know is that he's a tough man. Tougher than most. Maybe not as tough as Seth, but who is?

Me.

The lie barely registers as Seth's rugged, handsome face rises in my mind and curls my lips into a smile. He's my ever-shining light in this darkness I call life. A lone flame to guide me. God save the world if I ever lose him.

By the time I locate a coffee source, I must've walked halfway around the entire hospital. Thankfully, I have just enough change for the machine. It's a first in my sordid life of unfortunate events.

Twelve minutes later, I hand Seth his cup of black gold. Mine's a golden brown and sweeter than a kitten, chocolates, and flowers on Valentine's Day. A perfect blend for vending machine coffee.

I take a sip. "Any more revelations while I was gone?"

Seth scowls. "Not a one."

"Figures." I look around. "Anything for me to do?"

"We've got people following up on the missing nurse, and I think we've gathered everything we can from here." He slurps coffee through the sippy cup lid with obnoxious abandon, the sound almost a loud chirp. "Let's get this wrapped up. Lieut. Frost will want an update pronto."

"Sounds good. I'll see you back over there soon."

"Don't forget you're parked across the street at the morgue."

I point at my head. "Steel trap."

He laughs. "Nothing in and nothing out."

"Funny." I almost allow myself to laugh, but the weight of the day keeps me somber.

* * * * *

Several hours later, Seth, Detective Roland, and I sit around the table in the war room back at the police station. The windowless room smells of coffee and stale sweat. Unfortunately, it's not an unusual phenomenon. From what I can tell, I'm the only one who got any sleep at all last night, and that was limited to my twenty minutes of nightmares in the ER waiting room.

A handful of file folders lay open, their contents spread across the table. One folder sits in my lap, perched against the side of the table, but I can't keep my mind focused on the Night Mauler case. Every thought pulls me back to Isaiah's confrontation. To the video.

How did the Shadow Priests find him after all these years?

The answer is simple. Smacks me right in the face. Digging up my past led them right to him. His blood *is* on my hands. If he dies, the blame will fall solely on my head. If he lives, how will I face him knowing he suffered because of me? Then again, how can I not face him?

I need answers.

Officer Doug Spalding hobbles into the room. I don't need to look up from the deep pit I'm staring into to see that it's him because his cane clicks against the tile floor with each step. A pile of papers and pictures land on the table with a smack, pulling me from my thoughts and drawing my attention.

Doug looks at Seth. "We've got a positive ID on the female perp at the psych ward. Trista McClure. Fifty-six. Lives in Salt Lake City, Utah."

"Good work, Doug," says Seth. "How did you manage to track her down?"

"Not gonna lie, it took a great deal of effort." Doug leans forward on his cane, favoring his left leg—the one that *didn't* have a hole punched through it by a tree branch. "We scoured every source available and even cross-referenced it with the name Dashna and finally got a hit from the missing persons database. Didn't expect that."

"Huh. That is a strange bit of luck." Seth snatches one of the pictures off the table. "Nice work."

Doug pulls on his right earlobe. "Thanks, but it's not quite as good as it sounds."

"What do you mean?" I ask.

"Trista McClure didn't exist eighteen months ago," says Doug.

Seth frowns. "An alias?"

"Yup, but what's more interesting is the fact that her prints were already in the system." Doug stands up straight and holds up a hand, fingers spread wide. "Five different states." His other hand rises, thumb folded down and cane dangling from his wrist by a tether. "Nine cases linked to homicides."

"Good," says Seth, "but I need the details, Doug. See if you can get those case files, and also find out who filed the missing person report. We need to speak to them."

Doug frowns. "Sure, but I don't see the point if she's already dead."

I grab the folder in my lap and slap it down on the table. Doug's eyes widen when they meet my glare. "Perhaps you might want to take a few seconds to think about what you just said. There's a potential that those nine victims might have some sort of tie to my father. Capeesh?"

A simple touch from Seth's hand eases the tension in my shoulders. Dissipates my frustration. It's exactly what I needed. How he always knows what to do astounds me.

Detective Roland interjects, "Or they could all be random killings."

"Yes," agrees Seth. "We need to know which scenario is the case."

Doug's eyes light up. "Gotcha. I'll get right on it." He scuttles out of the room, his cane tapping the floor a bit lighter than when he'd entered the room.

It's the first time I've seen Doug excited about something since his accident. There's nothing worse for a field officer than being relegated to a desk job. I don't envy him one bit. No one does.

Lieut. Frost's cologne precedes him entering the room. An inescapable cloud hellbent on killing us all with its nidorous aroma. His glower falls on Seth. "We got anything on the missing nurse?"

Seth shakes his head. "No, sir."

"Well, she couldn't have just disappeared. She was on duty this morning, for Pete's sake." He smacks the table with an open palm. "Find her!"

"Done," says Officer Mike Brex as he enters the room. Everyone's attention turns to him. "One of the other nurses on duty recognized her car in the parking lot and called it in. We found trace amounts of blood on the ground and on the car's rear bumper. Once we got inside, we found her stuffed in the boot with her throat slit."

"The boot?" scoffs Detective Roland. "You going British on us, Mikey?"

Lieut. Frost grabs a chair by its back and slams it into the floor repeatedly, emphasizing each word as he does. "What. Is. Wrong. With. This. Town?"

To my surprise, the chair stays intact. It's a first for just about anything within the walls of this dilapidated police station.

Mike takes a few steps back from Lieut. Frost. I'm not certain if it's Lieut.

Frost's mood or cologne that triggers his reaction, but I don't blame him either way. "It's the world, Lieut., not just the town. Crazy *is* the new normal."

"Truth to that," agrees Seth.

"Well, get this case cleaned up and closed by the end of the day." Lieut. Frost shoves the chair underneath the table edge and crosses his arms. "No sense in letting it linger."

Funny choice of word, given the death cloud that surrounds him. I snort and quickly cover it with a cough. Seth shakes his head, all too familiar with the way my mind works.

"Other than interviewing Mr. Mallard, assuming he pulls through, I think we've about got things squared away at the psych ward," says Mike. "I'm heading back there now to close up shop."

Lieut. Frost adjusts his glasses. "At least that's something positive. Get on it." Mike nods and exits the room.

Seth sighs and runs his fingers through his hair. He doesn't even know how sexy he is when he does that. "As much as I'd like to get the case closed this evening, there are several things we still need to look into." He picks up a picture of the false nurse from the table and stares at it. "This Trista McClure or whatever her real name is has apparently been quite busy."

"How so?" asks Lieut. Frost. He snatches the picture from Seth and glares at it as if doing so will reveal all her secrets.

If only it were that simple.

My mind clicks.

Just one touch…

"Multiple homicides across several states," says Seth. "This attack on Isaiah Mallard could be a coincidence, but I'm leaning toward the doubtful side."

"Nothing around here is ever straightforward." Lieut. Frost shakes his head. "Put this thing to bed as quickly as you can."

"Yes, sir," says Seth.

Lieut. Frost turns to Detective Roland. "Where we at with the mauling case?"

"Square one," admits Detective Roland. "Not only did Deborah and Charlie not find a single shred of evidence in their lab or the morgue as to who might've taken the body and the evidence, but every single traffic cam in the area around the morgue glitched during that same time frame. A full thirty minutes of lost footage."

For once, there's nothing Terry says that I can object to. I catch Seth's eye. "Sounds like some sort of government cover up, doesn't it?"

Seth nods his agreement. "But why?"

I glance over at Detective Roland for an answer I know he doesn't possess.

"Ernesto Vasquez was a lowlife," says Detective Roland. "A smalltime drug dealer. It doesn't make any sense as to why anyone would snatch his body."

"Button it up," says Lieut. Frost. "No sense in wasting any more resources or taxpayer dollars on it."

"Sir—"

He scowls at me. "It's not up for discussion, Bergman."

I completely disagree, and he's going to know about it. "Don't you think—"

Lieut. Frost's glare burns holes through the front of my skull. "I do. What we have is a drug dealer mauled to death in the woods. Doesn't get simpler than that. Besides, if some government spooks came in and hauled away the body and all the evidence, there's nothing we can do about it. End of story. End of discussion. Case closed." He turns back to Detective Roland. "Button. It. Up."

"But it's not—"

"Enough, Bergman." His tone could stop a charging bull. "One more word about it, and you'll be turning in your badge. Understood?"

Vitriol burns on the tip of my tongue, yet I somehow manage to keep my lips shut and nod curtly. Then, I force myself to say, "Yes, sir."

My gut tells me that there's far more to the story than what we know. Government spooks or not, there's no way I can let the case go unsolved with so many anomalies surrounding it. It's just not in my nature.

"Good." Lieut. Frost turns and exits the room.

I turn in my chair toward Detective Roland and he raises his arms in submission. "Hold on, this isn't my fault."

Rising slowly, I meet his gaze and harden mine. "Maybe not entirely, but you sure as hell didn't say anything to help our case."

Detective Roland's arm shoots out in front of himself, his hand flat and fingers spread wide. "You saw the look in Lieut. Frost's eyes. Once he gets that look, there's no changing his mind." It's a well-known fact, but it doesn't lighten my mood. "There's nothing we can do now but close the case, as instructed."

"So then what? It's all over? We forget about all the strange circumstances and findings?" I shove my chair under the table. "You're pathetic, Terry. I thought you had a backbone."

Seth rises from his chair and stands between Detective Roland and me. "Alice, you've got enough on your plate already. Just let it go."

He touches my arm and I swat his hand away. "This isn't some Frozen fairytale. You know I can't just flip a switch and move on."

"Not asking you to," says Detective Roland.

Seth and I recoil. "What?"

Detective Roland massages the back of his hand with his other thumb. "After everything that's happened with this case, you don't need to convince me that there's something off about it. We *will* close the case, but our investigation must continue."

Maybe I was wrong about Terry after all.

Seth shakes his head and sighs loudly. "You're both reckless." Then, with a wry smile, he says, "Count me in."

"Me, too." We all turn to see Kenny standing in the doorway.

"How long have you been standing there?" questions Detective Roland.

Kenny grins. "Long enough." He sits down at the table and pulls a clear evidence bag out of his backpack. It contains the shredded, blood-spattered notepad from Ernesto Vasquez's satchel.

Detective Roland scowls. "What the hell you doing with that?"

"You don't see it?" Kenny slides the bag across the table.

The three of us lean in and examine the notepad. A good portion of the top sheet has been torn off, but it's not just that. The page underneath has blood smeared across it but no spatter.

"Whoa…" I look up at Kenny. "Someone tore that page out *after* the attack."

His eyes beam. "Exactly!"

Detective Roland stands up straight and rubs the back of his neck. "What the hell does that mean?"

"I'll show you." Kenny retrieves a folded sheet of paper from his backpack and unfolds it on the table. The paper is blank except for a three-inch-wide section scribbled over with pencil. "On a hunch, I took a rubbing where the page was torn off on the notepad."

Kenny slides the paper forward. Ten digits emerge from the smudged graphite.

"A phone number?" asks Seth.

"Yeah," says Kenny. "Tracked the number to an old pay phone over on 8th and Atrisco."

"What's over there?" I ask.

"Mainly a homeless hangout," says Kenny. "It's right across the street from the shelter."

Detective Roland says, "Not the best part of town."

Seth shakes his head. "Good work, Kenny." He looks over at Detective Roland. "Like you said though, what the hell does it mean?" Detective Roland shrugs.

I push my hair behind my ears. "It means there's more going on with this Night Mauler case than we thought."

"I'll look into Ernesto Vasquez's phone records again," says Detective Roland. "See if he called that number the night he died or any time before."

"I need to go check on my father and run a few errands." I pull Seth's phone from my back pocket and shove it toward him. "Thanks for letting me borrow this."

Taking his phone, he says, "Sure you don't still need it?"

"Positive. I'm headed to get a new one right after the hospital."

Seth stuffs the phone into his jacket pocket.

Kenny reaches into his backpack and fishes out my broken phone. He holds it up. "You certainly did a number on this one."

"Might want to think about getting a case for the new one," says Detective Roland. "It'll save you some cash and a headache in the long run."

I snatch the phone from Kenny's hand and shove it in my pocket after eying the shattered screen. "I'll keep that in mind."

Kenny jumps up from his chair and grabs his backpack off the table. "I can help you pick out the perfect one. Then we can go check out that *thing* we talked about."

I roll my eyes. "It's not a secret, but we might as well get it over with before nature intervenes."

"Gonna check out the trail?" asks Seth. Kenny nods, a sheepish grin on his mug. "You guys need a lift?"

Kenny holds up a set of keys and rattles them. "Got it covered."

I guffaw. "Not a chance in hell, *intern*. We'll take my car."

Kenny shrugs. "Was worth a shot."

"Can't say you didn't try, kid," says Seth. He picks up the evidence bag and rubbing Kenny made. "I'll get these checked back into evidence."

"Thanks, Seth." I round the table and push Kenny out the door. "Let's go find that smoking gun."

CHAPTER SEVEN

KENNY BANGS HIS HEAD and drums his fingers on the dash as we cruise down the road, immersed in the heavy rhythms and growling vocals of *Hopeless Ambition* by the band For Today. The more time I spend with the kid, the more I appreciate his love of life and positive outlook in the face of adversity. His musical taste is a bonus as well, the current selection from his collection. I totally dig For Today, despite knowing they're a Christian band, and will be adding them to my workout playlist.

Three songs later, we pull into the Desert Springs Nature Preserve parking lot. Unlike two days ago, the place is deserted.

Kenny looks up when the car rolls to a stop. "Thought we were going by the hospital to see your father?"

"Didn't want the rest of our daylight escaping before we got out here. Besides, my mother would've called if anything had changed."

Kenny laughs. "You get calls on that broken phone of yours?"

I'd already forgotten about my phone. "Zip it wise—" I catch myself, almost forgetting his age. "I'll pick one up tomorrow. Now get out of the car."

"Yes, ma'am." He throws his door open and catches it with his foot just before it crushes his head as it boomerangs back.

"Call me ma'am again, and I'll make sure that door doesn't miss the next time." He nods but doesn't catch my glare with his back turned.

I grab my backpack from the trunk and squeeze my shoulders through its shoulder straps. The fit is a little tight over my jacket, but it'll have to do. Reconfiguring the straps takes several college degrees and a load of patience, and I'm all out of the latter.

"You got the coordinates of that webcam?" I ask as we enter trailhead 4A.

Kenny pulls his phone from his pocket and waves it at me. "Sure do. It's 2.7 miles ahead if we stick to the trail. 1.6 miles if we trudge through the forest."

"There will be no *trudging* on my watch."

Kenny grins. "Hoped you'd say that. The longer hike will give us more time to talk."

He reminds me of a young male version of Veronica. It's both endearing and annoying. "Looking forward to it."

Kenny doesn't catch my sarcasm. "Same."

About three seconds of peace passes before he starts in about everything around us. Trees, birds, soil, elevation. You name it. If nothing else, it keeps my mind off all the walking and my father's condition. Well, sort of.

"...and that's how you know when you're dealing with an aggressive predator," says Kenny.

I stop in the middle of the trail. "Say that again."

Kenny rounds back. "Which part?"

"The aggressive predator."

"Right. I was saying that you can easily tell if you're dealing with an aggressive predator by searching the surrounding area of its kill. More than likely, if it's hunting for sport, you'll find other kills as well."

"And you think this Night Mauler falls into that category?"

"Dunno. Did you find other kills?"

"Not that I'm aware of."

"Based solely on nature, I don't think our Night Mauler hunts for sport. Why would it have just watched the woman who found the body and not killed her as well?"

"Maybe she didn't pose a threat or wasn't a challenge."

Kenny shakes his head. "I think you're making assumptions based on human perception. From what I gathered listening to Detective Roland, the young woman—"

"Samantha George," I interject.

"Right, Ms. George. She was fit and quite the runner. The victim on the other hand was a big fellow but completely out of shape."

"You're saying that Samantha would be more of a challenge to take down based on her agility and potential strength versus the chubby guy who couldn't run to save his life."

"Exactly. After all, he's the one who was scared enough to carry a gun and a knife."

The more Kenny talks, the more I realize just how smart he is. "Play your cards right, and you just might make detective one day."

He snorts and shakes his head. "As much as I admire you and what you do, being a cop isn't in my future. A salary like that would never allow me to afford the type of care Kellie needs."

"I know. It was a jest. Your computer skills could land you a job almost anywhere."

"Who knows? There's always the FBI or CIA. MI6 or Mossad, if I want to travel."

"Not with Kellie."

He grimaces. "Right. Every decision I make must include her."

We continue down the trail in silence, and my thoughts swirl around what Kenny told me the day we met. I've never met Kellie, but I'd do almost anything for him to see her smile again as well.

I'm not a fool. I know I can't save the entire world, but that doesn't mean that I can't help make Kenny's life easier. All avenues in life lead to money, and that's something I do have to offer. Living with Mother, who refuses to take a dime of my money, and getting a full scholarship to Desert Springs College have allowed me to save most of the money I've made working for DSPD. Seven years of paychecks sit in the bank collecting dust.

But would he accept money?

Kenny's phone starts beeping faster and louder with each step until it becomes a solid hum. "That means we're within three feet of the webcam."

We both stop and look around. Kenny spots the camera first and points it out. Its camouflage shell blends right in with the bark of the tree it's strapped to.

"Good eye, Kenny." I turn and face the same direction as the camera.

The difference in lighting between dawn and the angle of the afternoon sun makes everything look out of sorts. It's disorienting, even with knowledge of the webcam position. But then I spot the tree where we caught those yellow eyes watching Samantha George.

I point across the trail. "Over there."

"You're right." He chuckles. "And you say I'm the one with a good eye."

I take my flashlight from my belt clip and click it on. "Follow me, and watch where you step."

"Right behind you." Kenny shakes his phone and two LED lights come on. The modern flashlight.

We move through the brush methodically, examining every inch of ground and sprig of grass, weed, and plant. As we round the tree trunk, my heart sinks. Sitting next to our suspect tree is an old stump that sits about three feet high and is roughly two feet in diameter. A perfect spot for any animal to perch.

Kenny sighs. "I swear we were on to something."

"So did I."

A small crack runs across the top of the stump, about an inch wide in the middle and around nine inches in total length. Closer inspection of it sends my pulse soaring.

I nudge Kenny with my elbow. "Look at what's caught in the crack."

He leans closer. Cocks his head. "A red hair…"

"Exactly. It could prove that the animal that killed Ernesto Vasquez is the same one that watched Samantha George."

"But that evidence was stolen. They'll have nothing to compare it to."

"True, but the first hair was distinct enough that a fair comparison can easily be made."

"Okay."

I stand up straight and turn away from him. "Grab the extraction kit out of my backpack so we can bag it."

A minute later, Kenny dons a pair of latex gloves. The large-sized gloves droop from his hands like excessive skin on a person who's lost an extraordinary amount of weight. But they fit better than the medium-sized ones that were too short for his long fingers. Using a pair of tweezers, he fishes out the red hair from the crack and bags it.

After returning the bag and kit to my backpack, Kenny looks toward the trail. "It's the perfect spot to watch the trail from."

The spot is perfectly shaded, even in the daylight. "Almost too perfect."

Kenny nods and turns back toward me. "Now what?"

"Let's search this area some more and see if we can find additional evidence of what this thing might be."

He sweeps his hand to the side. "Lead the way."

I check the time on my phone. "We've only got about an hour of decent light left. We'll cover more ground if we split up." I point to the left. "Head back that way, and I'll go the other way."

"You got it," he says with a grin.

"Just holler if you find something."

"You, too."

We head off in opposite directions, our flashlights serving as the only reliable source of light in this densely populated section of forest. Ten minutes in, I've found nothing but a few hoof prints from a deer and a handful of snapped twigs, and those were likely broken by the deer as it passed through the underbrush.

Twenty minutes later, I'm ready to pack it in, and that's when I hear Kenny's call. "Detective Bergman!" He sounds like he's a good mile away. "You've got to see this!"

It takes another ten minutes to locate Kenny *after* he sends me his GPS location via Google Maps. When I come up next to him, I see that we're standing at the edge of a natural spring. The running water is shallow and only about a foot wide, with many sections of it flowing beneath the fall debris.

I sweep the area directly in front of us with my flashlight beam but see nothing obvious. "What exactly are we looking at?"

Kenny kneels and points the light from his phone to the other side of the spring, about four feet to my left and another foot beyond where we stand. "See it?" he whispers.

The light shakes in his trembling hand, but not enough to distort my view of the distinct paw print pressed into the soft ground, parallel to the stream of water. Its shape is similar to those I've seen of a dog or coyote, but wider and a bit longer. More akin to what I imagine I'd see from a wolf.

I pat Kenny on the shoulder. "Good eye. Let's photograph the paw print and take a casting."

He shakes his head slowly and takes my flashlight. "There's more. Look about a foot beyond the paw print on this side of the spring."

Kneeling next to him, my eyes follow the flashlight beam until I finally see what's gotten him so worked up, and it leaves me gasping for air. "Auh!"

The hairs on my nape stand on end, and goosebumps spread like a virus across my skin. My heart pumps faster. Louder in my ears.

The second depression in the soft ground crashes my mind. Leaves me kneeling there with my mouth gaping as I wait for it to boot back up. "My God…"

"Right?" He shines the light farther upstream. "It's not an anomaly. The tracks continue for a fair distance before disappearing."

I grab Kenny's arm and force him to look at me. "This stays between us for now. Do you understand?"

He nods. "Who would believe us even if we showed it to them?"

"I'm not sure." A few names come to mind, but I'm not sure they'd understand either. "Probably no one."

I slide my backpack off my shoulders and dig out the casting kit. "Take as many pictures and as much video as you can. I'll cast as many of the prints as I can."

Both of us set to work and spend the next hour photographing, videoing, and casting the dozen prints straddling the spring even as dusk transitions into nightfall. By the time the casts set, we're left in total darkness and a long way from the car. With the night comes the sounds of the forest, many of which seem more ominous than they probably are.

Several times on the way back to the car, we hear rustling in the bushes and spot glowing eyes in the deep shadows, but none of them appear to be the ones we fear seeing. After what we just discovered, I can't help but wonder if the Night Mauler lives somewhere far closer to civilization than anyone imagined. The thought leaves me shuddering from head to toe.

CHAPTER EIGHT

THE SIGN ON THE door of Rico's Cane Shoppe is turned to closed and the lights are off inside. The door rattles when I bang on it with my palm. After a dozen seconds without a response, I beat on it again. Pressing my forehead against the glass, I peer into the dimly lit store. No shadows stir and nothing moves inside, but there's a faint light emanating from the edges of the black curtain that leads to the back of the store.

It's 09:24 according to the glowing red digits of the clock hanging on the wall inside. The posted hours on the door specify 9am as the opening time. It's unlike Rico to close the store during business hours or be late opening. After what happened with my father yesterday morning, I'm a tad paranoid that the Shadow Priests might've come for Rico, too. My sweaty palms prove it.

Thinking back on the day Rico took me down to the basement that shouldn't exist, I recall a delivery door at the back of the shop. Rounding the back corner of the building, I spot two vehicles. I'm fairly certain that the red Jeep Cherokee is Rico's, but I've never seen the blue Maserati GranTurismo. If I had, I would've pulled it over just to take a peek. The GranTurismo hood is still warm to the touch.

The back door stands ajar. Two distinct voices, both heated but muffled, filter through the crack. One is Rico's, but the other I don't recognize. A female with an accent I can't place. Drawing my gun, I ease the door open with my foot and slip through the narrow gap.

The traitorous door squeaks at the last moment, but it's the least of my problems. A silver-barreled pistol gleams underneath a single buzzing fluorescent light just before its muzzle presses against my left temple.

"Holster your weapon," growls the woman. She's standing in the shadows and out of my field of vision.

Adrenaline rushes into my veins as my gun slides into its holster. I've trained for this exact situation so many times. Practiced with Seth.

Arms raised, I take a deep breath and let my training take over. Each heartbeat brings with it a precise movement.

Thump-thump.

Head tilts forward and arm arcs back in unison.

Thump-thump.

Wrist cracks against wrist as I wrap my left hand around her wrist and push the gun away from my body.

Thump-thump.

Twisting around, I grab the gun with my free hand and slide my other hand forward, over the gun barrel.

Thump-thump.

Foot stomps hers as my right elbow collides with her sternum.

Thump-thump.

Grabbing the gun, I twist around and get it pointed straight at her.

Thump-thump.

Yanking the gun free, I retreat a few steps and aim for her eyes. "Move a muscle, and you're dead."

Click!

The sound is distinct. Unmistakable. A revolver hammer cocked.

And it's behind me.

"Could say the same of you, darlin'." A gravelly, male voice. Texas accent.

I'm such a fool.

How could I have missed detecting him? The smell of his aftershave hangs in the air like a thick fog. The woman steps forward and relieves me of her gun.

Across the room, draped in shadows, stands another man. The green, alligator skin cowboy boots are a dead giveaway.

Rico.

My eyes meet Rico's gaze. His flattened lips curl into a smile when recognition triggers. "Hijita! What are you doing here?" He steps forward and into the light. "Dakota, this is the one we spoke of before."

"The blind girl?" She moves into the light, next to Rico, and holsters her gun. Her dark eyes meet mine as she cocks her head.

"Detective Alice Bergman," I squawk.

"Yes, of course." Dakota's slender fingers wrap around Rico's wrist. A knowing touch he doesn't shy away from. "You never mentioned her beauty."

"Didn't I?" He winks at me and then addresses the man positioned at my back. "Ease off, hijo. We're all amigos here."

The man uncocks his weapon and skirts around me with a wide birth. The big guy flanks Rico's left. At least six-five, but it's hard to gauge with the big black cowboy hat perched atop his head. The brim's drawn low over his eyes, casting his features in shadow, but his two gold-capped teeth gleam in the light. A wad of snuff pushes out his lower lip. At least that's my guess as to what it is.

"Girl's got some skills," says the man.

Rico nods. "She does, but that was nothing—"

"I'm not here to discuss my skills," I say, cutting Rico off. "We need to talk." I glare daggers at Dakota and then the man in the cowboy hat. "Alone."

"No worries." Dakota pulls the bulk of her long, black hair over her shoulder and runs her fingers through it before tossing it back behind her. "We were just about to leave when you came knocking." She rises on her tippy toes and kisses Rico's cheek, her gaze still locked on me. "It was good to see you again, my friend."

"Likewise." Rico takes her hand and lifts it to his lips. With a light kiss on her knuckles, he says, "Don't be a stranger."

"Never." She withdraws from Rico. "Let's go, Jake."

Rico proffers his hand toward Jake, and the big man takes it. "Cuida de tu mamá, hijo mío."

"Si padre." Jake tips his hat toward me as he walks past. "A pleasure, darlin'."

Dakota trails Jake, her dark gaze never breaking from mine as she draws near. "I'm certain we'll meet again." Her minty breath lingers in my nostrils even as she exits through the back door.

Moments later, the Maserati roars to life. Shakes my chest with its power. What I wouldn't give to be behind its wheel. Tires grip and rip the pavement, peppering the door and outside wall with rocks as the car accelerates out of the alley with heavenly thunder.

Rico closes and locks the door. Not sure how he walked right past me without detection. I'm certain it had nothing to do with the car of my dreams that just took off. Or my closed eyes as I imagined my fingers wrapped around its leather steering wheel.

"Tell me what you've come to talk to me about this time, hijita." His eyes glisten in the light.

My gaze falls toward my hands as they fold together in front of me. "My father, this new case I'm working, and also the Shad—"

"Not here." A finger rises to his lips, and his other hand touches my shoulder.

I glance over at the row of cabinets lining the wall to my left and gesture toward them with my head.

Rico nods. "It's the safest place for us to talk. No one can hear us within its walls."

A strange and absurd thought manifests in my mind, and I can't shake it.

I need to search my house, office, and car for bugs. And Seth's condo.

* * * * *

Everything in the basement is just as I remember it: dozens of pedestals with glass enclosures featuring items straight from a science fiction magazine, and a ten-foot, transparent cube at the center of the large room where I first wielded Esther, my trusty white cane with special powers. I could spend weeks here exploring each item, but they aren't the reason why I came.

Rico and I settle on the last step of the stairway once the entrance above finishes closing us in. I'm not claustrophobic, and the room is gigantic, but it doesn't prevent my chest from tightening or my lungs from wheezing. It's pathetic, but there's nothing I can do to change it.

"Let's start with your father," says Rico. "Who is he, and what's happened?"

It takes twenty minutes to fill Rico in on all the details surrounding my father, including his paranoia and incarceration in the psychiatric ward. Then I tell him about the attack my father suffered at the hands of the Shadow Priests and the threat they made on my life. By the end of the detailed account, my eyes are wet with tears and my heart is bitter once again.

How could Mother keep his existence from me for so long?

"I can see it in your eyes, hijita. You're blaming yourself for the attack, aren't you?"

"My father survived decades before I exposed him. How am I not to blame?"

"You couldn't have known they were watching. Besides, I'm certain your father has no regrets in meeting you." He leans forward and rests his hand over mine. "I certainly don't. And, for the record, you're not alone in this war. There are more of us than they think."

"There are?" I ask.

"Dozens," he says with finality.

Among billions of people…

Futility overwhelms me, but I keep my mouth shut, knowing anything I might say about it would do neither of us any good. Instead, I move the focus of the conversation back onto my father. "Do you know him? My father, that is."

Rico scratches his stubbly chin. It sounds reminiscent of high grit sandpaper against wood. "Isaiah Mallard…" He rises from the step and paces back and forth in front of me. "The name isn't familiar."

"What about Philip Isaiah Sudermann? That was his birth name."

"Hmm…" He shakes his head slowly. "Not ringing any bells. I've known many of our people over the years, but apparently not him. Stands to reason as to why I knew nothing of you."

"*Our* people? You say that like we're from some remote African tribe."

Rico stops pacing and faces me, his head cocked to the side. "After what you've seen and experienced, you're still not a believer?"

I shrug and wipe the moisture from the corners of my eyes. "How can I believe any of it? It's as absurd as some omnipotent, omnipresent, all-knowing god watching us with rapt fascination like we're some sort of botched science experiment."

Rico bends down, his hands on his knees, and nods knowingly. "There was a time when I believed the way you do, hijita."

My gaze focuses on the tattooed letters across his knuckles. *Jesus Freak.* Two words, one on each hand. "What changed your mind? What pushed you toward the absurd? Toward God? What made you a 'Jesus Freak?'"

His eyes gleam in the fluorescent light. "If you live long enough, you'll see and experience things that warrant no explanation outside of the existence of a heavenly creator."

Two strands of hair cut loose from behind my ear and fall across my left eye. A quick puff of air from my lips only worsens the situation. I sweep back the greasy strands with my finger and wonder when I last showered. "You don't think we're here by accident?"

"Do you feel like an accident? I certainly don't. Think about it." He stares at his hands as he flexes them. "How could we not have been designed?"

"I don't know. If there is a god who created everything, then why are things so messed up?"

"Sin, hijita. When sin entered this world through the first man, Adam, God punished all of creation by allowing death to enter as well. That decay corrupts all of creation, right down to every last living cell."

"Yeah, I've been to Sunday school. Heard all the tales. But I think it's all random. That's what creates the chaos and decay."

Rico raises his hands and looks to the ceiling. "Ay yi yi. Nothing is random."

"Says you."

He runs his hand through his hair and pulls on its stringy ends. "Think of it this way. When you go to an art gallery and look at all the paintings and sculptures, do you think about how some random event spontaneously conjured them?"

I laugh. "No, because each piece has an artist."

Rico slaps his thigh. "Exactly! They were created *with* design. Same as we are. God created each of us uniquely. Can't you see it?"

I'd never contemplated life in those terms, but it did seem to have some truth to it. Either way, I didn't come here to have a philosophical or religious debate. "God aside, how do you *know* this other world exists?"

Rico kneels on one knee before me and stares into my eyes. I've never seen such intensity in them. Such longing. But there's more. A deep sorrow. "I was born there, hijita—" Tears streak down his cheeks. "—and one day I hope to return."

If I hadn't been sitting, my legs would've collapsed underneath the weight of his sorrow. "But… how?"

His eyes close as he sits back on his foot. Several moments pass in silence before he finally speaks. "A decades-long war devastated our world, and a new king rose to power when it came to an end. At first, we cheered for his rule, but then he turned on those of us born with magic—the *zhiftäd* or *gifted* in English—and threatened life as we knew it, vowing to eradicate us."

"Just like the Shadow Priests hunt us."

"Precisely. From the king's eyes, the previous war would never have taken place if we hadn't existed. A large portion of the population agreed with him. Because of this, several militant groups formed and began hunting us. Desperate to preserve life, a group of powerful wizards conjured three portals between our world and this one to try and help some of the *zhiftäd* escape the king's wrath."

It doesn't take a genius to see that Rico believes every last word of his tale, but I just can't get on board with it, let alone wrap my head around it. "Don't take this wrong, but it sounds more like a tale from a fantasy novel than reality."

Rico chuckles and nods his head. "Yes it does—" His smile fades and his eyes sober. "—but where do you think those tales come from?"

"I guess I've never thought about it."

"Most legends are rooted in truth." He leans forward and proffers his hand. "Let me see your wrist again."

I offer my left arm to him with a hint of reluctance. Not because I'm afraid to show him the mark, but because of what he might tell me about it. "As I said, it's just a birthmark." My words hold about as much confidence as a bottomless glass.

Ragged breaths escape from Rico's lips as he traces each raised line on the inside of my left wrist with unspoken reverence. His thumb glides around the outline of an eye and across the sickle's curved blade. The birthmark rises above my skin like a raised scar, and gooseflesh pimples my arm.

"What does it mean?" My breath is almost as ragged as his.

Rico's eyes narrow into slits. "Because you were born into this world, your symbol is unique. But I assure you that it's the mark of..."

He releases my arm and stares at me until I'm squirming on the step with anticipation of his next words.

Spit it out, already.

"A wizard," he finally finishes.

The entire world screeches to a halt as my mind refuses to accept his words for truth. "Either you're messing with me, or I didn't hear you correctly."

"I said wizard, and I meant it. At some point, you must come to terms with the fact that you're different. If it helps to think of yourself as gifted and not as a wizard, then think in those terms, but it is truly no different."

Am I gifted, or is it a curse?

Rico continues, "If I'm not mistaken, the mark on your wrist means you possess an ability to see past death and into a person's past—" He cocks his head. "—but you already knew that, didn't you?"

The weight of his gaze is far too heavy for me to hold, so I peer down at my wrist. The symbol is still raised. "Yes, and it matches my father's... but how did you know that? Do you have a mark as well?"

"The answer to your first question is a good guess based on all the symbols I've seen in my life. And, to answer your second question..." Rico unbuttons the left cuff of his shirt and rolls back his sleeve, exposing the inside of his wrist. "All of us who are gifted do."

The reddish-brown mark, an eye within a diamond or four-pointed star, blends well with his skin tone. Our eyes meet as my heart hammers in my chest.

"Yours isn't the same as mine," I say, stating the obvious. "What does it mean?"

"In the most simplistic of terms, I am a seeker."

I take in all the glass cases around the basement with renewed vision. "How does it work?"

"Items from our world call out to me. It's like I'm some sort of magnet that they're drawn to." He balls his hands and crashes them together. "My gift didn't work this way in the other world. There, I would think of an object and feel a pull toward its location."

"So why haven't you been able to find the Shadow Mirror?"

Rico groans. "As far as I can tell, the Shadow Mirror doesn't come from our world. It must've been created in this world."

I look back down at my wrist. "What else does it mean? Is this the reason I was born blind? Because I'm a freak?"

"A freak? Nothing could be farther from the truth." His fingers touch the underside of my chin and gently lift my head until I'm forced to meet his gaze once again. "Your ability is a gift from God, hijita. It is his way of showing you how special and unique you are."

"Mother would disagree with you. If she knew what I could do, she'd disown me and label me a spawn of Satan."

"I only know your mother in passing, but I find that hard to believe. I've never seen anyone protect their child as fiercely as she did you. As with God, her love for you is unconditional."

I roll my eyes. "Tell that to Father Rogallo. He claims that me gaining my vision was the work of the devil. Deep down, I think Mother feels the same way."

And so do I.

"And yet she still loves you more than life itself." His brow wrinkles. "Are those two things compatible? Can they both be true?"

My heart pounds in my chest like a war drum. I'd never thought of it like that. How could Mother love and serve her god and still care for someone possessed by or in allegiance with her mortal enemy, the devil? The two must be mutually exclusive. "I guess not."

"Very good." He rejoins me on the step and clasps his hands together. "What else is weighing on your mind?"

Where do I start?

I shift on the step so that I can face Rico. "You and my father have a way of skirting every conversation concerning the Shadow Priests. It's time you tell me what you know of them. Who are they? Where do they come from? How can I stop them from killing us all?"

"Let me start from the beginning… or at least the beginning of what I understand to be true." Rico clears his throat and then wipes his mouth with the back of his hand. "Back in 1748, a man named Josiah Clarkson stumbled upon the Shadow Mirror in Oxford, England. When he discovered the mirror's true power—that it showed him people with unnatural abilities—, it scared the devil out of him.

"Years later, he met up with several individuals who shared his disdain when shown what the mirror could do. Those men and women came together and formed the original Shadow Priests. The sole purpose of their cult was to hunt down and exterminate anyone not of this world—what we call the Shadow World. Their belief was that if they didn't perform this service, their world would be overrun, and humans would eventually be bred out of existence."

"I'm still not buying into this *other world* business, but for argument's sake let's say it's true. Based on this *truth*, are you saying that you and I aren't human?"

"Others like us have studied themselves, and there are no genetic differences between humans of our world and humans of this world. As far as we understand it, the difference lies within our minds—or rather our brains. We use portions of our brain that native humans seem to lack access to. Beyond this, there is no distinguishable difference."

I hold up my left arm. "With the exception of these marks."

"That's only true for those of us who are gifted."

"And you know others like us?" Rico nods. "Can I meet them?"

"It's not for me to decide," says Rico, "but I'm sure you'll meet many more of us over time."

So I've met others already? I need to start paying more attention.

"Fine. So how does this Shadow Mirror help them track us down if we're no different from them?"

"I'm uncertain of the history behind the Shadow Mirror, but I can tell you that it only shows them children and those like us."

"All children? And how do you know that?"

"Yes, all children. I saw it once and confronted the woman who had it at the time. Certain she had the upper hand on me, she divulged more than she should've. Basically, the mirror doesn't distinguish between children who haven't gone through puberty yet and those like us. That's why they study many children for years before making a move. Thankfully, they made a sacred vow to never kill anyone native to this world."

That's why Russell waited so long to try to kill me.

"Why didn't you destroy the mirror right then?" I ask.

"Trust me, I would've if it were possible. But I was far outnumbered and barely escaped with my life. When I returned to the location, everything had been cleared out, just like what happened with you."

"And you've never seen the Shadow Mirror again?"

"As far as I know, no one had until you."

"If only I'd known what it was." I stretch my legs out and brood over the lives that could've been saved. Anger rises in my chest. "Where can I find them? How can I stop them?"

"I can't answer that." Rico's expression turns grim. "If I could, they'd be dead already," he says through gritted teeth.

"We will find them." My stomach lurches.

If they don't find us first.

"I know five names. How many do you know or have known?"

"What you're asking is how many I've killed." He pulls a small black book from his inside jacket pocket and hands it to me.

My pulse races as I crack it open and scan the names. Dozens. Hundreds. Pages of them. Each entry contains a name, location, physical description of the person, and what they do for a living.

"Every name I've ever known to be associated with the Shadow Priests is written in there. An X next to their name means they're dead. The data is a compilation from many sources, not just mine. Make yourself a copy if you'd like, but I'll need it back."

I study every page for several seconds and then hand it back to him. "No need."

Rico gasps. "You've memorized it, haven't you?"

I shrug. "Photographic memory. A curse and a blessing."

"You are a wonder…"

"You might want to add Russell, Reagan, and Morgan to your list. Russell's the only one who's dead."

Rico retrieves a pen from his pocket and writes down the names I gave him in the book. I provide as much detail of each as I can, explaining that Reagan and Morgan are in possession of the Shadow Mirror. At least as far as I know.

"I didn't see an entry for a Dashna in there," I say once Rico's finished writing. "Ever heard the name before?"

"Don't think I have."

"She's dead, too. Along with her sister. Not sure what her name is, but she was using the alias Trista McClure. She's the one who attacked my father. I don't know anything else about either of them."

Rico scribbles their names into his book, stands tall, and stretches his legs. "Have I answered all your questions to your satisfaction?"

"For now… but there is something else you might be able to help me with."

"Lay it on me, hijita."

"Did you hear about the mauling at the Desert Springs Nature Preserve a few days ago?"

He nods. "Who hasn't?"

"Well, there are several things about the case that have come into question."

"Really? I thought it was an open-and-shut case. A straightforward animal mauling." He sits back down next to me. "What is the media not telling us?"

"They certainly can't be trusted to tell the truth, but it's not like that." I lean close and continue in a hushed tone, "What I'm about to tell you isn't known knowledge outside of the police department. Promise me that what I'm about to disclose won't leave this basement."

He pats my knee. "Nothing we discuss ever leaves my lips without your consent."

"Good."

"So what's got you worked up about this mauling?"

"First off, someone stole the body and all the lab work from the morgue."

His eyebrows rise. "Well that certainly doesn't happen every day, does it?"

"Never in the history of the morgue has it happened. Sane people don't just go around stealing dead bodies."

"I suppose not. That'd be a nasty business for sure." Rico turns the plain silver ring that clings to his left ring finger. "So who do you think stole it? Obviously not the attacker, right?" He chuckles.

"Funny you bring that up. On the surface it looks to be a routine animal mauling, so the answer would be no. However, there's nothing routine about this case."

His eyes grow wide. "Really? How so, besides the body thief?"

"Trust me, it gets more interesting and disturbing. First, our CSI techs discovered several anomalies before all the files and samples were removed from the lab and wiped from the hard drives. Dozens of red hairs were found on the victim's clothing and embedded within the deep gashes carved into the victim's chest."

"You'd expect that kind of evidence in a mauling though, right?" asks Rico.

"Yes, but the thick, porous hairs match no known species of animal. The closest match the CSI techs found was from a Siberian wolf."

"A Siberian wolf in Desert Springs, Arizona?" Rico shakes his head. "What would the odds of that be?"

"Zero, I'd say, but it gets stranger still. The DNA results from the saliva extracted from the victim's neck wounds came back as a mixture of both wolf and human."

"Wolf *and* human saliva?" He whistles. "Wow, that is something. Surely those samples must've been contaminated in some way, right?"

I nod. "That would be the rational explanation."

He leans back against the stairwell wall and studies me for several seconds. "But you're not sold on that, are you?"

"Ask me that a thousand times and I'd say yes nine hundred and ninety-nine of them."

Rico shifts on the step and leans closer. "So what makes this case the one exception?"

"To be honest, it started off as intuition."

"And you get these feelings a lot?"

"Yes, and I'm rarely wrong when I do... but there's more to it than that. The young woman who discovered the body said that she felt like she was being watched several times during her morning run before discovering the body. She swore she saw a pair of yellow eyes watching her from the shadows when she stopped to take in her surroundings several times."

"Perhaps it was nothing more than her sensing death ahead," Rico offers. "We humans have an innate ability—"

I raise my hand. "Let me stop you there."

"Fair enough," he says with a frown.

"One of those times she happened to stop in front of one of the many webcams located throughout the preserve. The moment was caught on video."

Rico turns and faces me on the step, his brow furrowed deep. "And you found something?"

"Yes, but not enough to go on."

He leans in closer, his gaze intense. "Don't hold back on me now, hijita. What did you see?" The smell of cherry tobacco on his breath rises in my nostrils. It's not unpleasant.

Closing my eyes, I watch the video play back in my mind. "Two yellow eyes watch the woman from the shadows and blink out when she looks in their direction."

He latches onto my arm, his large hand easily wrapping around it. "You must've discovered something more significant in the video than just the yellow eyes. Am I right?"

I shake my head. "Nothing conclusive other than what looks to be a pointed ear."

Rico sighs heavily and releases my arm. "Well that's unfortunate."

"No doubt. However, there was one other detail that we initially found interesting about the eyes. Well, not the eyes themselves but their positioning in relation to the ground. When we calculated the distance from the ground to the eyes, we came up with a number close to six feet."

"Six feet?" he repeats.

"Yeah. We wondered what kind of wolf could stand six feet tall, too."

"Not even dire wolves or wargs stand that tall."

"Not even in Middle-earth?" I say with a snort.

He scowls at me. "Joke all you want, but I believe Tolkien knew the truth."

"Anyway, there are none that tall. But what if…" As the words swirl in my mind, they become more absurd. How can I bring myself to say what I'm thinking without sounding like a crazed fool?

"We're the only ones here, hijita. Even though I have a good idea of what you're probably thinking, I'd like to hear it from your lips so that I don't influence your words."

I shake my head. "It's foolish."

"You're talking to a man who claims to be from another world ruled by magic. How foolish can it be?"

He's right, and I know it, but it doesn't make it any easier to voice my thoughts. "Fine. What I'm saying is…" I lean forward on the step, place my elbows on my knees, and pull my hair back with my hands. "Ugh. This is going to sound completely absurd, but do you think it's possible that a human who looks like an animal could've attacked the victim?"

"You think you've got a werewolf on your hands?" Rico chuckles. "This coming from the girl who doesn't believe in a god?"

"Ugh! That's not what I meant by that." I nudge him with my elbow. "I was thinking of something more like an escaped science experiment. You know, some sort of genetic hybrid. I've read about so many strange experiments going on around the world." I face him again. "Do you think it's possible?"

His eyes sparkle, and for a moment I think it's not just a trick of light. "Science could play a part in it, but there might be a better explanation. Something more obvious."

"And what would that be?" I ask.

"A log or stump hidden behind the bushes. Perhaps this wolf of yours was perched atop it."

"Believe it or not, we did think of that."

"And you went back and checked?"

I roll my eyes. "Yes…"

"Ah, so you did find a place for it to perch."

"We did, and also found a red hair on top of the stump as well, but that doesn't explain the human saliva in the victim's wounds."

"True." He scratches his chin. "Perhaps someone coughed or sneezed on the sample and was afraid of admitting to it."

Doubt creeps into the corners of my mind and lurks in the shadows. "I don't know…"

Rico stands and helps me to my feet. "Either way, I'd suggest you leave it alone. Wolves are dangerous creatures, especially if they feel threatened." He presses the button on the wall and the shelves above begin sliding to the side, our conversation obviously over.

My gut tells me that Rico knows more than he's letting on, and I want to push him further on it, but I also sense that now isn't the time.

"Thank you, Rico." I begin climbing the stairs. "I'll take your warning under advisement," I say, knowing full well I won't stop until I find answers.

Kenny's discovery of the tracks in the forest might lead us to nothing, but I can't shake the feeling that there's something more sinister afoot.

Maybe Seth can add some perspective.

CHAPTER NINE

THE UNUSUALLY LARGE LUNCH crowd at Wired Coffee relegates Seth and me to the back corner of the shop. It's the perfect location, given the sensitive nature of the conversation we're about to have. A few minutes later, Kenny arrives.

"So what's this about?" asks Seth after Kenny settles into his chair.

I look to Kenny, and he gives me a nod. "Kenny found something very interesting last night when we were at the preserve."

Seth scowls at me. "And why didn't you present it at our morning meeting?"

"Once you see it, you'll understand."

Kenny pulls a laptop out of his backpack and sets it on the table where only the three of us can see it. "I uploaded all the pictures and video footage this morning and ran some initial analysis on it. Based on my findings, the tracks we found were left by a single entity."

I gasp. Seth scowls deeper. "Mind explaining what it is you're trying to say?"

Kenny brings up an image of the paw print we discovered at the preserve. "This is the first item of interest. Based on size alone, we're looking for a giant species of wolf that hasn't existed for millennia." He superimposes his hand over the paw print, and they are remarkably similar in size.

Seth scratches his head. "The scaling is accurate?"

"To the nanometer," Kenny confirms.

"This beast must be massive."

"You saw the carnage at the preserve," I say. "Imagine the strength it would take to bring down a 260 pound man and rip him open like an aluminum can."

"Point taken, but I still don't see what the secrecy is all about."

I place my hand over Seth's on the table. "Just sit back and listen and it'll be quite clear."

Kenny continues, "Now check this out." He pulls up another image. "This foot is a size twelve US."

"I'll take your word for it." Seth leans closer to the monitor. "Looks like both images were taken in the same area."

"Good eye, Detective," says Kenny.

"What kind of person would be out in the forest barefoot?" asks Seth.

"That's a good question, but not *the* question," I say and nod at Kenny. "Show him the video footage."

Kenny pulls up the video he took of the spring and the prints. We all watch with rapt attention as the camera sweeps along the narrow stream of water, capturing the footprints and paw prints that straddle its foot-wide body.

"Someone was with this wolf beast…" Seth's voice trails off.

"That's what we thought at first, too." Kenny pulls up another video of the same area, but this one's taken in the daylight.

My head whips around to face Kenny. "You went back?"

He grins and shrugs. "Needed to be sure of what we were looking at."

"You're an intern, Kenny. You can't be risking your life like that, especially when you've got Kellie to think about."

"Who's Kellie?" asks Seth.

"My little sister." Kenny refocuses on the laptop screen. "I went back and redirected the spring's flow so that I could get a better idea of what we were really looking at. I wanted to make sure that we weren't missing data underneath the debris and water stream."

Kenny plays the video. The leaves have carefully been pushed away from the area and the stream redirected, as he said. What his analysis reveals is far more shocking than I'd imagined.

"There aren't enough prints for a set of either," says Seth, alarm in his voice. "Right paw prints and left footprints."

"Exactly," says Kenny with excitement. "As I stated earlier, we've got a single entity. Part human and part beast."

"That's not possible," says Seth. "You must've missed the other prints."

"I thought so at first, too, and that's why I had to go back. The stream is only a foot wide, a distance easily straddled without effort. Based on the gait and distance between prints, they are definitely from a single source."

A single source…

* * * * *

After a long shower and a short nap, I head across town to RingBack, our local cellphone store. Two hours later, the young woman helping me finally returns from some back office with my new Motorola phone in hand.

She smiles, revealing a mouth full of metal. "It was touch and go at times, but I managed to salvage all of your data, contacts, photos, and videos. They're loaded on the phone and ready to go."

"Thank you—" I read her name tag with a quick glance. "—Stacy."

"You're welcome, Ms. Bergman." She puts the phone in a bag with all the additional accessories and hands it to me. "I hope your visit and my service were satisfactory."

"As well as expected." I turn to leave, and she follows me across the store.

"There's a survey on the bottom of your receipt. I'd really appreciate it if you filled it out. Helps with promotions."

"Consider it done," I say and exit the store before she has a chance to delay me further.

The phone springs to life inside the bag, uttering ghastly noises and vibrating harder than a massage chair. I dig into the bag and extract the phone. Its notification window displays fourteen missed calls, twelve text messages, and a half-dozen voicemails. Most of them are from Mother, so I return her call after I climb into my car.

"Hello, Mother. I just picked up my new phone a few minutes ago. How's Isaiah doing?"

The badgering begins immediately. "Why aren't you here? You've been gone the past twenty-four hours and left me here all by myself to deal with your father. I've been worried sick for the both of you. God knows I prayed all day and night. Where are you? Are you on your way back over here?"

"I'm sorry I left you alone, and I hate what's happened to Isaiah, but you know I still have a job to do."

"Your job can wait."

The woman makes me want to bash my skull against the steering wheel. "For what? Is there something I can do over there?"

She sighs loudly. "I suppose not. Due to the stress Isaiah's body has gone through with the attack and subsequent surgery, the doctors have limited his visitors to just one for now."

I nearly toss my new phone across the car. Instead, I take a deep breath and allow the anger to settle. "Well, that settles it then. There's no point in me going over there just to sit in the waiting room by myself when I can be working the case with Seth."

"All you ever do is work," she groans.

I stare vacantly through the windshield, oblivious to the people passing by on the sidewalk. "Don't you want to know who attacked Isaiah and why?"

"Yes, of course, but why can't Seth handle it on his own? From what little he told me, I've gathered that it was a random act of violence."

"That's where you're wrong, Mother." I lean my head against the driver's side window. Its cold touch soothes my burning cheek. "At least on the second count. Seth and I watched the attack footage from the security camera in Isaiah's room. The people he claimed were after him are real. He's not insane. At least not for that reason."

"Dear God… is it true, Isaiah?" Her voice is distant. Silence hangs on the line for several seconds before Mother returns to our conversation. "Is he safe here? Will they come after him again?" Panic fills her voice.

"The woman who attacked him is dead, so I think he's safe for now."

Mother sighs with relief. "Praise the Lord."

"And what have the doctors said? Will he recover?"

"They say it's a miracle he survived and believe he'll make a full recovery, but it will be a long road ahead. He continues to teeter on the edge of consciousness and groans incoherently from time to time."

Fighting demons in his sleep.

My phone says we've been on the line for twenty minutes. "Look, Mother, I need to go. Will you be home later?"

"I'm not leaving Isaiah's side until he's ready to walk out of here."

"Fine. I'll tell Vee to stop in and check on you this evening before her shift. I'll have her bring you some food, too."

"Please do, but the food isn't necessary. The nurses here have been very kind to me."

"Good. I'll come see you in the morning."

"Sounds good. I love you, Alice. Be safe, and may our Lord Jesus Christ watch over you."

"Um, yeah. You, too." A girl with fiery-red hair and a green trench coat saunters past my car on the sidewalk as I hang up with Mother.

The girl from the cafe.

My heart thunders and my palms moisten as I climb out of the car and shut the door. I start to call out to her but think better of it. The last thing I want to do is scare her off, so instead I set my phone on silent and follow her down the sidewalk.

She crosses several streets and traverses a handful of back alleys before entering the North Highlands High School campus. The buildings themselves hold little meaning for me since I was blind during my three years attending the school. However, stepping foot onto the school grounds floods my mind with memories, many of which I'd gladly delete from my data banks if possible. Outside of my friendship with Veronica, little else positive ever came from this place.

Why has she come here, especially at dusk?

The girl enters the looming sports complex ahead and disappears into the darkness. From what I recall, there's a corridor that surrounds the gymnasium that leads to the girl's and boy's locker rooms and several other torture chambers—cardio and weight-lifting rooms, wrestling room, volleyball courts, etc.

A solid minute passes before I follow her in, completely aware of the several dozen places she could ambush me inside. In my mind, the front door squawks as it closes behind me, a thunderous noise that quakes the ground and alerts everyone within a three-mile radius of my presence. The reality of the noise is a mild squeak, yet it still sets my pulse racing, and several deep breaths do nothing to settle me.

Ten paces ahead, light spills across the floor through two small glass panes and from underneath the closed gymnasium doors. Peering through one of the windows, I see a group of people sitting in chairs in a circle at the center of the gym. Fourteen chairs in all. One of them is occupied by the girl with fiery-red hair. I quickly pull back from the window when she turns and looks my direction. I'm certain she didn't see me, but how did she know I was there when no one else seemed to notice my presence?

She must've heard the front door.

Even with my ear pressed firmly against the door, I can only hear murmurs of conversation. There's no way she could've heard me come in.

Unless she's not human.

I push the absurd thought aside and pull up memories of the building's layout. Around the side of the gymnasium and through the girl's locker room lies another entrance. That one's an open doorway and partially blocked by the bleachers from what I recall. It's my best chance of getting close and hearing what's being discussed.

Two minutes later, I'm crouching next to the bleachers inside the gym.

From this spot, I hear the familiar voice of a man. I'd recognize it anywhere.

Dr. Strong.

Based on the current discussion, it sounds like he's conducting some sort of group therapy session. But why are they meeting here? Why not hold the sessions in his office building? Maybe the participants feel more comfortable meeting in a neutral place. Somewhere less clinical. Either way, the reason is irrelevant to why *I'm* here.

"…and that's why I miss her," says an older man.

The attendees pass a tissue box around the circle until it reaches the man. He takes one, wipes his eyes, and then blows his nose into it. A dozen seconds of silence fill the gym. A vacuum that threatens to pull me out of the shadows and into the circle.

Dr. Strong, his back to me, breaks the silence. "Thank you for sharing, Karl."

The group mimics him, "Thank you, Karl."

Reminds me of the AA meeting I attended once at Mother's church. Long story short, Mother caught me having a sip of wine one evening when I was fourteen, overreacted, and forced me to attend. From what I remember, it was a bit cultish but nevertheless helpful. She'd have a stroke if she knew how much Seth and I drank sometimes.

Dr. Strong turns to his left. "I'm glad you decided to make an appearance this evening, Lindy."

The girl in the green trench coat chews on her fingernails, her head tilted downward. She nods slightly. Her gaze levels, and she looks straight at me. Right through the bleachers. "Took the long way tonight, I guess." Her voice is surprisingly gruff.

"Is there anything you'd like to share with the group tonight?" asks Dr. Strong. "Perhaps continue where you left off on Monday?"

She shakes her head. "Not tonight. Feeling a little weird."

"Very well," says Dr. Strong. He turns and addresses the entire group. "Does anyone else have anything to say before we call it a night?" The thirteen participants all shake their heads. He nods and clasps his hands in front of himself when he stands. "Then you're all free to go. I hope to see every one of you tomorrow night." He looks to Lindy. "On time."

Lindy glances my direction and then turns and hurries away. By the time I wrap back around to the front of the gymnasium, she's disappeared into the night. Dr. Strong is the last one still inside. Through the window, I see him pack up his things and start stacking the chairs.

I push through the door and head toward him. "You got a permit for this little gathering?"

He spins on a heel, his eyes wide. "Alice?"

"Sorry, Dr. Strong. I didn't mean to sneak up on you like that."

The right side of his mouth curls up. "It's quite alright. What brings you here?"

"A homicide case, but I'm more interested in what it is you're doing here."

He grabs his jacket off the last chair and folds it over his forearm. "Dr. Modine, the school's principal, asked me if I'd be interested in starting a group therapy workshop a few weeks back. With everything that's been happening lately, she thought there might be some people interested in talking about the things going on in their lives, whether it be anger, grief, trust, trauma, stress, or anything else. So far it's been a great success."

I grab the last chair and add it to the stack. "Looked that way, given the number of people in attendance. But I noticed quite a variance in age. Are the older ones staff members from the school?"

"No, these workshops are open to anyone." He slips his jacket on and hauls the strap of his leather satchel up and over his head and onto his shoulder. "Over the years, I've found that people tend to open up more when there's a wide age range of people. Perhaps it lets them know that life can dish out problems no matter what stage you're in and no matter how old you are."

"With you at the helm, I'm certain it will continue to be a success."

He cocks his head and touches my arm. Makes me flinch, and it doesn't go unnoticed. "You should join us for a session or two. Never hurts to open up a little."

Even though I'd just been thinking about needing more therapy, the thought of a group session scares me. Then again, it might give me a chance to learn more about this Lindy girl. "I'll think about it."

"Perfect. We meet here Monday through Friday at 6pm. It's good seeing you, Alice."

"Likewise. I won't keep you."

The night has settled in beyond the outer doors, bringing with it a bitter wind that nips at my ears when I step out into it. The trek back to my car is uneventful, but it leaves me winded and frigid. As my car door swings open, I realize I'm not alone.

My hand slides over to my holstered gun.

"You don't need that." The gruff voice tells me it's the girl.

Lindy.

Alarm bells ring in my head. *"Draw your weapon,"* they cry. *"You don't know what she is."*

The thoughts are absurd, and I shake them out of my head as I turn and face her. She stands five paces away, hood drawn over her head and arms wrapped around herself. She seems harmless enough.

But those eyes.

Her eyes seem to glow in the darkness underneath the shadow of her hood. Two yellow lanterns. Haunting. Otherworldly.

Tension eases from my shoulders as the seconds pass, but the cold night leaves my jaw stiff. "Is there something I can help you with?"

She looks around but doesn't approach. "That's funny. I had the same question for you."

There's no doubt as to why she's approached me, but how did she know I was following her? She never once looked back.

I take a step toward her. "It's Lindy, right?"

She backs away. "Don't pretend like we're friends, *Alice.* Just tell me why you were following me."

She knows my name?

Realization clicks in my mind. "You were still in the gym when I spoke with Dr. Strong, weren't you?"

"What difference does it make? We know each other's names now." She looks around again, more nervous than before. "That doesn't tell me who you are or what you want."

"I just want to talk. Can I buy you a cup of tea? Maybe a bite to eat?"

"Why? So you can profile me, *Detective*?"

The girl's smart. "I recognized you from Wired Coffee the other day."

"I see. So it's a shoplifting charge you're after? We both know that's not true." She hugs herself tighter. "I tried to pay for the tea and the broken cup when I went back in, but the woman insisted it'd been taken care of. Who would've done such a thing?"

"That was my partner's doing. Besides, I never cared about some spilled tea or a broken cup. I'm more interested in you, Lindy." I move two steps closer. "I've never seen anyone with such unique and beautiful eyes."

Lindy pulls her hood lower. "Take a picture. It'll last longer, creep."

"Look, I get the hostility over me following you to the school, but there's no need for it."

"Here's a tip for you, Detective. Next time you want to follow someone, make sure you're downwind. Your perfume is strong enough to put down a rhinoceros."

"My perfume?" I lift my shirt and take a whiff.

Lindy wrinkles her nose. "Navy. You could do worse, I suppose."

It's been several days since I last wore perfume. Plus, I've showered. But the girl's right. Navy's my go-to scent.

I back up, shut the car door with my hip, and approach Lindy. She straightens but doesn't back away this time. From what I can tell, the top of my head barely clears the tip her nose. She must be around six feet tall.

She has the eyes and the height.

"I'm Detective Alice Bergman." My proffered hand is met with an uneasy stare, so I curl my fingers in. "You prefer a fist bump?"

"Lindy Baker, and I prefer neither," she quips.

"Fair enough, Lindy Baker. How about that cup of tea?"

"We're still not friends."

"True, but that doesn't mean we can't get to know each other and become friends."

"You'd be the first." She looks around again, a hint of fear in her eyes. Feels strange. "Look, I can't be here anymore. I need to get home."

I gesture toward my car with my hand. "I can drive you home if you'd like."

"Not gonna happen."

"Okay, just thought I'd offer." I reach into my coat pocket and retrieve a business card. "Take my card. If you ever change your mind and want to have that cup of tea, give me a ring."

Long, bony fingers covered with translucent red hairs reach for the card. Sharp, pointed nails protrude from the ends of her fingers. Claw-like. They tap against the business card just before she snatches it from my hand.

I couldn't look away from those fingers if I stood inside a burning building with a beam about to fall on top of me. But then a loud gasp draws my attention to her eyes. They're wide with terror. She looks at me, drops the business card, and bolts.

Her unexpected reaction throws me off and leaves me stunned for several moments. When I recover, I call to her, "Lindy, wait!"

But the night swallows her whole.

CHAPTER TEN

VERONICA APPEARS BENEATH HER bedroom doorway, a silhouette against the bright light at her back. Pink satin pajamas swath her slender form head to toe. They've been her favorite pair since the day I bought them for her, and I'm not just saying that. It's rare for her to sleep in anything else.

She rubs her eyes and yawns as she stretches her arms above her head. "When did you get here?"

"About an hour ago." Guenter, Veronica's beautiful Maltese, raises his head from my lap and peers up at me with coal-black eyes, obviously unimpressed with the shoddy job I'm doing rubbing his back. "Sorry, little guy. My fractured mind just isn't up to the task tonight."

Veronica joins us on the papasan chair and nestles her head underneath my chin. "Two can play at this, Guenter."

I give her head a few obligatory strokes before settling into the curves of the chair. "Sorry I didn't call before coming over."

She shoves my arm lightly. "Girl, don't be silly. You're always welcome here. Night or day."

"I know." I really do, but we've been slowly drifting apart ever since the night I showed her the storage unit. The blame for that debacle rests entirely on my shoulders.

"I went and saw your father this morning after my shift." She continues when I don't respond. "He's doing well. Far better than expected already. He wasn't awake though."

"Mother didn't tell me you stopped by. She urged me to go over there and see him though, but I'm not ready."

"What's there to be ready for?"

My lower lip trembles. "Him seeing me."

What if he doesn't like the way I look?

"I'm not following you. He's blind, remember?"

"Are you sure he still will be?"

Veronica jerks upright and frowns at me. "Whoa. Are you trippin' right now? You're an anomaly, Ally, not the standard. A friggin' miracle. Blind people don't just wake up from trauma with eyesight every day. You know that."

"Yeah, I know, but he's not some random blind guy, either. He's my father."

"Ugh." She rolls her eyes. "You're still sidelined over the *other world* thing, aren't you?"

"Yes… no… maybe." I sigh deeply and stroke Guenter's head. "I don't know, Vee. The whole idea of it scares me. But it intrigues me, too."

"It's a load of bull if you ask me."

"Don't think I was."

Veronica growls and wiggles her fingers at me. "Keep it up, smart girl, and you'll earn yourself a dose of the tickle monster."

"I'm not a five-year-old."

"Then don't act like one. Leave the fairy tales to children."

"And the nightmares?"

Veronica rears back and then tackles me and Guenter in the chair. Guenter yelps and squeezes out of the awkward embrace. She holds me tight, her breath warm on my cheek when she speaks. "That's why we have each other, Ally."

"Besties forever?" I ask.

"And then some." She kisses my cheek and then rolls right over the side of the chair and crashes to the floor with a thud.

I snort, and Guenter leans over the edge of the chair and barks. His little tail wags in a blur. "That's right, boy, your momma is a clumsy, neurotic mess."

Veronica groans as she rolls onto her back. "Forgot we weren't on the bed. And, for the record, you're the neurotic mess, Ally, not me."

She's right. For the most part, anyway. My mood swings can reach the moon at times, and the whiplash coming back down is killer. Hurts my neck just thinking about it. No matter how hard I try, my life is always in shambles.

But I'm still alive.

I rise from the chair and offer Veronica a hand up. She accepts and tries to pull me to the floor with her, but she's no match for my strength or mind. Like a prophet, I glimpsed the potential future and adjusted to subvert her attack. Or perhaps we just know each other too well.

"Dang, Ally. I know that look." Her lips turn pouty. "You're about to jet."

I shrug-nod. "Time marches on, and I've got a case to solve."

"Oh, yeah? What is it this time?"

"Nothing special. Just a werewolf on the loose."

She laughs. "Heard about the mauling. Hope you find your killer." She picks up Guenter from the chair and hugs him. "He certainly isn't it."

My thoughts focus on Lindy Baker. The girl's hiding something, and I need to find out what it is.

Perhaps she saw something, too.

I bend over and kiss Guenter on the top of his head before heading toward the front door. "It's only a matter of time."

"Don't let it keep you from going to see your father, Ally. He's still blind, you know, and it won't make you daughter-of-the-year if you do go see him."

My fingers rest on the door handle. "Don't you even dare try and push me into a relationship with that man. You said it yourself, he's nothing more than a sperm donor."

"That was like so many months ago." She meets me at the door and cups my cheek in her hand. "You might be able to fool yourself, but you can't fool me. I see the longing in your eyes when you talk about him. You want him to be the father you never had. Trust me, it's okay to let people in sometimes."

I push her hand away and sneer. "Is it? Look where it got me with you."

Veronica recoils with feigned hurt. "Ouch! You're vicious tonight, girl. Maybe you should call it a day and get some rest before you do some real damage."

"And maybe you should stop playing doctor, Nurse Gomez."

A smile cracks her lips. "Touché." She shows me out and lingers at the open door as I walk away. "Don't be such a stranger."

"Promise!"

* * * * *

Three hours later, a complete sweep of the house and my car turn up no listening devices. It makes me wonder if Rico's just a bit paranoid about being overheard, or if the Shadow Priests use some other method of spying. The Shadow Mirror races to the front of my thoughts.

Is that what Rico means?

With Mother staying at the hospital, and thoughts of disturbed men and women watching my every move, I don't want to be alone, so I head over to Seth's condo and let myself in. Every light in the place is blazing. It only takes a few moments to find him crashed out on his bed, fully clothed. It's likely the first bit of sleep he's had in several days, and I'm not sure how he does it.

His boots and socks come off without much of a fight, but his jeans prove to be a worthy opponent. Between me tugging at his jeans to unbutton them and grunting like a sow all the while, he rouses with a groan.

His hands reach for mine and push them away from his crotch. "Not tonight. Too tired."

I can't help but snort at the notion that he thinks I'm trying to seduce him right now. Sex might not be the furthest thing from my mind, but pretty dang close. "Relax, Seth. I was just trying to make you more comfortable."

He pushes his jeans down over his hips and rolls onto his stomach. Moments later, he's breathing heavy again. I grab his jeans at the ankles and yank hard. Perhaps too hard as they come flying off and send me staggering backward.

The wall meets me from behind and jars the air from my lungs, but the commotion doesn't faze Seth. When I glance over at him, I notice his boxers came off with the jeans. Carnal desire creeps into my mind as my gaze settles upon his bare backside. My lower lip slides between my teeth, my tongue caressing it.

Let him sleep, Alice.

Reluctantly, I shudder the desire to ravish him, turn off all the lights in the bedroom and adjoining bathroom, and close the bedroom door behind me. I'm sure Seth will wonder what happened to his boxers when he wakes up later. A smile parts my lips.

It won't be the first time he's woken up that way.

My thoughts turn to the Night Mauler case as I settle on the couch and pop the lid off an ice-cold beer I retrieved from the fridge. The cool liquid numbs my throat with the first swig and sets to work dulling my senses with each subsequent gulp. By the time I reach the bottom of the bottle, I'm sailing on a sea of tranquility.

The feeling fades as my laptop roars back to life, bathing me in its rays of blue spectrum light. With a few keystrokes, I dive down the rabbit hole and into oblivion, the search for Lindy Baker officially afoot. As with most searches these days, I start with Facebook and several other social media sites, but none of them turn up anything about the girl. I try several variants of her name but still come up empty. It makes me wonder if she even exists at all.

Did she lie to me about her name?

If so, she's used to referring to herself that way. Dr. Strong had called her Lindy as well, but that doesn't mean she gave him her real name either. After VPNing into the station, I search through criminal records for a Lindy Baker but find none. Several more searches on the name Baker give me a slew of results, but one in particular stands out: Lana Baker.

The woman's fiery-orange hair and yellow eyes are a close match to Lindy's, so I pull up her record. "Let's see what you've got for me, Lana."

Female. Six-foot-two. Known to be violent. My throat tightens with excitement.

Are you my girl?

Her record is extensive. A dozen charges of drug possession, a smattering of prostitution charges, several domestic abuse charges, four assault charges, one battery charge, and a handful of charges for child endangerment.

My heart breaks a little when I notice the coroner's report attached to her file. A quick scan of the document reveals that she died of an apparent overdose almost a month ago.

"Not my girl..." But it does give me an idea.

The Arizona Department of Protective Services (DPS) website loads in seconds, and I'm just about to fill out a request for information on Lindy Baker when I realize I've got no warrant and no idea if she's in the system. I close the webpage and drum my thumbs on my laptop. "How am I supposed to find out more about you?"

A strange window pops up on my screen. It contains a message stranger still: *"Open up your messenger app, Alice. This message will self-destruct in 4 seconds. ;)"* As stated, the window disappears after a few seconds.

"What the hell?" I sit there, my gaze frozen to the screen.

Another message pops up a few seconds later: *"It's Kenny. Open up your messenger app if you want to chat."* This one doesn't close until I press the "x" icon in the top-right corner.

When I get my messenger app fired up, Kenny's already messaged me.

Thursday, October 18, 2018

23:42

KP: *What are you doing working so late?*

Trying to find some info on someone but hit a roadblock. **:AB**

KP: *Maybe I can help. What are you looking for?*

DPS records. Forgot I needed a warrant though. :AB
KP: Who you looking to find?

I stare at the screen. Do I really want Kenny involved in what I'm doing? The more I think about it, the more I realize how nice it'd be to bounce thoughts and ideas off of someone besides Seth. I'm always in need of a fresh perspective. Plus, Kenny is assigned to help on the case.

The name is Lindy Baker. :AB
KP: Oh yeah? I know her. She went through the system?

The thought that Kenny might know her never crossed my mind. The chances of this conversation going south is fifty/fifty.

Not sure. :AB
KP: What put her on your radar?
To be honest, I'm not sure. Might be nothing. :AB
KP: Hold on a sec.
KP: Okay, you'll get a prompt in just a sec. Just press the "OK" button.

A message window pops up: *"Allow Kenneth Parker to control your system?"* There are two buttons: "OK" and "CANCEL"

After several seconds of debate, I press "OK" and wait.

I did it. :AB
KP: Sit tight. :D

My mouse cursor takes off and then dozens of command windows pop open and close faster than I can keep track of them. It's just like with the video software. After a solid five minutes, a PDF report pops up on the screen. Then another.

I recognize the logo on the header. They're Arizona DPS reports. My stomach climbs into my throat just as the messenger windows pops back up on top of everything else.

> **KP:** *You were right. She and her brother are both in the system.*
>
> *How often do you forget about Kellie? :AB*
>
> *I'm sorry. Don't answer that. :AB*
>
> **KP:** *It isn't my computer that accessed the system. ;)*
>
> *If I go down for hacking DPS, you're coming with me. :AB*
>
> **KP:** *So worth it. :D*
>
> **KP:** *Hope you find what you need in those reports.*
>
> *Thanks! No more hacking for the night. Promise me. :AB*
>
> **KP:** *No more. Scout's honor.*
>
> **KP:** *Oh! Sounds like Kellie's up. Gotta run!*

The message window grays out and shows Kenny offline. I close the app, hunker down on the couch, and dive into the treacherous world of Lindy Baker.

Lindy's file reads like a gritty suspense novel, and there seems to be no happy ending for her. She entered the foster care system seven years ago, at the age of ten, along with her brother Luca, age fourteen, after being removed from their mother's home.

So Lana is your mother…

I switch back to the criminal records database and save off a copy of Lana Baker's picture before continuing my research of Lindy. It might come in handy later. I save off pictures of Lindy and Luca as well and send them all to my phone.

Switching back to the DPS documents, I continue reading Lindy's record. It states that they separated her and her brother to increase their chances of adoption. Lindy landed in dozens of homes with foster parents over the first few years, but none of them kept her for more than a few weeks, each citing erratic behavior and bouts of self-mutilation while under their care. At sixteen, she emancipated herself and moved back to Desert Springs.

When I pull up Luca's file, it's nearly blank. Two months after entering the foster care system, he was placed with a family in Phoenix, Arizona. Three days later they found his bike abandoned at the edge of an arroyo. The rains had been heavy that week, and his body was never recovered.

After retrieving another beer from the fridge, I lean back on the couch and nurse it for a good fifteen minutes while processing everything that I've learned about Lindy. All the information swirls in my head, a maelstrom pulling me down into the depths of a violent ocean. I'm not sure what any of it means, if anything, but I'm more determined than ever to find out.

Why did you run, Lindy? Or what are you running from?

CHAPTER ELEVEN

THE MORNING SUNLIGHT POURS in through the eastern windows of Seth's condo, warming my bones and rescuing me from a world overrun by werewolves. Even still, their howls pierce my ears as though they've manifested just beyond the walls and beneath the floors of the condo. By the time I shake off the last cobwebs of sleep, I realize the horrendous sound is coming from the floor below us.

A yappy dog, not a werewolf.

Seth's bedroom door creaks open and Seth walks over to the couch I'm still crashed upon. He's still wearing nothing but a button-up shirt. He looks down at himself and then back to me. "Were you trying to solicit me last night?"

My eyes roll of their own volition. "It's seduce, Sherlock, and no I wasn't. You were too far gone for me to solicit you for anything, let alone sex. The boxers came off with the jeans."

Seth removes his shirt and tosses it at me. I catch it and pull it to my face. The smell is glorious. A mix of Drakkar Noir and Seth. My eyes caress his naked form as I inhale another breath.

His warm smile could melt the polar icecaps. "I'm headed for the shower. Wanna join me?"

"Now that's a solicitation." Every part of me desires to join him, but my phone says it's three past seven when I check it. I groan, "Don't have time this morning. Any other day, I'd carry you in there myself."

"Big plans?"

Lindy's face rises in my mind, but she's not a subject I'm ready to discuss. At least not until I can figure out what's drawn me to her. Right now I've got nothing to go on but a gut feeling.

"I've been guilted into going to see my father." I toss his shirt back to him and rise from the couch.

"Ah, right. It'll be good for you." He steps forward and kisses my cheek. "See you at the office later then?"

"Yeah, I'm sure we have a lot to discuss about the two cases."

"Yeah, I think we've got a few potential leads." He heads back to his bedroom, but not before I smack his bare butt.

I douse my face with some water from the kitchen sink and run my wet fingers through my hair. It'll have to do for now. If I time it right, I'll get to the high school just before the students arrive. The only question is whether or not I'll find Lindy there.

* * * * *

Sitting in my car outside the front steps of North Highlands High School and watching students arrive makes me feel like a pedophile choosing my next victim. Ten minutes before the warning bell, I finally locate Lindy's green trench coat in the undulating sea of rambunctious teens. She stands on the front steps, her back facing me, talking to a young man with shoulder-length, dirty-blonde hair.

The distance between the two of them is narrow. Much narrower than I would've expected based on my encounter with Lindy last night. She'd seemed so uncomfortable the closer I got to her last night.

Is there something going on between them? Or is it just me?

Exiting my car, I begin my approach, crossing the street and heading through an ocean of flesh and hormones. Several young men comment on my looks, and a few others offer me private lessons of their own—obviously thinking I'm a substitute teacher—as I push my way through the throng. Kids these days are far bolder than I ever was.

I'm half a dozen steps away when Lindy whips her head around and stares right at me. Her eyes widen and her mouth gapes for a moment, and then she bolts up the steps and into the main school building. There's no chance of catching her, but the boy she was talking to is still standing there with a confused look on his face.

"Excuse me," I say as I approach him. His gaze locks on my holstered gun when I reach into my back pocket and retrieve my credentials. I show him my badge. "I'm Detective Bergman."

He takes a step back but doesn't try to run. "Did I do something wrong?" His eyes dart about.

I shove my credentials back into my pocket. "Just take a deep breath and relax. I'd like to ask you a few questions. Is that alright?"

He picks at the cuticles on his thumb. "Guess so."

"Good. Let's start with your name."

"Rufin. Rufin Kuznik." He stares at his hands as though they might fall off if he looks away.

"It's good to meet you, Rufin." He nods, so I continue, "I noticed you talking with Lindy Baker. Are you two friends?"

He shrugs. "Not sure. I try to be, but she doesn't talk much."

"And how long have you known her?"

"Few months, I guess. She's come into my father's shop several times."

"Oh yeah? What does your father sell?"

"Flowers." Rufin finally looks at me. "Adolf's Flowers is the place."

"And what types of flowers does she like to buy?"

He scrunches up his face. "She never buys anything."

"Oh, so she comes in to see you?"

Rufin shakes his head. "I wish she did, but it's all about the flowers and the way they smell. She says their fragrance takes her mind away from the world. I tried to give her flowers once, but she wouldn't accept them. Said they were too beautiful to be wasted on her. But I disagree." He looks up at me. "Have you noticed how beautiful she is? Her yellow eyes melt my heart."

The young man is smitten with her, and it reminds me of Seth when we first met. "Have you told her this?"

His eyes grow wide, and he shakes his head fervently. "Never! I could never say anything to her. I'm no one."

His reaction makes me wonder if there were any boys that felt this way about me when I was in high school. I push the thought aside. "We are all someone, Rufin. Never sell yourself short. For all you know, she likes you, too. My guess is that she does."

"Why would you think that?"

"I was a young girl once, believe it or not. She'd find another flower shop to hang out in if she didn't like you. That's what girls do."

"Maybe you're right."

"Does she talk to anyone else at school?"

He cocks his head to the side and stares up at the cloudless sky. His lips pucker for a few seconds while he thinks about it. "Not that I've ever seen," he finally says.

"Well, there's your answer. It takes courage to tell someone how you feel, but I think you've got what it takes."

"What if you're wrong? What if she laughs at me or never talks to me again?"

"You move on knowing you tried. It's all you can do, and much better than living your life always wondering what might've been."

"I guess that makes sense." He grins. Shows off a faint dimple in his right cheek. "I can see why you're a detective. You're really smart." The warning bell rings, and he panics. "Oh, man. Oh, man. Gotta go before I'm late again!" He turns and rushes up the steps.

I return to my car and just sit there for a few minutes, allowing my brain to process everything Rufin told me. The more I think about Lindy, the more I wonder what the hell I'm doing stalking her. She's a teenage girl, not some cold-blooded monster. It's no wonder she runs when she sees me coming.

Unless she's hiding something.

* * * * *

Despite spikes of angst and apprehension with every stop and ding, the elevator ride to the seventh floor of the St. Thomas Medical Center west wing proves uneventful. In my heart, I know the fear is irrational, but my mind just won't let go of the past. The Braille Killer waits for me on every floor, in every shadow, and behind every door.

I know he's dead, buried, and gone, but sometimes I wonder if he's just a memory in my head or if some part of him lives within me, an imprint of his soul transferred through the psychic bond we shared after his death. Whatever the case may be, he'll never let me forget.

Until they're all gone.

Room W1748 lies ahead and to my right. Mother's voice carries into the corridor as I approach. My heart thunders in my chest and begs me to turn around and leave. It takes every ounce of willpower to keep my feet from turning back.

Pausing just outside the room, I think back to that first day after gaining my sight. Seeing Mother for the first time was one of the best experiences of my life. Everything about her was more beautiful than anything I had ever imagined. Why would I not have the same effect on my father? Am I not worthy of his gaze? His praise? What does it matter if I disappoint him? Why should I care what he thinks?

Because he's my father.

I *am* his daughter. He will love me no matter what, just like Mother does. Won't he? Then again, maybe fathers aren't wired the same way as mothers.

Seriously! Calm down.

After taking a deep breath, I round the corner and enter the room, but that's as far as I get. Mother looks up at me, but my father doesn't stir. His arms and legs are wrapped in thick bandages, along with his neck and a good portion of his head. A living mummy.

My stomach churns with sorrow and rage. Sorrow over what he went through and rage against those that seek to kill us. It further solidifies my determination to hunt down and kill every last member of the Shadow Priests, not that I needed additional prodding.

Mother scowls at me. "Well, don't just stand there with your mouth hanging open. Come on over and take a seat."

The plastic chair feels cold even through my jeans. "How's he doing?"

"Better than the doctors dreamed possible, but they tend to put their faith in themselves and their abilities and not in our Lord and Savior, Jesus Christ. Miracles do happen, mind you, but not without constant prayer."

"And you're the biggest prayer warrior I know."

"I do believe my prayers are helping Isaiah along the road of recovery."

"Has he been awake or said anything to you yet?"

"The pain medication they've been giving him has kept him under for the most part. The few times he has woken he's been quite groggy. The few words he spoke were unintelligible babble."

Mother's hand is cold when I take it into mine. "Thank you."

"What have I done?" A hint of suspicion gleams in her eyes. "Better yet, what have you done?"

"You've been sitting in this hospital for the last fifty hours watching over a man you loathe."

She stares at my father, and her eyes swell with tears. "I've harbored many feelings about Isaiah over the years, but loathing him was never one of them."

Could've fooled me.

"Look, what I'm trying to say is that you deserve a break. Go home, take a shower, and get some rest. You're not superhuman after all."

Mother wipes her eyes with a tissue she produces from thin air and then smiles. "Not yet, but the Lord has a new body waiting for me. Can't wait to give it a test drive."

"Seriously, Mother."

"I've never been more serious."

"Go home." I shake her hand for emphasis.

She sighs. "Very well. I will go home and take a shower if you promise to stay here with him."

I pull out my phone and look at the time. It's fifteen past eight. "I can stay until ten, but then I've got to get to work."

"I'll be back by half-past nine." She rises from her chair and gathers her belongings. "If anything changes with him, you call me immediately. Understood?" She doesn't move until I nod my agreement. "Good. I'll be back."

And I'll be waiting for you, Terminator.

I take aim at her back with my "hand" gun when she turns to leave and fire an invisible bullet right through her left shoulder blade and into her heart. But she keeps walking as though she felt nothing. That's when I remember machines have no hearts.

As soon as she exits the room, I scoot to the edge of my chair and lean on the bedrail. Isaiah's left eye flutters underneath a closed eyelid, but his right eye is concealed by a thick bandage. Each breath he exhales wheezes from slightly parted lips.

Even battered and bruised, he's a handsome man. I imagine he looks about the same as he did when Mother first met him, seeing as the years have been kind to him. Even though he's in his mid-forties, he looks young enough to be my brother rather than my father. I can only hope to age as gracefully.

Leaning closer to him, I whisper, "Father, can you hear me?"

He gives no indication that he has. Then again, why would he? Given his condition and the drugs coursing through his veins, I'm not sure what I expected. I close my eyes and rest my head against the rail for a few moments.

But then his hand grabs my wrist.

* * * * *

"Sh—" I clamp my hand over my mouth before alerting the entire hospital.

Isaiah releases my arm. "Go close the door." His voice is weak and gravelly.

"I didn't think—"

"We don't have much time. Hurry."

It only takes a few seconds for me to close the door. When I turn around, Isaiah's sitting up and unwinding bandages from his head and neck.

My breath catches in my throat, forcing me to choke out the words, "What the hell do you think you're doing?"

"Getting out of here—" He looks right at me. If I had any doubts as to him getting his vision back, they're gone. "—and you're gonna help me."

"Help you? You really are insane!"

"You know I'm not, and there's no way I'm going back to that loony bin."

"I saw what that woman did to you." The video plays back in my head. "You shouldn't be moving around. You shouldn't even be *able* to."

He grimaces. "Hurts like hell, but I'll survive."

"You unplug yourself from those machines and the nurses will be in here within a dozen seconds."

"This ain't my first rodeo, Alice. I know what I'm doing."

"I don't think you do."

He glares daggers at me. "You gonna help or just stand there?"

"I'm an officer of the law, for God's sake. Helping you will get me arrested *and* fired!"

"So you don't care about the truth? It's not worth you risking everything?"

I grab my head and dig my fingers through my hair. "The truth of what?"

"Don't play stupid with me. We're both smarter than that. Get me somewhere safe, and I'll tell you everything."

I take a deep breath. There's nothing I want more in the world than to learn everything he knows. For once, my mind and heart come to the same conclusion: how can I refuse?

"Okay. Fine. What do you need me to do?"

Seth's gonna kill me.

He points across the room. "Grab that wheelchair and help me into it."

Every moment and every action I take adds to the insurmountable guilt building in my mind. How did I wind up in this moment? If I continue down this path, how will I ever recover? Which action will push me over the threshold and prevent me from ever going back? Have I already reached that point?

I must be mad.

Darkness builds around the edges of my vision. Moments of time shatter into dust and fall into the abyss, creating holes in my memories. Isaiah sits in the wheelchair. But when did I fetch it? And how did we arrive next to the door?

The sound of my beating heart builds into a crescendo. Deafening.

Then the world screeches to a halt with a simple knock at the door.

Isaiah and I share a glance as we collectively hold our breath, as if doing so will somehow make the person on the other side of the door go away or disappear altogether. Only a fool would believe such nonsense, yet I cling to the thought with far more hope than should be allowed.

My eyes grow wide as the door handle arcs down.

Blood pumps faster through my veins, roars in my chest, and echoes in my ears.

Click!

The door latch disengages.

It's over. My career. My life. My relationship with Seth. Everything.

The door swings open, screeching like a banshee. Knocks against the wheelchair's footrest with a deep thud, sending concussive waves reverberating up through the wheelchair. Those waves pierce my hands, shoot up through my arms, and bury themselves deep within my shoulders. Shakes me to the bone until I can't hold on any longer.

"Alice?"

CHAPTER TWELVE

A FAMILIAR, GRUFF VOICE wheezes, "Alice, is that you?"

Radiating pain knocks against my forehead as my eyes fight to gain purchase beneath heavy eyelids. When they finally breach their prison of veined skin and membrane, their gaze is met with a sea of white tile. A long string of drool stretches from my gaping mouth to a sizable, gelatinous puddle on the floor.

Raising my head from the bedrail severs the tendril, sending it plummeting toward the puddle below. The splash it makes upon impact sounds in my ears, even though I know it's only audible in my mind. Isaiah's hand rests upon my shoulder, an IV anchored to the back of it.

We're still at the hospital.

A wave of relief washes over me, my job still safe for now. I shrug Isaiah's hand from my shoulder and grab a box of tissues from the roll-away stand next to the bed. "Yeah, it's me. Hold on a sec." Two tissues dry my sodden face, but several handfuls fail to mop up the lake on the floor. I'm certain I've only made the problem worse.

"Are we alone?" asks Isaiah.

When I finally look at him, I see that his left eye is still closed. "For now, but Mother will be back soon."

"Close the door and come around the other side of the bed so I don't have to turn my head to hear you."

Close the door!

A lump the size of Rhode Island rises in my throat. Cuts off my airway. I've lived through this scenario already, and it doesn't work out for either of us.

Get a grip, Alice. It was only a dream.

The door swings silently on its hinges, never once threatening to screech. Back at his bedside, I take Isaiah's left hand in mine. Seems like the right thing to do. His hand is warm and his grip stronger than I expected it to be.

It's the first time we've touched and really connected, and it takes all the strength I have to hold back a torrent of tears. How I've longed for a father's touch. *My* father's touch.

His left eye eases open. Blinks several times before remaining open. His greenish-blue iris is vibrant. Unclouded. Leaves no doubt in my mind that he's no longer blind when he looks up at me.

Tears spill from his eye, and he trembles. "My God, Alice, I never imagined I could have a daughter as beautiful as you."

Those words trigger an avalanche of emotions. A mountain of anger, shame, hate, guilt, and despair toward this man—twenty-six years' worth—comes crashing down around my feet in one felled swoop. For just a few moments, my small hand still cradled in his big mitt, I'm a little girl again, and the entire world lies at my feet. All I need to do is take that first step and choose my path.

But it was never to be, and the bitterness of that fact settles in once again. Roots itself deep within my heart where nothing and no one can ever dislodge it. Knowing I'll never be free of it sickens me. Turns my stomach. But there's nothing to be done. I'm the result of an overprotective mother and an absent father. It fuels my rage.

I swallow my anger as best I can, but it lingers in the back of my mind, ready to lash out at a moment's notice. "Thank you, but I'm not here to build a relationship. I'm here for answers, and we're running out of time."

His eye darts toward the door. "This isn't the place—"

"I don't give a damn who hears us. Do you understand? Besides, there's nowhere for us to go."

After a few moments, he nods. "Fine, but we need to talk quietly. What do you want to know?"

"Why do you insist that we're from another world?"

"Simple. We're not like the rest of them."

"So we have the ability to use more of our brain than most people. That doesn't mean we're from another world."

"Not by itself," he gruffs, "but there's so much more."

"How do you know? Where's the proof?" I ask.

"Get me out of here, and I'll show you."

My waking nightmare rears its ugly head once again. Attempts to paralyze me, but I won't let it. I am the dream master. "I'm not breaking you out of the hospital no matter what you promise me."

He sighs. "That's not what I meant. You have the power to get my case reviewed. You also have the ability to put me in protective custody."

"I—" The thought hadn't crossed my mind, but it could work. Given the fact that the woman on the video said that there were others, putting him into protective custody would be fairly standard procedure. Well, almost standard. Given that he's a mental patient, there might be a few more hoops to jump through.

"I'll see what I can do, but there are things we need to discuss now."

"I'm listening."

"How many Shadow Priests have you encountered?"

"Only two that I know of."

"Dashna and the woman who attacked you a few days ago?"

"Yes."

"What can you tell me about them?"

"Nothing about this last one."

"Obviously, but what about the first one? I'm guessing that's how you got your sight the first time?"

He nods and closes his eye. "It was the spring of '88. April 14th. My father and I were in New York at the time on a business trip. Rather, he was on a business trip. I tagged along because my birthday was that week and he promised to take me to an opera. There's nothing better than sitting back and listening to a good opera.

"Anyway, I mostly kept to myself in the hotel room during the days we were there, but that third day I was particularly bored and decided to find my way down to the pool and hot tub area. A quick call to room service afforded me a personal escort—no cost to my father or the company he worked for. The man took me down to the pool room and showed me where the restrooms were.

"After a solid ten minutes of insisting I was okay on my own, my escort returned to his duties elsewhere. I had the entire place to myself, or so I thought. I won't go into details, but suffice it to say a woman tried to suffocate and drown me in the hot tub. Somehow, I managed to overpower her and held her head under the water until she stopped struggling.

"I remember every last detail as though it were yesterday. I just left her body floating in the water and somehow found my way back to the room. The next two days I stayed in the room day and night, citing illness when my father tried to get me to go to dinner and see the opera.

"Over those two days and several more, I gradually gained my sight. Because of the incident in the hotel hot tub, I decided to keep the change to myself for a few weeks."

"And what about the woman? Was there ever an investigation?"

"Never heard a thing about it. Several years later, I went back to New York and made inquiries about it, but there was no record of anyone ever dying in that hotel either that day or any other for that matter."

"Someone covered it up then?"

Isaiah nods. "Yeah. Turns out it was my father."

"How did you find that out? Did he tell you?"

"No. A few days after we returned home from New York, my father began having blackouts and acted erratically at times as though he were someone else. A week later, I found him hanging from the rafters in the attic. He left a note on my nightstand, but it contained just two words: forgive me."

"My God…"

"Doctors claimed he had a mental breakdown, but I discovered the truth two years later when I prepped the house to sell it."

"What do you mean? What was the truth?"

"Taped to the underside of his old desk above the right-hand drawer was a manila envelope. Inside the envelope was a small, black journal book. The first page included a list of fourteen names. The last one was Dashna."

"All Shadow Priests?"

"Yes, and the other pages were filled with details about my father's mental state and how he started losing his mind after mind probing the woman I'd killed. Blamed it on her being a Shadow Priest. Said she'd set a trap for him and corrupted his mind. Each day he lost more of himself until he got to the point where he thought he might harm me. Knowing he'd never forgive himself if he did, he chose to take his own life."

"Did the journal say anything about how we can find them?"

"No, every time he tried to write details down about what he saw his words became incoherent and then illegible."

"I'm sorry, Father."

"So am I. He was a good father and a good man. I'd hoped to be the same kind of father to you, but I screwed that all up."

"No, Mother did."

"Alice, darling, don't ever blame Gladys for what she did. The way I carried on about cults and assassins and running for our lives because we're from another world is what got me locked up in the loony bin, not her. Sure, she signed off on the paperwork, but I left her no choice. I've never blamed her for it, and you shouldn't either."

"But she lied to me. Said you were dead. Told me you wanted to abort me. How messed up is that?"

"Look, I won't lay here and tell you she was wrong and that I would've done things differently if the roles were reversed, because I had knowledge she never did. I didn't know you'd be born blind, but I would've known why once you were. Your Mother's a good woman, and she has a big heart. Don't break it over me. I'm not worth it."

My thoughts return to the Shadow Priests and Milton Russell Puge, the Braille Killer. "I mind probed a Shadow Priest."

His cheek flashes red. "You did what?"

"His mind did have defenses and repelled me several times, but I found a way to get past them and was able to retrieve information from his memories."

"Then you got lucky."

"Maybe, or perhaps he was just weak."

"Either way, I forbid you from ever doing it again."

"Forbid me? You say that like you have some sort of authority over me."

"I refuse to lose you the way I did my father."

"But how will we ever find them and destroy them if we can't look into their minds?"

"I don't know, but the answer isn't risking your life."

"When I was in his head, I got glimpses of things and places when I told him to show me where the Shadow Mirror was."

"Then use that information. Don't try to extract more from another Shadow Priest."

"Well, it's quite inconvenient to be pressing my forehead against the foreheads of dead people anyway. Others tend to frown upon that kind of behavior, especially at crime scenes."

With part of his face covered it's hard to read his facial expressions, but his disgusted tone comes through clear. "Why would you do such a thing?"

"How else would I mind probe them?"

"How about just touching their arm or hand or something?"

"That works?"

"Yes." He shakes his head. "What the hell possessed you to press your forehead against the forehead of a corpse in the first place?"

"I don't know. There was this young girl. Sixteen. Blind. I felt drawn to her in a way I can't explain. For whatever reason, I leaned over her and placed my forehead against hers. That was the first time I ever mind probed anyone. I guess I just thought it had to work that way."

"Well, now that you know that isn't the case, I'd recommend you never do it again."

"Never again."

"Never again what?" Mother asks as she enters the room.

I jerk around, startled. My mind races to find something to tell her, and I blurt out the first thing that comes to mind. "I was just telling Isaiah about the time I ate escargot."

"He's awake?"

When I turn back around, Isaiah's eye is closed, and his mouth hangs open. He squeezes my hand and then releases it. I'm not sure what he's playing at, but I won't be the one to tell his tale.

"No, but I thought he might want some company anyway, so I've just been talking to him."

"Well, he certainly looks peaceful."

"Sure does. Look, I've got to get to work."

"Very well. Keep your phone on so I can get ahold of you."

"I will if I can, Mother." I kiss her forehead after she sits down and exit the room before the bitterness takes hold of me again. Surprisingly, Isaiah's words helped a lot.

Maybe there's a chance of recovery after all.

* * * * *

The moment I walk into Seth's condo, I know something's up. The place smells of lemon-scented Pine-Sol and Febreze, and the floors look shiny enough to eat off of them.

Then, the succulent aroma of seared flesh wafts in from the open balcony door. It pulls me right through the entryway and into the living room. My empty stomach rumbles and my mouth waters with anticipation of sinking my teeth into a juicy ribeye steak.

Out on the balcony, I discover a table set for two with real china, authentic silverware, and crystal stemware I'm certain Seth doesn't own. A white linen napkin lies over each plate, folded into a heart shape. A silver stand sits next to the table with a bottle of red wine bathed in an ice bucket. Two candles, tall and white, sit to one side, along with salt and pepper shakers and a bottle of Heinz Ketchup. The man knows me so well.

"You're just in time," says Seth as he steps out on the balcony. "Go ahead and take a seat. I'm just about to pull the steaks and asparagus off the grill."

As lovely as everything is, it puts me on edge. I hate surprises. "You don't cook, you don't clean, and it's not Valentine's Day. Did I miss some sort of anniversary?"

Seth opens the lid on the grill and pulls the steaks off of it. The asparagus sits in a grill basket of its own. He removes it from the flames as well and turns off the burners. "With all the chaos in our lives right now, I just thought we deserved a break from it all. A single evening to celebrate us."

Celebrate us?

I sit down. My pulse races. "I don't deserve all this."

He smiles as he approaches the table. "Figured you'd say that."

Seth takes my napkin, unfolds it, and places it in my lap. When he bends over me, I get a whiff of him and his cologne. My eyes nearly roll back in my head as my heart beats faster.

Let's skip dinner. It's what I want to say, but I'd never discount the effort he's put into this evening.

A few minutes later, Seth sits across from me, wine in our glasses and candles flickering with flame. The cool, calm evening couldn't be better, the city lights aglow below and beyond us. The subtle sounds of Marvin Gaye filter through the open doors into the living room and set the perfect mood.

The crisscrossed grill marks on the steak are exceptional, and the first bite melts in my mouth like a piece of heaven, washing away the stress of the past week. Paired with the wine, I can't remember a more exceptional culinary moment. All this from a man who never cooked a thing in his life beyond frozen pizza six months ago.

We eat in near silence, letting the night and the cloudless sky embrace us. How Seth always knows what I need even when I don't leaves me full of love and in awe of all he represents in my life. The way I shut him out and kept him at arm's length for so long shames me. Brings a tear to my eye. I wipe it away and blame it on the dry night air.

With the food consumed, Seth takes my hand and leads me inside. On a dance floor comprised of white ceramic tile, we hold each other and sway to the music as Marvin Gaye sings *Let's Get It On*. The lyrics stir feelings deep within.

My head against his chest, I listen to the rhythm of his heart. As we continue to turn and sway, it beats faster. Harder.

I pull back and take his hands as I stare into his beautiful, grayish-blue eyes. They're glassy with tears. "Is everything okay?"

He nods as his hands tremble in mine. He lowers himself to one knee and reaches into his pant pocket. Suddenly, my skin is on fire, and my chest begins to ache as I fail to breathe.

I'm not ready for this.

He pulls a small, black box from his pocket and stares up at me. Never has his gaze been so intense. I need to look away but can't.

I'm not ready for this.

The box snaps open. Breaks the spell I'm under. There in the box sits a ring. Platinum band. Diamond the size of Texas.

"Alice Marie Bergman, you are the light of my life and the keeper of my heart. There's no one else I want to spend my life with. Will you do me the honor of marrying me?"

"I… I…" Words fail me.

Every dark moment and secret in my life bubbles to the surface of my mind. Bombards me with the truth of who I am. What I am. A heartless woman with blood on my hands. How could anyone love me the way I am when I don't even love myself?

I'm not ready.

It's no secret that I love Seth more than life itself, but how can I stand here and pretend that I'm ready when I'm not? With multiple cases looming over our heads, my father in the hospital, and the Shadow Priests hellbent on killing me and those like me, how could I possibly settle down?

But it's Seth.

Deep within my heart, I know I'll never love anyone but him. He completes me in ways that no other man ever could. He gets me. Puts up with me. Loves me unconditionally. How could I possibly say no to him?

He snaps the box shut and rises from his knee. "It's okay, Alice. I know we've been in a weird place for the last few months, and I sprang this on you without any sort of warning. Take some time and think about it."

"I love you…" The words lodge in my throat. A lump that doesn't want to move up or down. I swallow hard and wipe tears from my eyes. "The answer will never be no… it's just not yet. There are too many things hanging over my head right now."

"I understand." Seth kisses my forehead. My nose. My lips. "Tell me when you're ready. I'll wait as long as it takes and won't bring it up again."

"Thank you." I gather myself and start to head for the front door, but Seth grabs my arm and pulls me back around.

"Don't leave, Alice." He wipes tears from my cheeks with his thumbs and kisses me deep. As we surface for air he says, "This changes nothing."

Sweeping me off my feet, he carries me into his bedroom. I cling to him with everything I have, afraid he'll vanish from my life if we separate for even a moment.

This changes everything.

CHAPTER THIRTEEN

SATURDAY MORNING. 04:17. *The Shortest Straw* by Metallica breaks through the silence, vibrating my phone right off the nightstand. Thankfully, Seth has carpet in his room. If it'd been my room with the concrete floors, I would've been replacing another phone.

Maybe I should get a case for it.

Leaning over the edge of the bed, I retrieve my phone and answer it. "Hello?"

"You with Seth?" The man grunts.

I check the caller ID but don't recognize the number. "Who is this?"

"It's Detective Roland."

"Sorry, didn't recognize your voice." I pull myself back up on the bed. "Yeah, Seth's with me."

"Good. How soon can you guys get over to 24th and Jackson?"

"Maybe thirty minutes, why? What's going on?"

"I think we've got another mauling, but this time it's in the alley behind Nolan's Tire Shop. I'd go there myself, but I'm on another call right now across town."

Another mauling?

"Don't sweat it. We'll be there in twenty." I hang up, nudge Seth, and spring out of bed. "Let's go, sleepyhead. I think the Night Mauler has struck again."

Seth groans as he rises and swings his feet off the side of the bed. "Why can't bodies ever be found in the middle of the day?"

Somehow, we manage to get out the door and on the road within seven minutes, albeit without coffee or breakfast. To my surprise, Seth shows restraint behind the wheel for once, opting to forgo the lights and siren as we head toward 24th and Jackson.

"This one's yours," he says, his eyes never leaving the road.

My fingers tighten around the door handle. "What do you mean?"

"We've worked together for several years now, and I always take control of the scene as the senior detective, but not today." He glances over at me and winks. "This one's yours."

My pulse rises. "Are you sure that's a good idea? Lieut. Frost doesn't—"

"Doesn't matter what he thinks. You're ready, Alice. You've been ready for a while."

Doubt creeps underneath my skin. Seeps into my veins. Flows into my mind. "Even after what happened with the Braille Killer case? I didn't think you trusted me anymore."

"One botched case over your entire career doesn't define you, Alice. Besides, had all the facts of your ties to the case been known, you never would've been allowed to work it with me."

Seth's right, but it doesn't change the fact that I still feel inadequate. "And what if I botch this one?"

"The only risk you run on this one is not following direction from Lieut. Frost. If he tells you to wrap it up, then do so without argument."

"That sounds simple enough, but you know me. I don't let things go."

He rests his hand on mine. "I'm not saying you *should* let it go, but you need to learn how to play the politics game. Work it on the side if you must. Lieut. Frost answers to higher authorities just like we answer to him. I don't think he's as hard-nosed as you believe."

Seth pulls around the side of Nolan's Tire Shop and parks alongside two police cruisers, just outside the wind-whipped crime scene tape strung between the tire shop and the Italian restaurant behind it. Officers Brex and Bartoli stand just beyond the tape, both men hunched over with their hands buried in their pockets.

A strong gust of wind rocks the car on its springs as it whips past us and rips through the alley, kicking up dirt, leaves, and an assortment of debris. Not the most ideal conditions for a crime scene. The morning air is bitter cold and bites right through my jacket the moment I exit the car. A hot cup of coffee would be most welcome right about now.

Officer Bartoli greets us as Seth and I step underneath the billowing tape. "Detective Ryan, Detective Bergman."

Seth nudges me, a gentle reminder that it's my scene. "Morning, Frank. I'll be taking control of the scene."

Officer Bartoli's eyebrows rise, his surprise obvious. He looks to Seth for confirmation, and Seth nods. "Very good."

"Which one of you arrived first?" I ask.

Officer Brex speaks up, "It was me."

"Good. Walk me through everything you saw and touched when you arrived. Bartoli, you'll be the recording officer."

"Yes, ma'am," says Officer Bartoli. He captures our presence in the log, including our arrival time.

"Make sure non-essential personnel stay behind the line." Officer Bartoli nods, and I turn back to Officer Brex. "The other end of the alley is secured?"

He nods. "Officer Janis has it blocked off with her patrol car."

"Perfect. Any suspects or witnesses detained?"

"No, ma'am. An anonymous call came in from a pay phone a few blocks from here. I arrived about ten minutes after that, followed by Officers Janis and Bartoli a few minutes later. It's been quiet ever since, aside from the wind."

"Very good." I turn to Seth. "Detective Ryan, can you get someone on that pay phone location? Dust for prints and check for cameras in the area?"

"On it." Seth exits the scene and returns to his car.

"You ready, Mike?" I ask.

"Absolutely," says Officer Brex. "Although you might want to get some floodlights set up back there. There's very little light and deep shadows."

"We'll get that going once Charlie from CSI arrives. For now, you can walk me through the steps you took upon arrival."

Officer Brex sweeps his arm toward the alley. "This is the only path used in or out, and I'm the only one that's been back here. Follow my lead and watch your step as we get closer to the body. There's blood everywhere."

We switch our flashlights on and head in. A few dozen feet into the alley sits a large dumpster that stretches half the width of the alley. Beyond that lies a form on the pavement. Together, our flashlight beams transform the dark alley into near-daylight conditions where we aim them, breathing life into the bloody massacre strewn across the asphalt. One glance at the victim leaves little doubt in my mind that we're looking at the handiwork of the Night Mauler, but I can already see that this kill is far more brutal than the first one.

The victim's chest is torn wide open, their ribcage split almost right down the middle. Broken ribs protrude from the carnage, an outcropping of bloody stalagmites. The scene triggers my nausea and sends my head spinning. Twice, I have to swallow back acidic fluid. The acrid taste burns in my throat and lingers on the back of my tongue. It takes everything I have to keep my stomach in check, but I'm a fighter.

After a few moments, I find my balance and dig deeper into the scene. Unlike the nature preserve, this location looks to contain a treasure trove of evidence. Bloody paw prints litter the area and lead away from the victim.

Nothing but paw prints.

It's both disheartening and a relief. My flashlight beam only extends so far, so I can't tell if the tracks continue down the alley or not.

"Did Officer Janis check her end of the alley for evidence before blocking it with her cruiser?"

"Yes. Unfortunately, the trail of bloody paw prints doesn't extend that far. And, given that it's asphalt and not dirt, we have no idea what direction the animal might've gone."

"Figures." I turn my attention back to the victim. "Did you touch or move anything?"

"No, ma'am." He shines his flashlight on the victim's throat. "As you can see, there was no need for me to check the victim for a pulse."

Unless this event marks the beginning of the zombie apocalypse, the male victim will not be rising from the dead in search of fresh brains. The thought reminds me that I still need to watch the movie *Zombieland*.

Focus.

The victim looks to be in his late fifties. Blond, close-cropped hair covers his head and transitions into a full beard, covering his rounded lower jaw and surrounding his mouth like yellowed moss. A dark bruise stretches across his brow, and his forehead looks like he took a massive blow to it, the shadows pooling in what looks to be a recent indenture.

Brass knuckles still wrap the fingers of his right hand, and a switchblade lies a few feet from his left. His black boots, black jeans, and dark-gray, button-up shirt—what's left of it anyway—don't match the expensive watch clamped around his left wrist.

"What about the green Honda Accord down the way? Did you or Officer Janis check it out?"

"I checked the vehicle with flashlight only. Officer Janis ran the plates. The car belongs to a Slavik Garin, and based on the DMV photo, I believe he is the victim."

Ninety minutes later, Charlie and Deborah wrap up photography, sketches, and gathering forensic evidence around the victim. From there they move on to the green Honda. A quick, yet thorough sweep of the car confirms that it belongs to the victim. The many questions that arise from the search all revolve around the arsenal of weapons hidden in the trunk.

Who were you, Slavik Garin?

The sun has yet to make an official appearance, but the sky's color pallet has transitioned from blacks, deep purples, and royal blues to a pinkish-red hue with streaks of oranges and yellows. The beautiful morning contrasts the horrific scene in every aspect.

Charlie stops on the way out, briefs me on the evidence collected, and assures me that the evidence will not go missing again. Either he or Deborah will keep watch of it during processing, and they will keep redundant backups of the reports, including one on a removable drive that will be personally delivered to me.

Seth returns, the man of perfect timing. "Got bad news. The phone booth was wiped down and there appears to be no cameras anywhere in the area."

"That's not what I wanted to hear." As disappointing as the news is, I have a plan. With any luck, the body will tell me everything I need to know, and it's not leaving the scene until I'm finished with it.

"It was worth a shot," he says.

I gesture toward the scene with my head. "Give me a hand with something real quick?"

Seth sighs and nods. He knows me well and understands exactly what's about to go down. He follows me back over to the victim.

"Wow, this guy really got it good," says Seth.

"Right? Much more brutal than the first one."

I give Seth a minute to survey the scene. Or maybe I'm giving myself a minute to gather the courage to dive into Slavik's mind. Either way, the time passes.

Seth exhales loudly. "I'm not seeing anything here but paw prints."

"Yeah, I was hoping for something more like what we found in the forest."

"What do you think it means?"

"Honestly, I'm not sure what to think." Slavik's dead eyes stare at nothing now, but I'm certain he saw something. "Maybe I'll have a better answer in a few minutes."

"Take a good look at the guy," he says. "You sure you want your forehead touching his?"

I retrieve a pair of latex gloves from my pocket and kneel next to the body, careful not to settle in any of the pools of congealed blood. "If it comes down to that, I'll gladly do it, but my father told me I can touch the body anywhere and get the same result."

He squats next to me. "Then what's with the gloves? Does it actually work through the latex?"

I pull the gloves on. "No, it has to be skin-to-skin contact. These gloves are in case someone comes over here while I'm doing my thing." I show him my right hand. "I poked holes in each of the fingers."

"Clever." He chuckles. "Speaking of which, I'm surprised you haven't come up with something better than *my thing* for whatever it is you do."

"My father calls it *mind probing*, but I'm not sure I like that any better."

"Irregardless of the name, you need to make it a quick trip."

"Regardless, genius, and I'm working on it. I don't need you rushing me into it."

He raises his hands. "Fine. I'll be here if you need me."

I gaze into his eyes for several moments and smile. "You always are."

A deep breath steels my nerve but does nothing to slow my pulse. Given the condition of the victim, my mind runs wild with thoughts of what horrors I'll be subjected to. But it doesn't matter. I'm going in no matter what. I must if we have any chance of solving this case.

Another breath, and then I close my eyes as I reach for his cold, dead hand.

Slavik Garin's cool skin rests against my fingertips, but the sensation I've felt each time before isn't there.

Maybe my father was wrong.

I'm about to give up and go for the forehead, but then his skin warms underneath my fingers and my pulse slows to a crawl. Time itself halts. My skin burns with a familiar fire, and I feel that shift in myself once again.

Strange. Alien. But it no longer startles me.

What does startle me is his hand. It grabs mine and pulls me down into his dark world.

* * * * *

Slavik squeezes his thick fingers into a set of brass knuckles as he walks down the dark alley. "Time to make good on a promise."

The shadows are deep, the way he likes it. Born with exceptionally large pupils, he's never had a problem seeing in low light. It's an advantage he's capitalized on for decades. This specific location, the alley that stretches between the backsides of Nolan's Tire Shop and Jimmy's Noodle House, is perfect for such "business" transactions. No cameras. No witnesses.

Slavik checks the time on his silver Rolex Daytona 'Big Red', a seventy-five-thousand-dollar watch commandeered from some guy whose name escapes him. A memento for his troubles. He keeps a little something from every person he sends to the afterlife. The luminous hands read 03:46.

Almost time to pay up, Jimmy Tuesday.

He's a bit early, as planned. The dozen extra minutes will give him time to recharge before the confrontation. A growing tradition.

Slavik can't remember when he had his last fix, and his veins are itching for it now. No matter what others say, it's not an addiction. The lift it provides allows him to function at a higher level. Sets his mind in the right frame. Gives him the strength needed to do his job more effectively. Who in their right mind would ever choose to go into a potentially volatile situation unprepared? Certainly not him.

I'm always prepared.

The needle kit is in his grasp when the silence breaks.

"Slavik Garin," says the gruff, high-pitched voice. "I've come to take your life."

Slavik turns around slowly. The brass knuckles dig into his flesh as he prepares to attack whoever threatens him. The shadows are deep, but the silhouette of a tall, scrawny form standing ten paces away is unmistakable.

But those eyes. Yellow lanterns in the darkness. It gives him pause, but only for a moment.

He smiles to himself. Two for the price of one tonight.

Slavik takes three steps toward the shadowy figure. He will close the distance and silence the threat, but not before extracting the information he needs. "Do I know you?"

"No, but you knew my mother. You killed her and made it look like an overdose."

He moves forward a few more steps. The stench of sweat thickens the air. Whoever hides beneath the cloak of shadows is scared.

They should be.

He reaches into his pant pocket and retrieves his trusty switchblade. It's spilled more blood than a skilled heart surgeon. Soon, it will spill more. "Sorry kid, but ODs aren't my thing. You're barking up the wrong tree."

"Liar," growls the shadowy figure. "You told her you loved her. Promised her a better life. Then you took hers from her."

Light glints off his switchblade when he shakes it at the shadowy figure. "Ah, now you're painting a picture I recognize. Your momma was worthless when she wasn't on her back. Trust me, I did her a favor."

Only four feet separates them now.

Another step, and it'll all be over.

His switchblade hand tremors with anticipation.

He licks his lips.

Takes a deep breath.

Rocks on his heels, about to lunge forward.

But he's several moments slower than the shadowy figure who lunges out of the darkness. The glimpse is brief, but it's enough to strike terror in his heart.

Thick, red fur.

A long snout lined with razor-sharp teeth. They glisten with saliva.

Everything is a blur and happens within an instant.

Something sharp, like claws, rips into his sides. Digs beneath his ribcage. The pain is excruciating. Fire in his gut.

The back of his head smacks against the asphalt when the two of them crash into the ground. Their foreheads collide upon impact, but the beast's is far denser. A sledgehammer.

The crack sounds in his ears. Blistering. A concussive shockwave. His head explodes with pain. More than he's ever known.

His vision blurs. Darkens. But he's never lost a fight. Refuses to lose this one. He must get the upper hand.

He swipes at the beast with blind rage, but his switchblade glances off the beast's thick hide as though it were merely a butter knife.

The beast grunts and roars. Pulls up and outward with ungodly strength.

Ribs crack.

For the first time in his life, Slavik screams.

But the scream doesn't last.

Sharp teeth rip into his throat.

He gasps for air, his brain starved of oxygen, but it's an impossible feat.

The beast rears its head. Blood and saliva drip from its jowls.

Hatred burns within its yellow eyes as it glares down at Slavik.

Slavik cannot keep track of the time that passes as they stare each other down, but then the light fades from his eyes, and the world around him falls into darkness.

✳ ✳ ✳ ✳ ✳

The alley rushes toward me from out of the darkness and springs back to life around me, leaving me gasping for air. Conflagration rages in my heart as my mind wars with what my eyes swear they witnessed. Despite everything I thought I knew to be true before delving into the depths of Slavik Garin's memories, I'm left speechless and mind fractured.

The implications of such revelations, if true, shake me to the very foundation of my soul. But they also bring meaning to what Kenny and I discovered in the forest. Not a deformed beast, but one partially transfigured.

Both human and beast.

"You alright?" asks Seth.

Am I?

Physically, yes. Otherwise, undecided. I nod, still breathless despite taking several deep breaths.

Seth stoops down and helps me to my feet. "Did you see anything?"

"Yes. Give me a minute to collect my thoughts."

I close my eyes and the beast is there. Standing in the darkness, eyes aglow. Fangs dripping with saliva. Claws, sharper than knives, itching to dig into my flesh again. One single instant. A flash of movement. Unnatural speed. Unparalleled strength. Drives me to the ground. Splays my ribcage wide open.

Again, I'm left gasping for air. My legs falter, but Seth is my rock. My strength. He prevents me from faceplanting right into the victim's open chest cavity.

"You can't keep doing this," he says. "It's obviously not good for you."

"I'm fine." It's a lie, and he doesn't buy it.

"Your skin is so pale that it's transparent."

"It's translucent, and I really am okay." Another lie. How many more must I tell? "These experiences just drain my energy, and I didn't have time to eat breakfast. That's all it is. I swear it."

"Still, you should be careful. What happens if you stay connected or whatever and run out of energy? It could kill you, right?"

Sometimes Seth's insights are truly astonishing. I would've never contemplated mind probing right into death, but now it will be at the back of my mind every time I dive into someone's mind.

I shrug. "Yeah, I guess so, but I don't want to think about it right now."

I push Seth back as my strength slowly returns to my legs. My muscles still tremble with fatigue, but there's no way I can allow him to walk me out of here. The others have seen me vulnerable too many times already. The last thing I need is for someone to tell Lieut. Frost that I'm incapable of doing my job when all I need is a bite to eat.

"I got a name for you to look into. Jimmy Tuesday."

"The owner of the restaurant right here? Jimmy's Noodle House?"

The gloves snap when I pull them off my hands. "Yeah. Our vic was waiting in the alley to ambush Jimmy when he was attacked."

"So this attack might've saved Jimmy's life?"

"Right. I'm thinking Jimmy's the one who made the anonymous call."

"We'll get him tracked down and rounded up for questioning."

"Good, but don't question him without me."

"Wouldn't dream of it, but Detective Roland might have other ideas. He's still the lead on this Midnight Mauler investigation."

"It's the Night Mauler. Midnight Mauler sounds too sixties horror."

Seth shrugs. "Whatever you say."

We start walking back toward the front of the alley, but Seth stops when we reach the dumpster. I can tell the cogs are churning because his lips purse.

Several moments pass. He obviously needs prodded. "What's going through your mind?"

"When you have these… experiences, do you sense everything?"

"Honestly, it seems to vary. With the girls, Sarah and Cara, I lived their experiences. I *was* them. Felt everything they went through. With Milton Russell Puge, the Braille Killer, it was different. I was aware of who I was while still being him in a strange way. This time, it was different still. It felt like I was a bystander or voyeur. I saw through Slavik's eyes and read his thoughts as though they were my own, but I didn't experience the pain of the attack or of his death the way I did with Sarah and Cara."

"Huh. I wonder what the difference is?"

"Me, too." A myriad of explanations race through my thoughts, but none hold together under scrutiny. "Perhaps my father will have an explanation."

"Maybe so. By the way, did you get a good look at the animal? Anything we can forward to the guys over at Game and Fish?"

There's no way I'm telling him we have a werewolf on the loose. In fact, I'm still finding it hard to believe myself. The alley was dark, and everything happened so quickly.

It could've been a person in a mask.

If so, why did they leave a trail of paw prints behind and not footprints? Better yet, what did they use to rip open Slavik's chest so quickly and effortlessly? No human has that kind of strength.

My throat tightens. Are we really dealing with an escaped science experiment? A human-wolf hybrid?

Or is it something far worse?

"Sorry, but the lighting was poor, and the attack happened in a flash. I've got nothing more to go on other than what we established with the red hairs and now the paw prints."

Seth nods. "I'll live with that for now, but I can see you're holding something back from me. To be honest, it hurts that you still don't trust me enough to tell me everything."

"Look, I don't understand this gift of mine any better than you do. For all I know, what I see is only partial truths."

"I know you too well, Alice. You don't believe that at all. If you did, you wouldn't want me to bother chasing down this Jimmy Tuesday for an obvious mauling case."

I shake my head and sigh. "Fine. You're right. There are certain aspects of what I saw that make no sense. I need to process them before I can even begin to articulate them in a meaningful way. Suffice it to say that I've told you everything I can for now. When I'm ready, I'll tell you everything. I swear, I'm not holding information back like I did with the Braille Killer case."

"I wish I could see what you see just one time so I could understand you better."

"Be careful of what you wish for."

Seth cocks his head. "Is that a threat?"

I tap my left temple. "This mind is a minefield. It's a threat to us all."

"Now that's the kind of truth I'm looking for. Keep it coming."

"Funny."

We walk back over to Officer Bartoli and give him a detailed account of everything we did at the scene, my touching of the body excluded. "Go ahead and get the coroner in there. Let's get this cleaned up."

Several reporters and cameras await us beyond the crime scene tape. My heart thunders as I give my first briefing and assure them and the public that everything that can be done to capture this wild beast is being pursued.

After Seth drops me off at his condo to pick up my car, I head to the one place I'm sure to find answers to what I witnessed: Rico's Cane Shoppe.

CHAPTER FOURTEEN

RICO AND I DESCEND the stairs into the basement below his shop. I'm starting to think this might become a regular thing we do. Besides my father, who might be less crazy than I thought he was just a few days ago, Rico's my only ally. Not in life, but in the battle that wages between us and the Shadow Priests. Seth and Veronica will always have my back in other matters.

Immediately, I notice the change Rico's made in the basement. To the right of the stairs he's cleared a ten-by-ten space, laid out a luxurious eight-by-eight rug featuring a majestic landscape of mountains, forests, and a valley of silver grass. A hint of some body of water can be seen below the silver grass, edging one end of the rug. Long couches border two sides of the rug, running perpendicular to each other and creating an "L" shape.

"You did this for us?" I ask.

"Yes, partially."

"I love the rug. Makes me want to drop everything and go live there."

His eyebrows rise. "Really? Then perhaps you should one day."

I study the rug further. "This place exists? Where?"

Rico settles on one of the couches and closes his eyes. "Its name is Arian Valley. One of the many beautiful places in Centauria. How I long to be there again." He stretches his arm out and strokes the air. "I remember the softness of its silver stocks as though it were yesterday that I walked through them."

The sincerity with which he talks of this other world brings me to the cusp of belief, but nothing short of concrete proof will tip the scales. It's the same with God. If the sky rolled back and a mighty being stuck his head into our world, I'd believe.

I perch on the edge of the second couch and stare right through the beautiful rug and into a dark alley. Right into the eyes of a beast that cannot exist. Yet my heart knows it does.

"You look quite shaken, hijita." Concern laces Rico's voice and shapes his face when I meet his gaze. "What troubles you?"

"There was another mauling earlier this morning."

"Two within a week. That is concerning."

"Yes, but that's not what's bothering me." I lean back on the couch and stare up at the concrete ceiling. "I saw the impossible today."

"And what defines the *impossible*?"

"To be honest, I'm not sure anymore. The immovable line I've always known to separate possible from impossible has started shifting. Or perhaps it's blurring."

"Tell me what you saw and perhaps we can work it out together."

If I can't bring myself to tell Rico, a man who claims to be from another world, what I saw, then who could I tell other than my father? I roll my head to the side and stare at Rico.

Just say it.

Finally, I blurt out, "A werewolf."

Rico doesn't laugh aloud, nor does he scoff at the notion. In fact, the only thing he does do is flex his hands. Perhaps I've stunned him.

Knowing I've dug a hole for myself, I scramble to save face. "It's crazy. Certifiable." I shake my head and laugh, more out of nervous fright than anything else. "I don't believe in werewolves, Rico."

The silence between us spans the length of the universe and draws my fingernails into my palms. I gather myself into the cushions of the couch, seeking solace from the impending onslaught I'm about to face, but the knit of the fabric is too tight. There's nowhere for me to hide.

Finally, after completing his trip across the universe, Rico breaks the silence. "Perhaps you should." His serious tone sobers me, but not as much as what his words imply. "As I said, many legends are born out of truth."

I pull myself from the folds of the couch and lean forward, my elbows resting upon my knees. "You know what this is, don't you?" It's more of an accusation than a question, and he clearly gets the gist.

"I believe I might, but it's only a theory as I have no evidence to back it up."

"Don't leave me in the dark. Help me understand what this is and how to stop it."

"In our world, Centauria, there are these ferocious beasts we call gnolls. Hideous, wolf-like creatures who can walk on their hind legs and talk like humans. Created through dark magic, they are cunning and devious and bred for killing."

The other world again…

I stare at the rug and wonder if such a place really exists. Silver grass aside, the terrain could match a thousand locations right here on Earth. "Assuming you and my father are not insane, and this other world exists, which I'm still having a hard time believing, you're saying these beasts came to this world with you?"

"Again, I have no proof of such an occurrence, but it wouldn't surprise me. Our enemies will do everything in their power to hunt us down and kill us, no matter how far we run."

"If what you're saying is true, how would these beasts go unnoticed?"

"This world mutates and distorts the magic of *our* world. Take me, for instance. I have the ability to hear objects from our world calling out to me, and each time they do it slowly leeches my energy until I'm forced to locate it and bring it here. This is far different from how it worked in Centauria. There, I controlled when I used my ability."

"And these gnolls?"

"I believe the magic that created them mutated as well when they came into this world. If I'm correct, these beasts reverted back to their natural human form but have the ability to 'shift' to their conjured form."

To my surprise, it kind of makes sense. At least in a theoretical way. The actual idea of any of this still leans toward the absurd, but I can't come up with a better narrative. It provides a good explanation of the paw prints and footprints in the forest as well, all things considered.

"With a full moon?" I ask. I can't remember what phase of the moon we're in right now.

"Again, truth in *legend*. I believe the cycle of the moon is the legend part of the werewolf story. I am of the opinion that these creatures have only been witnessed during a full moon because of the amount of light produced by it and not because the full moon brings out their darker form."

"So you're saying, for all intents and purposes, that they are werewolves?"

Rico shrugs. "Perhaps. Or, as you said the other day, this could be nothing more than an anomaly. An escaped science experiment."

I lean back on the couch again and give my brain some time to process what Rico's said. My mind circles around a thought that might blow Rico's theory. "Based on what you've said about these creatures, wouldn't there be an inordinate number of maulings if they did come here?"

"Not necessarily. The gnolls were created to kill, but it doesn't mean that they don't possess the ability to make their own choices. In our world, non-compliance would mean death, but in this world, away from their slave masters, many of them might choose to live differently. Here, in a normal human form, they'd be able to live among us without scrutiny. Without the prejudice of our world."

"This is all completely absurd." Even as I say it, my mind begins to contemplate all the possibilities and consequences of actual magic existing in our world. Perhaps many world issues could be solved and diseases eradicated with just a thought or a few special words. And how many mysterious things could finally be explained?

If only Harry Potter was real.

Then, thinking about my gift or curse—I'm still on the fence as to which side I lean toward—, I can't think of another word that would describe it better than magic. And, if it is magic, then why would any of the rest of it be a leap to believe?

How could it all be random?

The thought shudders my shoulders and leaves trails of goosebumps down my arms in its wake. My legs prickle and ache when I stand as blood begins to flow into them again. I hadn't realized they'd gone to sleep.

"And how would I go about tracking down a gnoll, assuming these beasts exist? What would I be looking for?"

"This is pure speculation on my part, hijita, but I'd venture to guess you'd be looking for a person with red or reddish-brown hair, longer fingers and fingernails, and probably quite tall. Yellow or yellowish-brown eyes, too. They'd want to fit in, but would likely still feel like an outcast. A loner, but not necessarily reclusive. It's possible they might seek solace in a church or through therapy for atrocities they might've committed in this world or before coming to this world."

Lindy… She keeps rising to the top of my list.

My voice jumps an octave. "Have you ever met one before?"

"A few, but as I said, never in this world."

"Well, at least what you've told me will give me something to go on."

Rico stands and meets my gaze. "Look, hijita. I've given you this information because I feel I've owed you an explanation of things for several months. However, I think you should put this behind you. Drop the case and don't look back."

Rico's holding something back. I can feel it. "What are you not telling me?"

He purses his lips and then sighs. "These beasts… if they've come into our world… they're very dangerous." Concern radiates from his stare.

Looking at him makes me weak, so I turn away and chew on my lip. "I can handle myself."

His hand touches my shoulder. A father's touch. "I'm sure you can in most situations, but these beasts have immense power and tend to be short tempered. Not a good combination."

An earth-shattering, groundbreaking thought occurs to me.

If what Rico says is true, then there must be truth in what the Braille Killer told me as well.

My heart races. A thousand horses galloping in my ears. The sound fills my head. Shakes my core. With only one way to know the truth, I blurt out, "I can't be killed."

"What?" Rico pulls me around to face him. "Who told you that?"

My cheeks burn with fire. "While I have my vision, I can't be killed. That is the truth, right?"

Rico sighs and shakes his head slowly. "Hijita…"

I pull away from him and take several steps back. My hands are shaking. Can't control it no matter what I do. "Two of the Shadow Priests confirmed it. That's why Russell, the Braille Killer, waited ten years to attack me again."

"God, I wish that were the case, but the only truth to it is a false belief. It's a gross misunderstanding of how magic works. In short, we are not immortal." He peers down at his tattooed knuckles and smiles. "At least not yet."

I grab his arm. "Then explain it to me. Why did they tell me that?"

"You and I—our kind—have an innate ability to heal quicker because of our nature." He scratches his head, clearly in search of the right words. "What I mean by *our nature* is the energy that runs through our veins. The *magic*. In this respect, we can recover from wounds that might kill a normal person, therefore making us seem immortal. This, among other things, is what fuels their belief that we cannot be killed except in certain circumstances. A simple misconception."

Memories of Sarah and Cara flood my mind. "But we can't survive suffocation."

"Right. There's no coming back from death."

"That only explains part of it. Where does my blindness fit in?"

"In truth, I'm not certain, but it most likely came about because of an encounter one of the founding members of their cult had with someone like you. Can you imagine how frightening it would be to witness a blind person *take* someone's sight by killing them? I'm sure something to that effect is what started the lore."

"I guess that makes sense."

Rico checks his wristwatch. "Let's just say that it's far more complicated than that and leave it there. Now, I need to get going. I've got a client to meet. I hope some of what I told you helps."

"As always, you've opened my eyes to something new. Thank you."

Rico presses the switch on the wall and the stairway up to the workshop begins sliding open. I climb the first step, and Rico grabs my arm. "Hijita."

The tall step allows me to stare down at him for a change. "Yes?"

"This case of yours." He frowns and pauses. "Don't go looking to stir up trouble. Let sleeping dragons lie."

"Wouldn't dream of it," I lie and then take the stairs two at a time.

A thunder of dragons couldn't hold me back.

CHAPTER FIFTEEN

THE WORLD MOVES AROUND me at breakneck speed and threatens to toss me to the wolves with a single misguided step. Roland and Seth huddle over several case files in the war room. They're the ones Seth ordered Officer Spalding to dig up about the woman who attacked my father.

As interested as I am in getting to the bottom of that case, the Night Mauler consumes my every thought. Yes, the Shadow Priests are everywhere, but this beast I hunt is an imminent threat to everyone in Desert Springs. The question I'm trying to answer is what ties the two victims together.

Officer Brex walks into the room. "We've got a Jimmy Tuesday waiting in Interview Room Two."

"Excellent." I rise from my chair. Seth glances up at me from his stooped position but doesn't move to join me. It's not his case.

Detective Roland straightens. "Let's go see what Jimmy Tuesday has to say."

Jimmy Tuesday paces next to the interview table when we enter. A caged animal, eyes wild with suspicion. Thanks to his presence, the room reeks of stale cigarettes, bad booze, and body odor.

The man wears dark-green slacks several sizes too big, cinched up with a brown belt at least a decade past its end of life, the once-brass-plated buckle gouged and tarnished. His white, wife-beater shirt is tucked into his pants unevenly, yellowed with age and stained a darker yellow underneath the armpits.

Thinning, disheveled black hair crawls down the sides of the man's cranium and coils around and over narrow shoulders. It's stringy, greasy, and drenched in sweat—same as the scraggly beard hanging from his jawline.

Note to self: never eat at Jimmy's restaurant.

Beads of sweat glisten on Jimmy's forehead and hang in his thick eyebrows. Guilt does that to a person. One look at the man tells me everything I need to know.

Detective Roland offers Jimmy a bottle of water, but he refuses. From the look in his eyes, I surmise he suspects it to be poisoned, his mistrust of police evident.

I gesture toward the chair sitting on the far side of the table. "Please take a seat, Mr. Tuesday."

"Jimmy Tuesday," he grumbles. The metal chair screeches across the floor as he pulls it several feet from the table before plopping down onto it.

Detective Roland takes the chair closest to the wall, and I settle down on the one next to him. Jimmy cranes his neck and scowls at one of the two fluorescent light fixtures that hang from the ceiling as though it might be responsible for him being here. His fixation with the light draws my attention to their incessant buzzing, the sound reminiscent of a neon vacancy sign outside a seedy motel. Feels like I'm there now, ready to make some nefarious transaction for drugs, sex, both, or something far worse.

Detective Roland starts the recorder and makes the introductions, and then I ease into the questioning. Okay, perhaps they'd qualify more as statements than questions at first, but I want to lay down the ground rules of what we already know so that Jimmy doesn't get the idea that he can just sit there and give us the silent treatment.

"You're the one who called in the body in the alley behind your restaurant, correct?"

He glares at me with round little black eyes. "Not sayin' nothin' to yous."

His New York accent shines through.

"Oh, so you *will* talk then? Glad to hear it."

Jimmy cocks his head and stares at me as though I'm an alien from another planet. "Huh?"

"It's called a double—" I shake my head. "Never mind."

What Jimmy needs is a good scare. A few lies might stimulate the conversation. "We've got you on camera at the pay phone. There's no point in denying it. The question I'd like answered is why you walked all that way to make a call when you have a phone in your restaurant and a cellphone in your pocket? What are you afraid of?"

He shakes a finger at me. "Jimmy Tuesday ain't afraid of nothin'."

Struck a nerve.

It's a start, but what I need to do is appeal to his wallet. "Look Jimmy, I know you struggle to make rent on your restaurant."

Jimmy scowls. "Says who?"

"Your landlord. I know you can't afford to be here, and honestly, I've got more important things to do than sit here and ask you questions all day. Will you please do both of us a favor and answer the handful of questions I have for you so that we can all get back to our lives?"

"Didn' do nothin' wrong."

"And we're not saying you did. You're a witness, Jimmy, not a suspect."

"Name's Jimmy Tuesday, not Jimmy."

"Very well. Can you tell me why you called the body in from a pay phone?"

"To avoid this." Jimmy spreads his arms wide. "Look, Slavik got what he deserved. Dirty rat-fink bastard."

Detective Roland leans into the table. "So you didn't like the guy?"

Jimmy sneers at Detective Roland. "Talkin' with the lady, not yous."

I stifle a snicker. "Did Slavik have it in for you?"

He nods. "Me and everyones. Called it insurance."

"He forced you to pay him monthly for protection. Is that it?" I ask.

"Weekly. That's why me and everyones on the block struggle to make rent." Jimmy curls and flexes his fingers. "Work my fingers to the bone just to scrape by."

"How long have you known Slavik?" I ask.

"Ten years. Maybe longer. Takes my money from the back door and then brings his girlfriend into the restaurant and lets her order the world. Then he refuses to pay a dime for any of it. Says it's a bonus." He spits at the floor. "Good riddance."

"Did you see what happened to Slavik?" asks Detective Roland.

Jimmy glares at Detective Roland but answers the question, "Nope. Saw the final deal, though. Can' say it didn' feel good knowin' he'd never be at my back door again."

"And why were you still at the restaurant at four am?" questions Detective Roland.

"Always am. Bar closes at three. Then there's cleanup." Jimmy points at Detective Roland. "Leave at four pronto every mornin'."

Detective Roland leans forward. "You see anything run off? Perhaps an animal with red fur?"

"Nah. Never seen nothin' round other than rats and cats."

I steer the conversation back toward Slavik's girlfriend. "Did you know Slavik's girlfriend?"

"Everyones did. Always flyin' high and flauntin' what she had. Low-cut tops left little to the imagination, and her shorty-shorts were shorter than should be allowed, her ass cheeks fallin' right outta them."

"You know her name and where we might find her?" I ask.

"Slavik always called her Firestorm, given her red hair I suppose."

Red hair?

I sit up in my chair, the interview suddenly much more interesting. "What else can you tell me about her?"

Jimmy cocks his head and looks to the ceiling for a few moments. "About a month ago, she got pissed at Slavik oglin' some other tramp, so she started flirtin' with some guy at another table. Went over and buried her tongue in the guy's mouth right in front of Slavik." Jimmy squirms in his chair, clearly disgusted.

"Bet that torqued Slavik," says Detective Roland.

"Bet yer booty it did. Slavik raged on that guy. Broke his nose and threw him through a table. Tore up a good portion of the restaurant. Slavik grabbed Firestorm by the arm and said, 'let's go, Lonnie.' She fought him tooth and nail. Feisty little tramp."

"Any idea how old she was?" I ask.

Jimmy scrunches his face. "Wasn' young, but her boobs didn' sag neither. Perky as two pineapples. However old that be."

Doesn't sound like Lindy.

"You're sure he called her Lonnie?" I ask.

Jimmy frowns and shrugs. "Lonnie. Lanny. Somethin' like that."

"Are you sure it wasn't Lana?"

His eyes narrow, and his head slowly bobs up and down. "Yeah, I believe that's the one." He tries it out for himself. "Lana."

I take my phone out of my pocket, pull up the picture of Lana Baker, and show it to him. "This her?"

Jimmy grabs my phone and pulls it close to his face. After several seconds, he grunts and says, "That be her."

My heart thunders with excitement as I take my phone back. "When was the last time you saw them together?"

"That was the last of her I ever seen. Slavik always came in alone after that day. Changed man. Harder, if that's possible. Swore off women, he said. Never thought I'd see it."

My body tingles with excitement. The final pieces of the Night Mauler puzzle are falling into place. Satisfaction curls my lips as I lean back in the chair, but the feeling is fleeting. Even though I'm beginning to think that Lindy Baker is the Night Mauler, I have no proof.

So what can I do to prove it?

Without a confession, I have nothing. Even if she provided one, no one would believe it... unless she shows the world her true self.

*The beast.** * * * *

Seth, Terry Roland, Kenny, and I meet up at Kicker's Bar and Grill at 17:00 to have a drink and discuss the Night Mauler case. We grab a corner booth and huddle around the table. The place is dead for a Saturday, but it's still early. A few hours from now, the place will be crawling with people.

A beautiful young waitress comes over and takes our drink order. Terry tracks her across the room with his eyes when she leaves. "This joint definitely has some appeal."

Kicker's did just open a few months back, and the decor fits its name with football and soccer paraphernalia throughout, but we all know his appeal of the joint lies within the flesh.

"How about we concentrate on the case," says Seth. "What did you guys learn from interviewing that Jimmy Tuesday character?"

Terry eyes me. "That's a good question. You seemed pleased with the result, Bergman. What exactly did you get out of it?"

"It won't hurt you to call me Alice during off hours, you know." He stares at me with a blank expression. I roll my eyes and continue, "I believe there's a link between the two victims. In fact, I know there is."

Seth's eyebrows rise. "Really?"

"Out of what we just heard?" asks Terry. "What the hell did I miss other than you going way off track about some tramp?"

What didn't *you miss?*

"I've done a bit of digging on my own, and what Jimmy Tuesday said pieced together a few things I'd been having trouble with. What I'm trying to say is that the two mauling victims are connected to each other and this Lana woman."

"How so?" asks Terry.

"It's simple. She knew both victims, and I'm certain they knew each other. The first, Ernesto Vasquez, was her drug dealer, and Slavik Garin was obviously her boyfriend. But Slavik was also a druggie."

Terry scoffs. "You've got proof of all this, or are you just pulling it out of your—"

Kenny cuts Terry off, "Circumstantial evidence. I cross-checked phone records before coming over here. Lana and Ernesto Vasquez spoke once every week like clockwork. About a minute each time. I didn't see a direct connection between Vasquez and Garin, but phone calls from Lana's number kept popping up right until Vasquez's death."

There's no way Kenny checked those phone records legally. The kid doesn't seem to know how to play within the rules. Reminds me of myself. He frowns when his eyes meet my stern gaze. I mouth, "Kellie," and he nods solemnly.

"So you think Garin used Lana Baker's phone to continue getting drugs?" asks Detective Roland.

Kenny shrugs. "My best guess. Lana certainly wasn't using the phone."

"If that doesn't say Vasquez was both of their dealers, then what does?" asks Seth.

Terry plays with the cardboard coaster in front of him. "And this Lana woman? Who is she?"

"Lana Baker. A lowlife drug addict. She's got quite the rap sheet."

Terry leans over the table and scowls. "You knew this going into the interview and didn't bother giving me a heads up?" His tone bites with accusation.

"No, Terry. I've been looking into Lana Baker's family for a few days. I didn't have the faintest notion that Slavik had been dating her until Jimmy Tuesday brought it up."

Seth sighs heavily. "Forget all of that." He eyes Kenny and then me. "Let me make sure I'm following what the two of you are implying. This Lana Baker woman owns some sort of wolf-like creature that does her bidding?"

I really need that drink I ordered. "Not even close. Lana Baker died from an apparent overdose almost a month ago."

Terry shakes his head. "Then what's the point of all this? It feels like we're spinning our wheels and getting nowhere."

I groan. "Look, I have no proof yet, but I believe Lana overdosed the same day she got into that scrape with Slavik at Jimmy's Noodle House."

Seth leans back in the booth and rakes his fingers through his hair. "Even if you're right, how does it tell us anything?" asks Seth.

Kenny interjects, "What it tells *me* is that someone close to Lana might believe that Ernesto and Slavik are responsible for her death—even if they weren't."

Finally, someone with a clue.

I exhale loudly and slap the edge of the table. "Thank you, Kenny."

The waitress returns with our drinks. A Cherry Pepsi for Kenny and three tall mugs of some Scottish dark ale. The name of it escapes me. Terry thanks the girl, his hand briefly touching hers when she sets his drink down. Her ebony cheeks flush with a red hue, enhancing her beauty. She looks back at Terry as she walks away. I admit, the man has skills with the women, and he's not half-bad looking, either.

But he's no Seth.

I pat Seth's leg under the table and smile when he eyes me.

"So what's the next step?" asks Seth. "We look into this woman's life? Find out who her friends and family are and see if any of them own a wolf with red fur?"

Terry snorts and raises his hands. "I'm sorry, but this circus isn't what I signed up for. I thought we were trying to find out who stole the body from the morgue, not who or what killed the victims."

"One could lead to the other," I say, "but I know it's not likely. Still, we owe these victims to get to the truth, even if it winds up being a random coincidence that they were connected to a woman."

"*Possibly* connected," Terry emphasizes. "You don't know for a fact that Ernesto was this woman's drug dealer."

I concede. "You're right, but I'm gonna find out."

"Still, these two guys were total thugs," says Seth. "A drug dealer and an enforcer for the mob or whatever. Do we really care about any of it other than finding the beast that killed them and putting it down?"

"Nope." Terry takes a long swig from his mug.

"Look, you guys can stop now if you want, but I'm not letting it go. *Any* of it." The froth tickles my upper lip when I finally take a drink of the ale. It's thick, nutty, and delicious.

Terry drains his mug and sets it on the table. "I'm out."

"You talking ale or the case?" asks Seth. I already know the answer.

"Both." Terry slides out of the booth and drops a twenty on the table. "I've got a life to live, and it starts with that waitress. You guys can do whatever you want." He walks away.

Kenny pops out of the booth and stretches his arms over his head. "I've gotta run. I promised my aunt that I'd be there by six to watch Kellie."

I still can't believe I ever suspected him of being a Shadow Priest. It's just another of many "Crazy Alice" events I'd love to erase. "Be safe, Kenny, and thanks for your help."

Kenny nods and drops a five on the table next to Terry's twenty. "See ya later, Alice. Detective Ryan." He heads toward the exit.

"Seems like a good kid," says Seth.

I nod and suckle my ale over the edge of the thick mug.

Seth strokes the top of my thigh underneath the table. "I know you, Alice. You're holding back again. Let me in."

Remembering how things went with the Braille Killer, I can't allow myself to fight this battle alone. Seth is my rock and loves me, warts and all. He deserves to know everything, even if it makes him think I'm insane. Sometimes I wonder if I'm the one locked up in the loony bin dreaming up all this craziness I call life.

It would explain a lot… but not everything.

I set the mug down, close my eyes for a moment, and then nod. "Fine, but you must promise me that you'll be objective about what I tell you and not have me committed."

Seth lifts my hand to his lips and kisses the back of it. "Nothing you say will change my opinion of you, and for the record, I'd have to commit myself as well because I refuse to live without you. Your madness is mine to bear."

"Okay then…" I drain my mug and take a deep breath, and then I delve into the nightmare I witnessed while mind probing Slavik Garin.

Once I finish my tale of madness, we both sit there and stare at the table. Were it not for the current setting, the silence between us would be deafening. Every part of me wants to wind back time and erase every last word I uttered for the last ten minutes. Even as I laid everything out for him, I found myself doubting my own words and memory. I willingly drank the Kool-Aid Rico served me and asked for a second glass. Dove headfirst into a world of madness.

Finally, Seth breaks free from his waking coma. "I believe you."

The world screeches to a halt as my mind finally wraps itself around what he just said. My heart flutters, and my stomach rises into my throat. Tears brim at the corners of my eyes.

"You do?" I choke out.

He strokes my cheek with his thumb. Wipes away the lone tear that escapes containment. "If there's one thing I've learned while being your partner, it's to trust your instincts. You're rarely wrong about anything."

"So that's it? Hook, line, and sinker? You bought the farm? Sold your life and joined my crazy cult?"

Seth raises his arms. "Whoa, don't get too excited just yet. I'm not saying I believe every last thing you told me, at least not at face value. After all, animals don't walk around on their hind legs and talk like humans. Plus — and I know you might fight me on this one — werewolves don't exist, no matter how realistic the *Underworld* movies make them seem. But there's definitely a logical explanation for everything you saw while brain probing."

"*Mind* probing, according to my father. Although I think I'll start calling it *mind tethering* since the former sounds a bit too alien encounterish."

"Call it whatever you want." He downs the rest of his ale and belches half-heartedly. "So where do we go from here? Dig further into the victims? Or this Lana Baker woman?"

My gaze meets the waning sun through the window. The sunrays have set the clouds ablaze in shades of yellow, orange, pink, and red. It's all beautiful, but the reds are what draw my eye. Crimson claw marks.

I slide out of the booth and add another twenty to the table. "Close. We need to find Lindy Baker, Lana's daughter, and I think I know where to start."

CHAPTER SIXTEEN

THE UNSEASONABLY WARM EVENING has renewed Desert Springs' night life once again. That, plus the annual "Fall Slam," an organized event between the restaurants, bars, and nightclubs where a prepaid pass gets you access to all of them for the entire evening. The combination of the two has the downtown streets crawling with people. The crowded sidewalks bustle with conversation and laughter.

Seth stares through the windshield of the unmarked sedan. "How are we going to find anyone in this chaos, let alone some scrawny girl?"

I admit the conditions aren't ideal, but I have a plan. "We get out of the car and walk around."

Seth scoffs, "You mean like real cops?"

I roll my eyes. "We are *real* cops."

"You know what I mean." He sighs. "This Lindy girl… she could literally be anywhere."

"Based on the encounters I've had with her, she won't be hanging around on the street, and she's too young for the bars. She's not one for crowds or attention."

Seth stares at me, his eyebrows hunkered down over the bridge of his nose. "Then why are we here?"

"I think this is her territory, so to speak. We know she frequents Wired Coffee, which is right down the street."

"Yeah, but they've been closed for hours."

"True, but there's another place she likes to visit right around the corner, and it's still open."

Seth shakes his head. "Why didn't you just start with that? 'Hey Seth, let's go check out this place right around the corner. I think Lindy might be there.'"

I smile and open my door. "That'd be too simple."

He shakes his head again. "Of course it would be."

We exit the car and enter the throng. It takes much longer than it should to reach the corner, and by the time we do, I'm starting to feel claustrophobic. Around the corner, the crowd thins out significantly, allowing me to breathe again.

According to Google Maps, Adolf's Flowers sits three doors down from the corner on the left-hand side of Third Street. A quick glance confirms its location.

I grab Seth's arm and pull him to a halt. "We need to be cautious."

He nods. "I know. If she is the Midnight Mauler, she's dangerous."

"You do that on purpose, don't you?"

"Do what?"

"Say things wrong."

His head jerks back. "What did I say wrong?"

I can't tell if he's joking or not. "You know it's the *Night* Mauler."

He frowns. "Isn't that what I said?"

"Never mind." I point across the street. "She might be over there at Adolf's Flowers."

"As in Adolf Hitler?"

"Yeah, genius, the guy named his flower shop after the Nazi leader." I shake my head.

He shrugs. "Why else would it be named Adolf?"

"It was a popular Polish name. It means noble wolf."

"Huh." He cocks his head. "Is that why the girl likes the place?"

"I seriously doubt she's made the connection. Anyway, I'm pretty sure she likes Rufin, Adolf's son."

"Gotcha. Makes more sense."

We approach the building from across the street and hold up behind a parked car. A daisy and a bee adorn the blue-and-green neon sign hanging in the flower shop's window. It's a quaint design, yet appealing. Another neon sign glows red below it, continually spelling out the word "OPEN."

The door to the flower shop swings open. I duck behind the car and pull Seth down with me. Through the car windows I see a young man dressed in black slacks and a white polo exit with a bouquet of red roses. He heads down the sidewalk and away from the crowded street.

I rise and motion for Seth to follow. "Come on, it's not her."

We cross the street and stop just beyond the shop window. Peering through the window, I see nothing but flowers. Display after display. Each one showcases a beautiful arrangement. Adolf is a master at his craft. From what I can tell, the shop is narrow but deep. Lindy could be anywhere inside.

"Guess we go in."

Seth nods and opens the door, which triggers one of those annoying doorbell noises.

So much for ninja mode.

He ushers me inside the aromatic shop. It's the first time I've ever set foot inside a flower shop, and I immediately understand the affinity Lindy has for such a place. The wide variety of flowers and the vast array of colors on display mesmerizes me. Far too many scents battle for the attention of my nose, rendering them all indistinguishable. It's a sensory overload.

A man approaches from deep in the shop. His broad smile welcomes us well before he speaks. "I see you are here for the first time." He chuckles, likely due to the looks of surprise on our faces. "I am no psychic, but I am an expert on flowers… and love." He halts before us, his hands folded behind his back, and bows. "I am Adolf. Welcome to my flower shop."

Seth and I return the man's bow. What else could we do?

"We're looking—"

Adolf holds up a finger and wags it. "Ah, ah, ah. There is no need for explanation. You two make the perfect couple. I have the perfect solution for your wedding flower needs. Follow me." He turns and marches back the way he came.

Seth looks at me and shrugs with a grin. "We're already here, and I did ask you to marry me, even if you haven't given me a real answer yet."

Guilt rises from my gut. With everything going on, I'd all but forgotten Seth's proposal. At least that's what I tell myself. Both of us know better. Seth turns and chases Adolf deeper into the shop, leaving me no choice but to follow.

"Blue lilacs to match your fiancé's stunning eyes," says Adolf. "She will be the envy of the world."

"Those are nice," admits Seth, "but I was thinking more along the lines of something in a shade of red to match her hair."

Adolf frowns, then nods his head. "Very well, I have the perfect choice."

"That's not why we're here, Mr. Kuznik," I say, much louder than intended. Seth and Adolf both face me, neither brave enough to challenge me with words.

"I'm Detective Bergman, and this is Detective Ryan. We're looking for a girl named Lindy Baker. Do you know her?"

Adolf's expression darkens. "Has she done something wrong?"

"That isn't a concern of yours," says Seth.

"If it involves my son, then it *is* a concern of mine," counters Adolf.

"I assure you that this has nothing to do with your son. Has she been here?" I ask.

Adolf nods. "She and Rufin are in the alley behind the shop at this very moment." He points in the door's direction.

I approach the open door with stealth and caution, Seth close on my heels. When I glance back, I see that Seth's drawn his gun and holds it low. I scowl at him and mouth "no guns." He scowls back and then holsters it.

God, don't let that be a mistake.

"You can come out, Father." I recognize Rufin's voice.

"It's not your father," growls Lindy.

So much for the element of surprise.

I step outside, hands raised. Seth follows my lead. "We just want to talk, Lindy."

Scorn burns in Lindy's eyes. "Why would you betray me, Rufin?"

"I didn't," Rufin pleads.

Lindy tosses a bouquet of lilies on the ground. Tears glisten in her eyes. "You're a liar."

She turns to leave, but Rufin snags her arm. "Lindy, please don't go."

Lindy jerks away and hunches over as she screams, "Why won't you just leave me alone?"

I'm not sure if she's talking to Rufin or me. Probably both. Either way, her tone sets the hairs on my nape on end. My hand slides toward my holster with expectations that the beast will manifest. "Everything's okay, Lindy. Just calm down."

She turns and bolts down the alley. Seth brushes past me and takes off after her before I have the chance to warn him. But what would I have said to convince him anyway?

Rufin backs up to the wall and slumps to the ground. "This is all my fault. I never should've talked to you." He lowers his head and sobs into his arms.

I kneel next to Rufin. "I'm sorry that just happened, but it's paramount we speak with her."

Adolf enters the alley and stares down at his son. "Rufin, this is not the way I taught you to behave."

"But I love her." Rufin sniffs and coughs. "Now she'll never speak to me again," he whispers.

"If she loves you, she will forgive you." Adolf proffers his hand to Rufin. "Take my hand and get up, son. Detective Bergman has questions for you, and you will answer them all." Rufin wipes his face with his shirt and then takes Adolf's hand.

Seth appears from out of the shadows, his face bright red and sucking wind. "I… wow… she's fast."

I chuckle, more from nervous energy than amusement. "That's why I didn't chase after her."

The four of us head inside the shop. Seth, Rufin, and I sit down at a small round table in the back while Adolf heads to the front of the store to lock the front door and roll down the steel security mesh gate. Apparently, stealing flowers is a big business.

Rufin stares at his hands. "What do you want to know?"

I place my hands on the table. "Tell us where we can find Lindy. Where does she live?"

"Our Lady of the Desert," mumbles Rufin.

"The homeless shelter?" asks Seth.

Rufin nods. "I've seen her come out of there before."

"She could've been there for another reason," I offer, but he shakes his head.

"It's not possible." He looks up at me. "Not when I saw her."

"What do you mean?" I ask.

"Everyone always comes out of there at seven in the morning."

"And that's when you saw her," I confirm. Rufin nods.

"Is there anything else you can tell us about her?" asks Seth. "Does she have other friends?"

Rufin shakes his head. Tears begin streaming down his cheeks again. "She has no one anymore."

"That's not true. She still has you." I hand Rufin one of my cards. "Call me if she shows up again. It's imperative we talk to her. Do you understand that?"

"Yes." Rufin pulls out his cellphone and enters the number into his contact list. "But I doubt she'll be back after tonight."

Seth and I share a glance and then head down the dark alley toward Main Street.

God, let her be at the shelter…

* * * * *

Fifteen minutes later, Seth and I pull up outside Our Lady of the Desert. The building looks nothing like what I expected. Its drab, brown stucco saw its peak a decade ago, and the building contains nothing of architectural significance. It has no porch and therefore no columns or arches to speak of. Given its name, I'd expected it to look more akin to a church. Instead, it looks more akin to a seedy motel, albeit one with a single set of doors.

Several people lie on the handful of steps leading up to a set of faded turquoise doors, all of them incapacitated in one manner or another. I can't imagine sleeping that way. It must be hell in the morning.

The two wooden doors, blistered with age and in need of a good sanding, stand closed. Several knocks later via a large brass knocker on the left door finally bring a portly man to the door.

"We're closed for the night," gruffs the man. "Filled up early."

The man moves to close the door, but Seth sticks his boot in the way. "We're not looking for a bed—" Seth flashes the man his badge through the crack. "—we're looking for a person."

The man sighs and pulls the door open. "Very well. Come inside, and we'll see if we can't find whoever it is you're looking for."

Once inside, the small foyer doesn't smell too bad or look too dirty, but the age of the building is evident with every surface and fixture. Run strictly by donations, the shelter likely scrapes by housing and feeding those they can with little to no money left over for renovations. It's sad to see people relegated to these kinds of living conditions, but the alternative of sleeping out in the elements is far worse, especially during the winter months.

It takes a few moments for the man to secure the door behind us. Once he does, he turns back and says, "Alrighty, give me the basics."

"We're looking for a red-headed girl," I say. "She's seventeen years old."

The man nods. "Yep, yep. Not too many gingers around these parts. Think I know just the one you're looking for. She's a good kid. Never been in trouble to my knowledge. Hope she's not now."

Seth's been scoping out the place since we walked through the door. "Is there another way out of here?"

"Fire safety demands a back door," says the man, "but it stays locked unless the fire alarm sounds. We have someone stationed at the door as well."

"Good." Seth looks around. "So where can we find her?"

"I'll take you to her. We keep the adolescents separated from the adults unless they're under four years of age. We also don't allow just anyone in the rooms with them—" He turns and winks at me. "—even those with badges."

"Can't be too careful these days," I agree.

"By the way, I'm Stephan Jorg, head of security." His laugh is jolly and warm. "Okay, one of those two things might be a falsehood."

Seth smirks. "So you're not Stephan Jorg."

Stephan continues to laugh as he beckons us to follow him. The building is a maze of doors, hallways, and staircases, some leading up and some leading down. Several turns, doors, and hallways later, we arrive on the third floor and halt in front of a semi-pink door with the number 36 affixed to it. As with the rest of the building, the door has seen better days.

"If we're talking about the same girl, she'll be in this room," notes Stephan.

"Thank you," I say. "We'll take it from here."

Stephan dips his head. "Very well. I'll wait here in the hallway so that I can escort you back out when you've finished." He knocks on the door, opens it, and steps back.

Rectangular windows set high in the outer wall give the room its only source of light, two squares of moonlight on the rough wooden floor. The effect casts the outer perimeter of the room in deep shadows. Additional light pours in from the dimly lit hallway when we step into the room.

It takes several moments for my eyes to adjust to the low light. Four sets of bunk beds nestle the walls, one against each of them, but the only one I'm interested in is the one in the far corner. More specifically, the lower bunk.

Huddled in the corner as far from the light as possible sits Lindy, her knees drawn to her chest. She clutches what looks like an old photograph in her hands. Her yellow eyes shine in the darkness, just as they had in the webcam video from Desert Springs Nature Preserve.

Seth stands just inside the doorway, his hand resting on his holster.

"Wait here," I whisper. He nods, but I can tell he doesn't like it.

Lindy growls as I approach. Deep. Throaty. Causes the hairs on my nape to stand on end. Instinct tells me to draw my gun, but I ignore the warning.

She's just a scared young woman.

I know better. There are two bodies that dispute the fact.

Pulse racing, I kneel next to the bed.

Stare into the shadows.

Meet Lindy's gaze.

Sweat dampens my palms.

Fear twists my gut.

I'm less than three feet away from a vicious killer.

CHAPTER SEVENTEEN

AN HOUR LATER, SETH and I sit with Lindy Baker in Interview Room One at the police station. She sits with her feet perched on the edge of the chair, her arms wrapped around her legs. Something about her unsettles me, and it has nothing to do with what her true nature might be. In fact, I'm unsettled because this all feels wrong.

Seth rests his forearms on the table. "Where were you between the hours of 1:30am and 4am on Monday morning?"

Lindy stares straight ahead and says nothing.

"How about between the hours of 3:30am and 5am this morning?" I ask.

Her gaze meets mine. Bright yellow eyes underneath the shadow of her hooded jacket. Sends chills racing down to my toes and stands the hairs on my arms on end.

How can she not be the monster we're after?

After a full minute of silence, Seth speaks up. "Lindy, you need to talk to us."

Her gaze breaks away from mine and focuses on Seth. "I've got nothing to say to you," she growls. "You're just like everyone else."

"I promise you that we're not," I say. "We're here to help you."

"Help me?" Her eyes flash with anger. "I've done nothing wrong, yet you pursue me as if I'm some sort of fugitive."

"Answer our questions, and you'll be free to go," says Seth. "Where were you?"

"At the shelter, like I am every night." She looks back at me. "Why are you asking me these questions?"

"I think you know why," says Seth. "Two dead men."

She frowns. "The ones who were mauled? What do they have to do with me?"

"Everything." Seth leans back and crosses his arms. "I don't think you were at the shelter either of those mornings."

"I'm not lying." She looks at me again. "Why won't you just leave me alone?"

Seth leans forward. "You know we can't do that, Lindy. We know what you did to them."

She scrunches her face. "What are you talking about?"

"They hurt your mother, didn't they?" Seth presses.

"My mother? You think they hurt her?" she scoffs. "She always dished out as much as she ever got, but I'm sure you read that in your police files."

Seth nods. "We did. She was a tough woman, but that doesn't change the fact that she was your mother. You still loved her and hated what they did to her."

Lindy seethes, spittle peppering the air with every word. "That woman was *never* a mother to me. She abused, neglected, and abandoned me, and I hated her for it."

"But you went back home after emancipating yourself," I say. "Why would you do that if you hated her so much?"

Lindy's gaze falls to the floor. "I had nowhere else to turn and didn't want to live on the street. When I came back, she greeted me with open arms. Made me feel like things had changed. I wanted to believe it so badly that I ignored all the signs pointing to the fact that she was the same person I'd left behind so many years before."

"That must've been hard to take," I say.

"She tried to get me to turn tricks for her. Introduced me to all the thugs in her life. I refused, and that infuriated her. She would've killed me if I'd still been the little girl she remembered, but the years of drug abuse weakened her, and my strength finally matched hers. Strength and strong will runs in the family.

"I thought everything would be okay if I just stayed out of her way, but she hounded me day and night. I never thought it would end. Then, the day she overdosed, I could finally breathe again. It gave me my freedom back."

"With your mother out of the picture, Ernesto Vasquez forced you to distribute for him, right?" asks Seth.

Lindy's head jerks up, her eyes wide. "No! I've never met Ernesto Vasquez."

"I don't believe that for a second," says Seth. "I think that's why you agreed to meet him in the woods in the middle of the night—"

Lindy jumps up from the chair, her arms raised in the air. "I don't know what you're talking about."

"—but you had other plans and took matters into your own hands, didn't you?" Seth finishes.

"You're insane!" She gestures toward herself with open hands. "Look at me. I'm little more than skin and bones. How could I possibly take down a giant man? He was mauled to death by a vicious animal."

Seth presses forward. "You might be scrawny, but your beast isn't."

Her hands curl into fists at her sides. "I don't understand." Tears glisten in her eyes. "I live in a shelter, and animals aren't allowed in there."

Seth rises from his chair and points a finger at her. "I know *what* you are, Lindy."

Tears stream down her face. Drip on the tile floor. "I'm just a seventeen-year-old girl," she pleads. "You know nothing about me."

I'll admit, she's quite the actress, turning on the waterworks at just the right moment. But then I see it. More than tears wet the floor. Tiny crimson pools.

Goosebumps crawl up my arms and legs as I watch blood drip from her clenched fists.

Seth is relentless. Thinks he might break her. "Don't I?" He sits back down. "How long did Slavik use you before you finally had enough?"

"He never used me," she growls through clenched teeth.

"But he tried, didn't he? That's why you had your beast butcher him in the alley."

"You don't know what you're talking about. I was at the shelter. Ask Stephan if you don't believe me." Lindy collapses back into the chair and buries her face in her hands. "Why are you doing this to me? I've done nothing wrong."

I place my hand on Seth's knee. "Can we talk outside?" He nods.

After offering Lindy a tissue, we step outside the room and move down the hallway, out of earshot.

"What's up?" asks Seth.

"I think you've grilled her enough for now."

"She's about to break. I can feel it." He glances back down the hallway. "Five more minutes, and she'll tell us where she keeps the beast."

I touch his arm. "No, Seth. Five more minutes, and you'll be lying in a pool of blood."

He scoffs. "Not a chance. No matter what you think you saw, she's no werewolf. I've got her scared."

"That's what she wants you to believe, but you're only gauging her demeanor by her face. You didn't see her hands, did you? She's so enraged that she drew her own blood with her fingernails—or claws."

Seth broods. "Fine. Maybe I don't have her scared." He motions back toward the interview room with his hand. "What do you want to do then? Cut her loose? Let her back out so she can have her beast kill again?"

She is *the beast.*

"Right now, we've got nothing to hold her on, but I think I can get through to her if you'll let me go back in there alone."

Seth sweeps his hand through his hair. "That's a stupid idea. If she controls this Night Mauler..." His eyes mist over. "You set her off, and she'll sic her beast on us. We'll never see it coming until it's too late."

"But I won't." I take his hand. Kiss it. "Trust me, Seth. I think she wants to talk, just not to you."

He shakes his head and sighs. "I know there's no point in arguing with you. I won't go back into the room, but I'll be right outside the door. If I hear even the slightest hint of a raised voice or a threat, I'm coming in and booking her. Got it?"

I laugh and kiss his cheek. "Not sure what you'd charge her with, but okay."

When I reenter the interview room, Lindy is staring at a photograph. She shoves it into her jacket pocket and turns toward the wall.

I sit back down at the table. "What's the picture of?"

"Why should I tell you?"

"Because I'm asking politely."

"You think I'm stupid? I've seen plenty of police shows. This good cop, bad cop routine is a waste of time."

"I promise you that's not what we're doing here, Lindy. In fact, that kind of tactic is illegal. Seth—Detective Ryan—becomes impassioned easily, especially when he believes something to be true, but he's honestly one of the nicest guys you'll ever meet."

She folds her arms. "Easy to say about a guy you're sleeping with."

My jaw drops. "What makes you think that?"

"I smelled him on you the first time we met." She turns and looks at me. "Don't deny it."

"Fine. You're right, but that doesn't change the fact that he's a good detective. The truth will come out."

"Maybe it will, and if it does, you'll see that it has *nothing* to do with me."

"I hope you're right." I get up and move my chair around the side of the table. Position it so that we're only a foot apart before sitting down again. "Look, I think we got off to a bad start. How about we begin again?"

"I told you before, we'll never be friends. You and I are from two different worlds."

I reach over and touch her covered forearm. "We're more alike than you think."

She glares at my hand but doesn't recoil. "What, you think us both being gingers makes us kindred spirits somehow?"

I smile and squeeze her arm. My hand nearly encompasses it. As I let go, I can't help but wonder how someone as scrawny as she is could ever muster enough strength to break a twig, let alone rip open someone's ribcage.

"No, but it's not a bad start," I say. "Like you, I grew up without a father."

She shrugs. "Everyone does these days. It's abnormal to have two parents."

"I agree, and it makes me sad. I hated my father for twenty-six years. Thought and hoped he was dead, but just recently found out he's been locked away in the loony bin since before my birth. To be honest, I'm not sure which is worse."

Lindy stares at her open palms, and so do I. There are several red marks across both palms but no visual wounds.

So where did the blood come from?

"My mother never told me who my father was," she says. "I'm not sure she even knew, given the fact that she was always high, wasted, or both."

"I'm sorry."

She looks up at me. "Don't sweat it, I haven't. Given the caliber of men in her life, I'm sure he's probably some lowlife thug rotting in jail or six feet under."

"Sometimes, not knowing is far better than the truth." She nods but doesn't comment, so I change the subject. "So how about that picture you were looking at? I could tell it means a lot to you."

Lindy retrieves the picture from her pocket and stares at it. "This is my only possession. At least the only one that matters." Tears well in the corners of her eyes.

"I can see that." What I don't see is a killer.

Have I gotten this all wrong?

She wipes her eyes with the back of her hand. "It's the only picture I have of my great grandma. My mother destroyed everything else in a drunken rage one night. Took everything we owned and threw it into a burning trash barrel. She would've burned this picture too, but I kept it hidden inside a hole in my bedroom wall."

I proffer my hand. "May I see it? I promise I'll give it right back."

Lindy hands me the picture. "She's the one on the left. I was only five when she passed away."

The picture is yellowed and worn with age, its edges tattered. Four women stand in front of an open field of golden wheat, arms locked over each other's shoulders. The woman on the left is a spitting image of Lana, Lindy's mother. The two in the middle, an older blonde and a black woman, are unremarkable, but the woman on the right with jet-black hair catches my breath.

She looks like the woman from Rico's.

My heart kicks at my ribcage as my pulse spikes. "Do you know who these other women are?" I ask, hoping for confirmation of what I already know to be true.

Lindy cocks her head and stares at me for several seconds. "You recognize one of them, don't you?"

"I believe so, but how did you know?"

"There's a hint of recognition in your eyes, but it's your racing heart that's a dead giveaway."

I glance down at my chest. "You can hear it?"

"A stampede." She points at the photo. "Great grandma wrote their names on the back."

Flipping the picture over, I see a date and four names scrawled in black ink. According to the ledger, the picture was taken on May 11th, 1972 in Lamar, Colorado. Three of the four names—Lora Murphy, Judith Penshaw, and Abigail Foreman—hold no meaning for me, but the fourth sends my pulse racing ever faster.

Dakota Barnes.

CHAPTER EIGHTEEN

SETH'S STILL WAITING OUTSIDE the door when I exit the interview room. "Well?" he says expectantly.

I shake my head and push past him. "She's a smart girl."

"No confession then?" He sighs. "Figured as much."

"I'm going to grab my stuff and drive Lindy back to the shelter."

"I'll go with you."

"That's not necessary." I put a finger to my lips and motion with my head. Seth follows me down the hallway.

"What's up?" he whispers once we're a good distance from the interview room.

"I'll handle Lindy. You need to collect samples from the interview room and deliver them to the lab."

He frowns. "Samples of what?"

"She bled all over the floor. Plus, there's the water bottle she drank from. I'm sure she lost a few hairs as well."

"You don't need to be alone with her. She might have some sort of whistle she uses to summon the beast. I'll get someone else to gather samples and come with you."

I close my eyes for a moment and take a deep breath. "This is important,

Seth. It's not something to push off onto someone else. The first body was stolen, along with all the evidence. Remember?"

He crosses his arms. "Yeah, I haven't forgotten."

"These samples may give us the proof we need to tie her to the victims."

"Okay. Fine." He raises my chin with his hand and stares at me until I meet his gaze. "You sure you'll be okay?"

"She's a young girl who might've killed the men she thought were responsible for ruining her life and taking her mother's life. I don't think she's out to kill everyone she meets."

"Maybe not, but I'm sure we're climbing up her list of potential targets."

"Either way, we can't leave this to someone else."

He grimaces. "I agree, but that doesn't mean I have to like it."

"Me neither." I rise on my tippy toes and kiss his cheek. "See you tomorrow?"

Seth's brow wrinkles. "You're not staying at my place tonight?"

"There's just so much going on right now. I need to sleep in my own bed for a change." Seth nods and I head toward our shared office.

"Love you," he calls to me.

The fifteen-minute ride from the station to the shelter is awkward to say the least. Lindy says nothing the entire way. When I drop her off, she doesn't look back as she climbs the steps to Our Lady of the Desert. After what we put her through, especially Seth, it's understandable.

She's a tough girl.

I sit and watch until she's let inside and then start driving home. At least that was the plan. But the picture Lindy showed me continues to weigh on my mind. As tired as I am, the last thing I need to do is go somewhere else, but I don't think there's any way I'll be able to fall asleep until after I pay Rico another visit.

My dash display says it's after eleven already when I pull around the back of Rico's Cane Shoppe, but Rico's Jeep Cherokee isn't there. I park next to the back door and thrum the steering wheel with my thumbs, trying to decide what I should do next.

Why am I here? It's late.

A lone yellow light flickers above Rico's back door. The three other shops in the small strip mall have lights above their doors as well, but all are in disrepair. Two of them hang from their wires and the other one houses a shattered bulb.

The entire building has seen better days, its beige paint chipped and peeling away from cinderblock walls cracked so bad in places that I can see light coming through the wall. In this desert environment, it doesn't take long for anything to fade, crack, or sun rot. The sun is brutal eight months of the year.

Rico's Cane Shoppe is the only store that remains open. If not for the basement, I'm sure Rico would've moved on to a better location. He's stuck now.

The red lettering painted on Rico's back door, the "freshest" paint on the entire building, reminds me of the business card Rico gave me. I retrieve it from the hidden pocket tucked behind my credentials and stare at the business name.

Steven's VCR Repair.

Rico told me to call the number day or night if I had information about the Shadow Mirror but never specified if I could use it otherwise.

Will he be upset if I call him now?

Then another thought strikes me.

Will this number ring through to him or someone else?

As with most things in life, there's only one way to find out, so I punch the number into my phone. My thumb hovers over the SEND button. Once pressed, there's no going back. Suddenly, I'm Commissioner Gordon, contemplating whether or not I should use the Bat Signal.

Just make the call.

I swallow hard and press SEND.

A single ring, and the line clicks open.

My breath catches in my throat.

"Steven's VCR Repair. How can we help get your tape rolling?" The male voice isn't Rico's, but I'm certain I recognize it. The deep Texas drawl sends chills racing down to my toes.

"Jake?"

"It's Steven, ma'am, just like the name implies. There ain't no Jake at this number. Do you have a VCR emergency I can help you with?"

I feel like I need some sort of secret pass phrase, but Rico never gave me one. "It's Detective Bergman."

"A pleasure, ma'am. How may I assist you?"

"Rico gave me this number. Said to call it day or night."

"We do twenty-four seven repairs every day of the year. You got a stuck head or a tape jam? Perhaps your kid stuffed their PBJ inside? That one's always a doozy, but we can fix anything."

I'm getting nowhere, so I say the one thing I'm certain will grab his attention. "I've got information about the Shadow Mirror."

"Hold your horses, darlin'." Three distinct clicks sound in my ear, followed by a loud screeching noise and other tones reminiscent of an old dial-up modem. I pull the phone away from my ear just as the horrific sound cuts out.

Ten seconds later, a woman's voice shatters the silence. "Detective Bergman?" I know her voice, too.

"Dakota Barnes." My hand tightens around the steering wheel. "You've got a lot of explaining to do."

She ignores me. "What do you know of the Shadow Mirror?"

"We talk in person or not at all. Meet me at Rico's within the hour." I pull the phone away from my ear and move my thumb to hit END, but then her face appears on my screen.

"Wait," she says.

My mind reels, uncertain as to how she converted our phone call into a video stream. "Wait for what?"

"It's not possible for me to meet you in an hour." She pulls her phone back from her face, giving me a view of the looming metal structure behind her.

A twinge of jealousy sends my voice soaring several octaves. "You're in Paris?" I've always wanted to visit the Eiffel Tower.

"Yes, on business. I can meet you at Rico's tomorrow night." She glances down at something. "Twenty-one hundred hours?"

Tomorrow night…

The timing is far from ideal, but I need to see her reaction in person when I tell her about the picture. Faces can lie, but the body never does. For so many reasons, I need to know the truth. "I'll see you then."

CHAPTER NINETEEN

TWO IN THE MORNING. Sunday. My phone blares *The Shortest Straw* by Metallica. Second day using it, and I'm already rethinking my new ring tone. It takes a few moments for me to acclimate to my surroundings before I grab the phone. A local number displays on the screen, but I don't recognize it.

I answer it. "Hello?"

"Help me," the voice rasps.

My sleepiness vanishes. "Who is this?"

"Rufin," he whispers. "It's here, Detective Bergman. The beast. I think it killed my father, and now it's after me."

I pull on my pants with the phone smashed between my ear and shoulder. "Where are you at?"

"In our apartment above the flower shop. Hurry! I don't think I've got a lot of—"

Bang!

Bang-bang!

"Rufin!" The line goes dead. I call right back, but it goes straight to voicemail.

Pulling on a shirt and stuffing my feet into my boots while running out of the room produces the expected result. I hop-slip on the floor and catch the doorjamb with my left shoulder. Several expletives fly off my tongue as pain shoots down my arm and numbs my fingers. Thank God Mother isn't here to hear me. She'd be in the hallway with unnatural speed, lecturing me about Jesus and how he hears every word we utter. She'd die seven times over if she knew some of the thoughts I have.

Only thirty seconds pass before I'm sprinting to my car. Once inside, I jam the key into the ignition and twist with such force that the top of the key breaks right off. I curse the day even as the engine roars to life. The car jerks and bucks backward when I give it gas and shove it into reverse. Tires squealing, my headlights burn holes through the dark night as I speed down the narrow residential road, but my gut tells me this day's about to get several shades darker.

Adrenaline pumping, and my grip tight on the wheel, I barrel toward Main Street. My mind swirls with questions and fear, but my primary thought revolves around Lindy. What would make her go back and attack Adolf and Rufin?

It's a stupid move.

Seven minutes later, I pull up in front of Adolf's Flower Shop. The shop is still locked down tight, the window intact and the metal security mesh gate in place. No light filters through the front window, but there's a light on upstairs. Jumping out of my car, I make a quick call to Seth and ask him to notify dispatch of the situation, something I should've done right from the start.

Gun drawn, I sprint around the side of the building and into the back alley. In my peripheral vision, I glimpse a flash of red at the far end of the alley, but it disappears around the corner by the time I look over.

"Wait!" I yell and start to pursue the beast, but then an engine fires behind me. I swing around and take aim at the white van facing me. It sits about twenty yards away. Through its windshield, bathed in the light of its dashboard lights, I can just make out a bald-headed man in the driver's seat. He looks right at me.

The blood drains from my face, and my breath catches in my throat. I know that face behind the van's wheel. It's one I'll never forget.

Reagan.

I move forward and squint to get a better view of him, just to be certain, but the van's headlights blast me. The bright lights disorient and blind me momentarily, but it's far too long.

Tires squeal. Kick up rocks that ping off metal dumpsters and doors.

The light intensifies as the van careens wildly and then heads straight for me. The alley is narrow. Far too narrow for me to avoid the oncoming van. I turn and run, holstering my gun in the process.

The engine roars louder, and the air warms as the demon breathes down my neck.

The door to Adolf's Flower Shop stands wide open just a few paces ahead. But will I make it in time? There's no way I can chance a backward glance. Throwing myself forward and to the side, I tuck and roll across the asphalt. The impact jars me, and little rocks bite into my shoulder.

The alley twists around me as I tumble through the open door, not a moment before the van rumbles past. A black cloud of exhaust fumes fills the flower shop. Stings my eyes and burns my lungs.

Scrambling to my feet, I thrust myself back into the alley, my gun drawn once again. I take aim at the van as I sprint after it, but I'm already too late. Its tires squeal as it rounds the corner at the end of the alley and merges onto Main Street.

By the time I reach the end of the alley, I'm sucking wind hard. A red taillight glows in the distance as the van speeds away, the roar of its engine fading. Doubled over, it takes a minute for me to catch my breath and breathe again, my lungs full of fire and a twinge in both my sides. When I finally do, I call the van in.

Twisting around in a circle, I see no movement of any kind. Deep shadows fill the distances between sporadic streetlights. The beast could've gone anywhere.

Or she could be watching me right now.

The hairs on my nape stand on end as I will myself to see into the shadows. Then another thought sends my pulse soaring once again, and my tired legs can't carry me back to the open door of Adolf's Flower shop fast enough.

She could've doubled back to finish the job if Rufin's still alive!

* * * * *

Gun drawn and flashlight in hand, I enter the back door of the flower shop. All is quiet except for my heart raging in my ears. As my flashlight beam sweeps the deep room, I take stock of the chaos. Glass shards, rocks, water, and remains of flowers are literally everywhere. What I don't see among the debris is blood.

To the left of the small table at the back of the shop lies the remains of a door, half of it ripped off its hinges and torn to shreds. A steep, narrow stairway lies beyond the doorway and ascends to the upper floor apartment. Gray carpet, worn with age and use, covers the treads. Several are spotted with fresh blood.

I do my best to preserve evidence as I creep up the stairs with caution, but Rufin's life still hangs in the balance. I keep one eye on the treads and one eye ahead. The last thing I want to do is track blood through the apartment.

The seventh, ninth, and twelfth steps creak and groan under my weight. If Lindy is waiting for me up ahead, she knows I'm here now. Then again, she would've smelled me long ago.

A narrow hallway, little more than two feet wide, runs perpendicular to the awkward landing at the top of the stairs. The split hallway leads to four separate rooms, two to my left and two to my right. Three of the four doors are closed. Only the farthest one to my left stands open.

Light bathes the hallway carpet and part of the wall from the open door, and shadows continually crawl up the wall. A dull hum and a consistent squeak tell me there's a ceiling fan on in the room. The trail of blood from the stairway leads in that direction. Or rather, comes from that direction.

Knowing I've got nothing to lose at this point, I call out Rufin's name, but the boy doesn't answer. After about thirty seconds of listening and hearing nothing but the ceiling fan, I'm fairly confident I'm alone. Or at least the only one still alive.

With my eye still on the open door, I carefully ease open the first door down the left hallway. A quick sweep with my flashlight confirms it's an empty bathroom. I pull the bathroom door closed and move toward the open door ahead.

Squeak!

The jarring noise leaves me gasping.

Bam!

My heart thrashes against my ribcage as I jerk around and face the landing. The sound came from downstairs.

Snap!

The bedroom light behind me zaps out, causing the shadows to deepen beyond my flashlight beam.

Someone's tripped the breaker.

I draw a deep breath and let it out slowly.

Squeak!

The stairway. Is it the seventh step, or one closer to the top?

Squeak!

A low growl rumbles from the stairway. Yellow eyes glow in the light of my flashlight beam. Flashes of Slavik's death bombard me. Suddenly, the gun feels useless in my grasp.

I should've brought Esther.

I take a step back and plant my foot, keeping my flashlight and gun trained on the beast. "This needs to end, Lindy. No more bloodshed."

The beast's ears perk up, and it turns its head back toward the stairway. A moment later, it bolts down the stairs.

Thump!

Thump!

Bang!

Yelp!

The gunshot echoes from downstairs. Startles me. But not as much as the mournful yelp.

Several seconds pass as I hold my breath and strain my ears for the faintest hint of movement.

"Alice!" Seth's voice nearly stops my heart. "Are you okay?"

"Upstairs!" I yell, aiming my gun at the landing just to be safe.

Three stairs squeak as Seth rumbles up the stairway. His head pokes around the corner, gun at the ready. We both lower our weapons.

"I think I wounded it," he says, "but it still managed to get up and scurry off."

"We need to go find her!"

"Brex and Janis are on it. They arrived right after I did and saw it bolt down the alley."

My stomach lurches. "If they find her, they'll kill her!"

"No matter what you think, that beast isn't Lindy," says Seth. "Trust me. And we're all better off if it is killed."

I nod, but I don't agree with him. I looked straight into her eyes. Saw exactly what Slavik did. "Fine."

"Are Adolf and Rufin okay?" he asks.

"I don't know, but I doubt it. Didn't get a chance to search the apartment yet."

Seth shines his flashlight past me. "Why are there spent bullet casings lying on the carpet?"

Just past the open doorway, I see them gleaming in Seth's flashlight beam. Three .22 caliber bullet casings. "Maybe Adolf got off a few shots."

My mind flashes back to the alley and Reagan. It can't be a coincidence.

Seth pushes past me and heads for the open door, gun drawn. I turn and follow him.

Beyond the open door lies a bedroom. Sparse, save a rickety eight-drawer dresser to the right of the door and a four-poster bed shoved against the far wall. No closet. Nowhere to hide except underneath the bed, but it sits high enough to see that the space underneath it is empty. The blood trail leads right to the foot of the bed.

A form lies atop the bed in a heap. As Seth and I move closer, it's clear that the body has no head. The sheets and bedspread are saturated with blood.

Seth looks around and frowns. "Where the hell is his head?"

It only takes a few moments for my flashlight beam to locate a steady stream of blood running down the left-hand bedpost at the foot of the bed. "Found it." Adolf's severed head is skewered atop it, his dead eyes staring into the abyss and his mouth agape. What the hell did he do to deserve such a brutal death?

"I'm calling it in," says Seth as he holsters his gun and takes out his cellphone.

I nod, knowing he means CSI. "Okay. I'm going to check the other two rooms."

Back in the hallway, I head over to the first door on the other side of the landing and ease it open. A second bathroom. Empty as well.

Something bangs against the fourth door as I approach.

"Rufin? It's Detective Bergman. Are you okay?"

No response. I place my ear to the door and hear whimpering. The handle turns when I test it, but something prevents me from opening the door. Rufin must've barricaded himself inside.

I knock loudly. "Rufin? Are you in there alone? The beast is gone."

"Are you sure?" he asks.

"I chased it away. Do you think you can open the door for me?"

A few moments later, something scrapes across the floor beyond the door. Then the door opens just wide enough for Rufin to peer through the crack.

His gaze meets mine. "You're safe, Rufin."

He opens the door farther. "What about my father? I heard him scream."

"Let's not think about that right now. How about you and I go downstairs?"

"I'm not a child, Detective Bergman." He peers down the dark hallway.

"He's dead, isn't he?"

I nod, knowing a lie would do neither of us any good. "I'm sorry, Rufin."

"Let me see him," he says.

He pushes past me, so I grab his arm and pull him back around. "There's nothing for you to see in there."

"He's my father!" Tears wet his cheeks and stain his shirt.

"I know, but I can't let you go in there right now. This entire apartment is a crime scene now."

He drops to his knees and covers his face. "This is all my fault."

"Don't ever think that. None of this is your fault." I urge him back to his feet and usher him toward the stairway with my flashlight beam and an arm around his back. "Come downstairs with me and tell me what happened."

Detective Roland meets us at the foot of the stairway. "What the hell happened in here?"

"That's what we're trying to sort out."

"Officer Brex said it was another mauling."

I nod. "Detective Ryan is upstairs."

"Good. Don't go anywhere."

"Wouldn't dream of it." I lead Rufin outside and into the alley where we can get some fresh air. It's a bit nippy but welcomed given the gruesome scene inside.

Officer Jaramillo arrives moments later, the click of his cane preceding him. "What can I do?"

I'm surprised to see him in the field. "Secure the perimeter. No one comes in or out until we get this sorted out."

"Yes, ma'am." He returns to his patrol car at the end of the alley. Officer Bartoli blocks the other end of the alley with his patrol car and helps Officer Jaramillo cordon off the entire section of the alley.

After about fifteen minutes, Rufin and I head back inside and sit down at the table in the back of the shop. "Tell me what happened after Detective Ryan and I left earlier this evening."

Rufin wipes his face on his sleeve and clears his throat. "After you left, I sat in the alley for several hours crying about Lindy. My father eventually came back out and told me that I needed to come inside and forget about her. He said that she wasn't worth my time or affection and that people like her were little more than human garbage. I argued with him for at least fifteen minutes about it, but he wouldn't listen. He just kept ranting about her being worthless and forbade me from ever talking to her again.

"I was so upset with him that I wanted to run away, but he's all I have left." Rufin pauses and tears stream down his face again. "All I *had* left." He tries to hold back a wave of sobs, but the effort just makes his nose bubble with snot. A stack of napkins sits on the small counter behind us. I grab one and hand it to him.

Rufin blows his nose into the napkin and then wipes his face with his sleeve. "I'm sorry."

I place my hand over his. "It's okay. Just take your time."

Rufin stares at my hand for a solid minute before continuing, "When we went back inside, about two in the morning, we weren't alone. This beast with red fur appeared out of nowhere and cornered us in the shop. My father and I made it to the stairway, and he locked the door behind us. By the time we made it up the stairs, the beast had clawed its way through the door.

"My father told me to get inside my room and barricade the door. He was going for the gun he kept underneath his pillow. Neither of us made it more than a few paces before the beast appeared on the landing. I've never seen an animal or whatever it is move so quickly. It looked between the two of us and rose on its hind legs like a bear. I've never been so scared in my life. It took everything I had to keep from wetting myself."

"No one would've blamed you if you had," I say.

"I didn't want to leave my father alone with the beast, but then I swear it said something to him." Rufin squeezes his eyes shut. "I know it doesn't make any sense. It's not possible for something like that to happen, but I saw it with my own eyes and heard it with my ears."

He looks at me and trembles. "Maybe it was the adrenaline pumping or something. I don't know. But the beast had yellow eyes, just like Lindy's. Its red fur reminded me of her red hair, too. I don't understand."

"I'm not sure what you saw, but I promise we'll get this figured out."

"It was her. I just know it." Rufin puts his hands over his face and cries. "Why would Lindy attack us? Is it because I told you where to find her? I was only trying to help. I love her. More than anything. Why would she do this to us?"

I reach over and rub Rufin's back. "I don't have an answer, but I won't stop until I get to the bottom of it."

"She came after me as well. Told me I was no better than my father and deserved to die. Why would she say that to me?"

"And you're sure it was Lindy?"

Rufin shakes his head. "I'm not sure of anything, but who else could it have been?"

"I don't know, but we'll find Lindy and bring her in."

"What am I supposed to do now?" He looks around. "Everything I had in this world was inside these four walls, and now nothing's left."

"For the time being, we'll take you down to the station where you'll be safe and where you can make an official statement."

Rufin looks back toward the stairs. "Can I go back up and see my father first?"

"That's not possible, Rufin. As I said before, this entire place is a crime scene. We can't have anyone going back through the shop or the apartment until we have our team sweep it for evidence. You understand that, right?"

"I guess so, but I don't want him to be left alone. The last words we had with each other were not ones I wanted to be our last. I still love my father. I hope he knew that."

"There's no need to worry about that. I'm certain your father knew how much you loved him." I rise from the table and touch Rufin's shoulder. "Everything will be okay. Let's get you out of here."

* * * * *

In a perfect world, the police station wouldn't be bustling with activity at 06:49 on a Sunday morning, yet here I am sitting in the war room trying to sort out what happened at Adolf's Flower Shop. I'm wired, coffee running through my veins and pumping nervous energy all the way into my toes as I await word from Brex and Janis.

"Tell me you have good news," says Seth when Officer Amy Janis walks into the room.

Based on her expression, I already have my answer, and it settles my nerves.

"I've never seen anything move so fast. It put all those parkour video guys to shame, leaping over and bounding off walls, cars, and buildings." Officer Janis gestures with her hands. "We weren't prepared for that."

Seth slouches in his chair and exhales. "I was really hoping to put an end to this thing."

"You and me both," says Detective Roland as he enters the room.

"Thought you were done with this case," I snap.

"Wish I was." He rubs the back of his neck. "Nothing about it makes sense. Should be a few simple maulings, but then we get an eyewitness account like Rufin's. The poor kid must've lost his mind."

"So you don't believe what he thinks he saw?" asks Seth.

Detective Roland scoffs. "Do you?"

"Not at face value," Seth admits, "and I'm finding it hard to imagine a scrawny young girl taking on those men and tearing them apart with her bare hands."

"I hear you," agrees Detective Roland.

"Not to mention the fact that I shot at an animal and not a girl," Seth finishes.

So you think.

My mind returns to Reagan. Why would the Shadow Priests be after Lindy? Better yet, how do they know about her?

"Anything come up on the white van with the broken taillight?" I ask.

"Believe it or not, we picked up two teenagers cruising down Main St. in it," says Officer Jaramillo. "They claimed to have found it abandoned on the side of the road with the engine still running. Unfortunately, there are no traffic cameras in that area."

"As I said before, there was a bald man driving the van, not some teenager."

"They knew exactly where to ditch the van," says Detective Roland. "We've got to get better coverage in this city."

"Fat chance," I say. "Look at this place. It's falling apart around us."

"Guys, come check this out," says Kenny.

The entire room gathers around Kenny and his laptop.

"I've been running searches for video feeds around the shelter but didn't find any. After that path failed, I decided to do some poking around on social media sites and came across this video uploaded the morning of October 15th, the day Ernesto Vasquez was killed." He presses play on the video.

It's a wide shot of two young Latino men in their late teens or early twenties. They're laughing and carrying on about the mamacitas they'd scored with earlier that night at some abandoned warehouse rager. A typical brag video popular with the college crowd.

Then the video cuts to a closeup of one of the men rubbing his close-cropped hair feverishly and looking around with wide eyes. *"My God… my God. Thought I was trippin' or something. I'm sure you didn't notice anything out of the ordinary in that first video clip. I didn't either at first. Now that I seen it, it's got me scared out of my mind."*

The man pulls on his face. *"Ugh! Not sure what to do or even what to think of it. You guys gotta check this out."*

The video cuts back to the first clip, but then zooms in on the four-story building behind the two guys. The video is very grainy, its quality just a step above watching VHS on a 4K TV. At first, there's nothing but the building in the video, but then some humanoid shaped thing shows up in the bottom of the frame and starts scaling the side of the building.

Back on the man. He continually shakes his head. *"I just… I can't…"* He grabs his head and squeezes it between his palms. *"Holy—"* The video cuts off.

Kenny plays back the last part of the video several more times, pausing the last time on the grainy image of the thing crawling up the side of the building. He leaves it up on the screen so we can all get a closer look.

"Do we have any idea where that video was shot?" asks Detective Roland, his brow deeply furrowed.

"Because the video was taken on a cellphone, the GPS coordinates are embedded in the video. Turns out it was filmed right here in Desert Springs." Kenny pulls up Google Maps. He's already preloaded the coordinates. "Just off 8th and Atrisco. The building in the video is the backside of Our Lady of the Desert."

"The homeless shelter," Seth and I say in unison.

I look at my phone. It's 07:09. "Damn."

"What's the problem?" asks Seth.

"The shelter's already cleared out."

"Makes our job easier," says Detective Roland. "Let's get a warrant and get in there. If she's been hiding something, there'll likely be evidence."

"You work the warrant, and Bergman and I will head to the shelter," says Seth. "We're already familiar with the head of security over there." I chuckle and he scowls at me.

Detective Roland pulls out his phone. "I'll draw up a warrant and personally call Judge Serno. Should have it within the next hour or so."

"Sounds good," says Seth. He motions toward the door with his head. "Let's roll."

CHAPTER TWENTY

THE FRONT STEPS OF Our Lady of the Desert are deserted when Seth and I pull up. It's Sunday, and a nice day at that, so there are several options around town for a free hot breakfast.

Stephan Jorg answers the door on the third knock. Recognition lights his eyes. "Detectives, what brings you back?"

"We've got a few questions about Lindy Baker, the red-headed girl we picked up for questioning the other night," says Seth.

"Yes, of course." Stephan pulls the door open wide. "Please, come on in." We step inside, and he closes and locks the door behind us. "Ask away."

"Was she here last night?" I ask.

Stephan steps over to a small desk and fingers through an open book. "Here it is… yes. She checked in last night around ten forty and didn't leave until we opened the doors at 7am."

"And how about the nights of the 14th and 19th?" asks Seth.

Stephan thumbs back a few pages and then several more. His head bobs as his finger scans the pages. "Yes, and yes." He looks up at us. "She's here most every night. As I said before, she's a good girl. Never makes any trouble."

Seth crosses his arms. "We've got a search warrant being drawn up as we speak, but would—"

Stephan waves his hand. "I appreciate your adherence to the letter of the law, but there's no need for that. We've nothing to hide here. Take your time searching around the place. There are no locked doors in this building other than my office."

"Very good."

I look around the drab foyer. There's little furniture other than a short wooden bench nestled against the west wall and the small desk to the north, where Stephan stands. A single mural on the far east wall depicts a large gathering of people down the side of a hill and into a valley. The people are eating and distributing fish and loaves of bread. A bearded man sits at the top of the hill, cloaked in white linen.

The feeding of the five thousand.

"Is Lindy always in the same room?" asks Seth.

"Yes, of course. Our *regulars* always are. Would you like me to show you the way?"

"We'll manage," I say.

Stephan dips his head. "Very well." He points toward a doorway to our left. "Through there and the third door on the right is my office. If you need anything at all, please don't hesitate to let me know." With that, he turns and exits the foyer.

After a few wrong turns, Seth guides us to room 36 on the third floor. The door stands open. Even with two small windows in the outer wall and a central light fixture, the room is bathed in shadows.

Seth and I snap on latex gloves, switch on our flashlights for better coverage, and set to work scouring the room for hairs, blood, or anything else that might link Lindy to any of the three crime scenes. I head straight for the closest window to Lindy's bunk, and Seth heads over to the bunk itself.

The single-pane window, about four feet wide and eighteen inches high, is water stained and smudged with dirt and grime from decades of neglect. A good cleaning would improve the lighting in the room tenfold. The window uses an old hand crank mechanism to open and close it, but the handle is missing. Rust coats the small metal arm that pushes and pulls the window open and closed, and its end is broken off and jagged.

Three screws are driven down through the window frame and into the jamb, securing the window from opening. However, a fingernail easily turns all three of them. Upon closer inspection, I notice several red hairs caught within the chipped and peeling paint of the outer window frame.

"I think I've got some—"

Seth grunts, and then metal scrapes against wood as he pulls the rust-coated bunk bed several feet back from the wall. "Me, too." He rounds the end of the bed and squats down in the corner between it and the wall. When he rises, he clutches what looks like a blanket in his gloved hand.

Back in the light, Seth holds up the blanket. Bloodstains cover a sizable portion of it. "I think we might've found what we're looking for."

I point at the window. "We've got several red hairs on the outside of the window, too."

"Can you get to them?"

"Think so." I set to work on removing the three screws.

An hour later and still short one warrant, Seth and I drop off the two pieces of evidence to Dr. Deborah Dages at CSI and return to the police station.

"You two are back already?" asks Detective Roland when we walk into the war room. "I was just about to take you the warrant."

"Didn't need one." Seth pulls out a chair and sits down. "Ended up recovering a bloody blanket from underneath the girl's bed. Dr. Dages over at CSI has it now. She's running the sample against the blood of the second and third victims as well as that of the girl. Said she'd call over here as soon as she's done. Maybe a few hours. Also found several red hairs on the outside of one of the windows."

"Good work. Now let's pray we get a match," says Detective Roland.

I sit down at the table and pray we don't.

* * * * *

My phone buzzes in my pocket.

"Is this Detective Bergman?" asks a female caller as soon as I accept the incoming call.

Rising from my chair, I exit the war room and step out into the hallway. "Lindy?" I whisper.

"Yeah." Panic shrills her voice.

I head farther down the hallway, glancing around to make sure no one will overhear me. "We've been looking all over for you. Where are you at?"

"It doesn't matter. I saw all the police around Adolf's Flower Shop."

"We found the blanket under your bed, Lindy. You need to turn yourself in before the blood analysis comes back. You run, and it'll only make things worse."

"I haven't done anything wrong. Is Rufin okay?"

"I'm sorry, but I can't disclose information about an ongoing investigation."

Lindy gasps. "You must tell me!"

"You were there." I head toward my office. "Look, Lindy, you need to tell me everything. Rufin claims that you attacked him and his father."

"I swear, Detective, it wasn't me," she pleads. "I would never hurt Rufin or his father."

"Just tell me where you're at, and I'll come pick you up."

Silence hangs on the line for several seconds before Lindy finally says, "I'm outside your house."

She knows where I live? My skin prickles.

"I didn't know where else to go after leaving the flower shop," she says, "and I don't trust anyone."

Think, Alice.

Mother's still at the hospital, so the house is empty. It's as good a place as any for her to wait. "There's a key under the pot on the back porch. Let yourself in, and don't go anywhere. I'll be there as soon as I can."

"Okay, but what's going to happen to me?" she asks.

"That all depends on what you tell me. We'll work it out when I get there. And Lindy... don't tell anyone else where you're at."

"No one else knows but Kenny."

"Kenny who?" I ask.

"Parker." My mind draws a blank, but Lindy fills it in for me. "Your intern. He's the one who convinced me to call you."

What the hell does Kenny have to do with all of this?

"Look, I don't know what's going on, but I'm heading there now."

"Thank you," says Lindy.

I end the call and head to my office. When I get there, I'm not alone. Lieut. Frost sits in my chair and leans over my desk. He glowers at me as he wags a cellphone.

I freeze. "Sir? Can I help you with something?"

Lieut. Frost's eyes flash cold blue ice. "Sit down, Bergman."

I take a seat in the chair on the opposite side of the desk. "I don't understand what's going on."

Seth and Kenny enter the office, and Seth closes the door. Kenny pulls up a chair next to mine.

"Where's Lindy Baker?" demands Lieut. Frost.

Kenny shrugs when I shoot him a glare. Finally, I meet Lieut. Frost's gaze. "Don't you—"

"Think long and hard before you lie to me again," he snarls.

My pulse races as my eyes focus on the cellphone he clutches. The truth smacks me in the face. "You cloned my phone?"

"Detective Ryan did."

Daggers of betrayal pierce my heart. Seth looks away when my gaze meets his. "Why would you do that to me?"

"I didn't give him a choice." Lieut. Frost places the phone on the desk. "I've been listening to many of your calls over the last two months and was convinced you were finally playing by the rules, but then you told Detective Ryan you had 'a play going down' and that you needed 'interference.' That alone concerned me, but Detective Ryan assured me that it had to do with gathering intel on a case."

I lean over the desk. "Sir, I can explain everything."

He clasps his hands and leans forward. "I had decided that today would be the last day I monitored your calls—" He shakes his head. "—and then you receive a call from the single person we're trying to find. I prayed to God that you'd do the right thing and report the call, but you chose not to."

"I *literally* just got off the phone with her. At what point between then and now was I afforded the opportunity to report anything to anyone?"

Lieut. Frost scowls. "You're telling me that you were going to report it? I call bull."

Honesty's the only thing that might save me. "No, and I'll tell you why."

He leans back and crosses his arms. "I'm all ears."

"I'm convinced she's not the one we're after. You were listening in on the call. Did she sound like someone who knew about Rufin?"

Lieut. Frost shrugs. "She's a good actor, unlike you. Didn't you ask yourself why she called you? Why she showed up at your house? You don't find that a bit odd *and* disturbing?"

"I didn't need to because she explained it. Weren't you listening—"

"Of course I was. That's why Kenny's in here." Lieut. Frost's death ray glare focuses on Kenny. "What the hell have you gotten yourself into, son?"

"Me... I... uh." Kenny shakes his head and squeezes his eyes shut. "I know Lindy. She's a sweet girl once you get to know her. I don't think she's involved in any of this, and that's why I called her and told her she needed to talk to Ali—Detective Bergman."

"It doesn't matter what you think," says Seth. He looks at me. "Remember those samples you asked me to collect from the interview room yesterday?"

"Yeah," I say.

"Deborah came in and processed them last night. She compared them to the samples we gathered from the second victim, Garin." He tosses a folder on the desk. "Just got the report in a few minutes ago. The hairs, blood, and saliva samples were all close enough matches to concern her."

I rifle through the half-dozen pages. "But they weren't exact matches?"

"Because of the conditions in the alley and the fact that our interview rooms are not cleaned thoroughly, there was some cross-contamination, so a definitive match couldn't be made."

"Of course not." I turn my attention back to Lieut. Frost. "You're the one that said this was an open-shut mauling case. Why are you suddenly convinced a scrawny, seventeen-year-old girl killed three grown men, two of them more than twice her size?"

"I've seen the strength some strung out perps exhibit firsthand. A girl like Lindy Baker, high on meth, crack, speed, or all three could've gotten close to both men without causing too much alarm. After all, they both knew her, right?"

He has a point, but it still doesn't add up. "Ernesto Vasquez had a gun, and Slavik Garin had a switchblade and brass knuckles. Do you really believe she took them out without either of them getting in a good blow of their own? Not just that, but how do you explain Garin's ribcage being torn wide open? Even someone strung out doesn't possess that kind of strength. They'd have to use some sort of device, and we found no evidence of anything like that. Just claw marks. On top of it, I'm pretty certain Lindy isn't a user."

Lieut. Frost sits up. "I watch you, Bergman. You're a good detective, and your intuition is unrivaled. It's the single reason you're still here. Do you think Detective Roland went along with continuing the investigation without my approval? He's too smart for that, and so am I. You're a bulldog. Once you sink your teeth into something, there's no getting you to back off until you're satiated."

He shakes his head. "I'm honestly baffled by these maulings, and now we have a witness that claims this beast talks. I'd chalk it up to the witness being terrified out of his mind or the perp wearing some sort of costume, but your initial reaction to the case gave me pause. What do you know that you're not telling us?"

The Night Mauler is a werewolf!

That's what I want to scream, but I'm not ready for another psych evaluation, so I'll give him the next best explanation I have. "This is just a theory as I have no proof, but the pieces are beginning to fall into place."

Lieut. Frost weaves his fingers together behind his head and leans back. "This had better be good."

"I believe the beast we're after is an escaped science experiment. A hybrid creation of man and wolf." Over the next ten minutes, I explain how we're close to Nevada and Area 51 and how the first body was stolen from the morgue and the evidence removed.

Lieut. Frost sighs heavily. "You're telling me that we're chasing an honest to God werewolf?"

"Essentially, yes," I say. "Why do you think Kenny and I kept this theory to ourselves?"

He eyes Kenny. "You knew about this, too?"

Kenny's smile fades. "Yes, sir. It's all quite crazy, to be honest, but do you have a better explanation?"

"I knew, too, sir," Seth admits.

Lieut. Frost glares at all three of us and shakes his head. "What the hell is wrong with you people?"

"I admit it's audacious," says Seth, "but Alice and Kenny found evidence to back up their theory at the preserve."

It's ludicrous, genius.

"What evidence?" demands Lieut. Frost.

"It's cataloged. Pictures, video, and castings of tracks found in the forest." Seth forces air from his nostrils. "Trust me when I say it's compelling *and* beyond belief."

Lieut. Frost turns back to me. "How so?"

"The left half of the tracks are human. The right half are large paw prints reminiscent of a wolf's."

He shakes his head. "Preposterous."

"Agreed," says Seth, "yet indisputable."

"Science experiment..." Lieut. Frost leans back in the chair again and stares at the ceiling for several seconds before turning his gaze back on me. "So what the hell does this Lindy girl have to do with everything going on then?"

"That's what I'm trying to find out." I hold Lieut. Frost's gaze for several moments before continuing. "Maybe she's befriended this beast or something. I don't know, but you need to let me do my job, sir."

Lieut. Frost sighs. "I swear this job is going to be the death of me."

Of us all.

"One more thing, sir. I must speak with Lindy—" I glance over at Seth. "—alone."

"You think she'll spill her guts to you?" asks Lieut. Frost.

"She reached out to me. I think she wants to confess something, even if it's just that she saw something or knows who is involved."

"I agree with Alice," says Kenny, "and I think she's the only one Lindy will talk to."

Lieut. Frost sets his glasses on the desk, signaling the discussion is over. He pinches the bridge of his nose. "I must be out of my mind today. I'll let you conduct your one-on-one, but I've got two conditions." He looks to Seth. "First, you will setup a one-block perimeter around Detective Bergman's house. We can't allow the girl to run since she might be involved somehow."

"She won't," I say, "but I'm willing to live with that condition."

"Figured you would, but you won't like this next one." He stares me down for several seconds before continuing, "Once you have your little chat with her, you bring her in."

"Sir, I can't—"

His cold glare freezes my tongue right in my mouth. "You will, or I'll bring her in right now."

"Yes, sir," I concede. What other choice do I have?

"Good." He stands and claps his hands together. "Let's make it happen, folks."

CHAPTER TWENTY-ONE

AN HOUR LATER, I walk through my front door. The living room sits empty, but my pulse spikes when I glimpse Lindy sitting at the kitchen table. Despite everything I think I know and my gut telling me to trust her, my mind still refuses to believe her innocence.

What if I'm wrong about her? What if she is the Night Mauler?

Another look at her quells the storm brewing within my chest and quiets the voice of doubt in my head. I've never seen so much fear in anyone's eyes before. She's trembling so much that it quakes the table.

I sit down opposite her. Stare into her beautiful, wild eyes. "What happened, Lindy? Tell me what you've been keeping from me."

Her long fingernails dig into the table as though its surface is made of clay. The raw power is remarkable. Terrifying. Makes me rethink everything again.

She lowers her head and closes her eyes. "I don't know where to start."

"How about you start with the truth? If I'm not mistaken, you can change into some sort of wolf-like creature. Right?"

Tears roll down her cheeks. "I can, but I never do. It hurts too much, and the only way to relieve the pain once shifted is by spilling blood."

My throat tightens. Pulse rises. "So you've killed before?"

Her gaze meets mine once again. "Yes, but it's not what you think. The one time I did shift into my wolf form, I went into the forest and killed a doe. In the moment, I'd never felt anything so good. Such relief from the pain. It was like ecstasy. But when I shifted back, I saw what I'd done. The doe was torn apart as though it were made of nothing more than bloody cotton balls. The sight of it sickened me. I never wanted to do it again and never have."

Either she's telling the truth, or she should be up for an Academy Award. Searching her eyes, I see no deceit. "I believe you… so who is behind the maulings?"

She shakes her head. Tears drip onto the table and snot hangs from her nose. I get up and retrieve a box of tissue from the living room and return to the kitchen table.

Handing her a tissue, I say, "I know that you know, Lindy. You need to talk to me."

She blows her nose and wipes her face. "It's… my brother. Luca."

"Your brother's alive?" I ask. She confirms with a nod. "I thought he drowned when he was fourteen."

"Everyone thought that because it's what he wanted them to believe. He tracked me down a few weeks after he faked his own death. Followed me to every foster home. That's why I did what was necessary to get out of each home. I feared someone would discover him. He's always been a little off."

"So what made him decide to go after Ernesto Vasquez and Slavik Garin?"

"It's my fault. All of it." She gets up, tosses the used tissue in the garbage can, and stares out the window. "Luca demanded that I tell him who supplied drugs to our mother."

"And you told him," I say.

She turns and looks at me. "I didn't want to, but he can be very persuasive. That day in the coffee shop…" She blinks back tears and buries her hands in her armpits. "When I saw the news report about the mauling, I knew it had to be him. I confronted him about it the next day, and he didn't even try to deny it. He told me that Ernesto deserved to die for his role in our mother's death. Luca said Ernesto was the one who took our mother's life by dealing her the drugs in the first place."

"I don't quite understand. The two of you grew up together, so why are his feelings toward your mother different from yours?"

"He was her boy and loved how aggressive he could be. His wild streak made her proud. But I was her disappointment. She thought I was weak. A runt of the pack, so to speak. In fact, she used to call me runt."

"So why didn't he return home after faking his death?"

"Right before child services took us away, she made him promise to look after me. At the time, I thought she might actually care about me, but I later realized she was only looking out for herself and our family secret."

"I see." I get up, fetch two bottles of water from the fridge, and hand one to her. "And what about Slavik? What made Luca go after him?"

Lindy's gaze falls to the floor. "That's my fault as well. A few days later, we were arguing about Ernesto and the fact that it was wrong of Luca to kill him, but Luca wouldn't listen to me. He pressed on about how justified he felt in doing it. I couldn't take it. Couldn't listen to him gloat about spilling another person's blood. Impassioned by the moment, I let it slip that Slavik was the one who had actually killed our mother."

"You're sure Slavik killed your mother?"

She nods and sits back down at the table. "I saw him doing it, and I didn't even try to stop him. I'm just as guilty for her death as Slavik is."

I rip the lid off my bottle and down a third of it in one giant gulp. Big mistake, the frigid water igniting my nerves and scrunching my eyes.

"Brain freeze?" asks Lindy.

The only response I can offer her is a nod as I fight the pulsing pain of icicles lodged in my brain. After battling it out for a solid minute, the pain begins to fade. My brain finally thawed, I manage to ask, "Did Slavik threaten you?"

"No." Lindy rubs the gouges she made in the table. "He didn't even know I was there. He would've killed me if he'd known. Anyway, the night my mother died, she and Slavik fought like I'd never seen before. I knew right then that it was over between them. Made me happy and sick at the same time."

Eying my water bottle, I notice a small iceberg floating atop the water's surface. It explains the brain freeze. I bring the bottle to my lips and manage a small sip. It's not much of a victory, but I'll take it.

"What happened after that?" I ask.

Lindy finally opens her bottle and suckles it before answering. "Desperate to escape reality, my mother took a sizable amount of heroin and became catatonic. When Slavik realized it, he lit her up with several more doses and then left the house. It only took about ten minutes for her to stop breathing. She never woke from it."

"I'm so sorry you had to witness that, Lindy."

"I felt nothing as I sat and watched her take her last breath. My own mother. What kind of person am I?"

"It's not your fault."

"Everything is. When I told Luca what Slavik had done, he went ballistic. The next morning, I heard about Slavik. Even though the man was a sadistic bastard, the guilt over his death tore me up inside. Twice, I dialed your number but then canceled the call. I was afraid to tell anyone what happened because I knew I'd be blamed for it."

"That's on me," I admit. "I've been hounding you right from the start despite my gut telling me that you didn't seem like the type to butcher anyone. I'm glad I was right about that, but I'm not the one who needs convincing. Do you have proof of your whereabouts on those two nights?"

"Our Lady of the Desert keeps a log. If you check it, you'll see that I was there before the killings and didn't leave until the morning."

"We're aware of that, but it's not good enough. They searched your room at the shelter and found a bloody blanket underneath your bed. What will be discovered once it's been analyzed?"

Lindy chuckles. A sweeter laugh than I would've expected. "Nothing useful."

Her response catches me off guard. "It's not Luca's blood from when he was shot early this morning?"

Her eyes grow wide, and concern fills her voice. "Luca was shot?!"

"We think so, but he escaped." I finish off my water, the mini iceberg still trapped inside the bottle. "If that's not Luca's blood, then whose is it?"

Lindy pokes at her bottle with a jagged fingernail. "One of the girls at the shelter. She had her first period a few nights ago and was scared out of her mind. I helped clean her up and gave her my blanket. Stuffed hers under my bed. To be honest, I'd forgotten about it."

"That solves one issue, but we've also got a video of what I'm guessing is your brother scaling the shelter wall in the middle of the night."

"I begged him to stay away from the shelter, but he wouldn't listen. He climbs up to the window several nights a week and watches me sleep, but I never let him in. If the other girls saw him, they'd freak."

"Well, they think you control some sort of beast, and the video of him climbing toward your window doesn't do you any favors."

"I understand how it looks, but what am I supposed to do about it?"

"Not sure, and it's not enough to hold you for long." I cap my bottle, iceberg included, and toss it into the recycle bin next to the fridge. "Do you have anything else I can use to prove your innocence?"

"Yes… Kenny. We were on the phone the night Slavik was killed."

Why didn't Kenny say something? Then another thought strikes me. *Is he the reason she doesn't accept Rufin's advances?*

"Good." I hesitate a moment as I mull over asking her a more personal question, but I need to know if Kenny can be trusted. "Does Kenny know about your… what you are?"

"No way! No one does other than you and Luca. Kenny and I don't talk about things like that. Our friendship is completely platonic. He's like a big brother to me. Stuck up for me at school several times a few years back."

"I see. I'm glad he's your friend."

"Me, too."

"Well, hopefully that'll help clear you from being a suspect, but we have a bigger problem."

She looks up at me, her eyes wide. "We do?"

"There's no good way to tell you this, so I'm just going to say it. Your brother killed Rufin's father."

"What?" Lindy's eyes fill with tears as she breaks down and bawls. It takes a few minutes for her to calm down enough to speak again. "Why would he do that? What did Adolf ever do to him?"

"Apparently, Luca was hiding in the alley while you were talking with Rufin. When you ran off, Detective Ryan and I persuaded Rufin to tell us where we could find you. Sometime after we left, Rufin and Adolf got into an argument about you. Adolf wasn't nice in his assessment of you. I guess that must've pissed Luca off. Luca went in and killed Adolf and destroyed the shop."

"And Rufin?" Her voice quavers.

"He's okay. But he thinks it was you who attacked them."

"I don't blame him. I haven't been very nice to him."

"Lindy, you know what needs to be done. We need to find your brother and bring him in before he kills again."

She nods, tears still pooling in her eyes. "I think the blood has altered his mind. He craves it more and more with each kill. I warned him after he killed Ernesto, but he said he would never go back to his human form. He is the beast now, and nothing would change that. The look in his eyes scared me, but I didn't know what to do about it."

"It's okay. He's your brother. I can only imagine how difficult it must be for you to be talking to me now."

She growls and digs her nails into the table again. "He's not my brother anymore. At least not in his current state of mind. The last time I confronted him, I thought he might attack me as well. I've never seen so much rage in his eyes."

I lean forward and slide my hand toward hers, but she doesn't take it. "Where can I find him, Lindy?"

Her eyes fill with tears again. "I hate what he's become, but I don't want him to be killed."

"For your sake, neither do I, but I can't allow him to continue killing innocent people."

"I know… but you'll never bring him in alone." Tears trickle down her cheeks.

She's right, but what choice do I have? Seth and Detective Roland won't hesitate to use lethal force if needed. There must be another way.

Rico…

"Lindy, I have a friend who can be trusted. He understands these kinds of situations and is the one who told me about those like you and your brother. I think he might be able to help with your brother. Would you be willing to go with me to see him?"

She wipes her eyes with the backs of her hands and shrugs. "I guess so. I don't know what else to do, and I'm not sure Luca can be reasoned with."

I smile. "We will find a way."

"That's what Kenny said, too."

"He's a good kid." I proffer my hand. "Can I borrow your cellphone?"

"Sure, but what's wrong with yours?" She fishes an old flip phone out of an inside pocket in her jacket and hands it to me.

"My phone is compromised."

Lindy jumps to her feet and knocks over her chair, her eyes wide and wild. "This is some kind of setup, isn't it!"

I slowly rise from my chair. "Calm down, Lindy. It's not what you think."

"I trusted you!" She backs away from me until she's cornered.

"The only chance I had of keeping you safe was to allow them to surround the house. Otherwise, they would've stormed it."

She sinks to the floor and buries her head between her knees. "Why did you tell them I was here?"

"I didn't. Some bad decisions on my part several months ago created trust issues at work. My lieutenant had my phone cloned and overheard our conversation earlier. I didn't know until after I hung up with you. I swear none of this was my intention, but it was the only move I could make."

She looks up at me. "You could've called me back and told me to run."

"That would've been bad for both of us. You know that." I cross the kitchen, kneel next to her, and embrace her. She doesn't fight me. "You need to trust me."

"How can I when you're making it so difficult?"

"They don't know who Rico is, and I want to keep it that way. That's why I need to call him using your phone."

Lindy nods and takes a deep breath. "Okay, but you're sure we can trust this Rico?"

I pull back and wipe a tear from her cheek with my thumb. "I think he's the only one we can trust right now. I've known him most of my life. He's one of us."

One of us…

Those words sound strange coming from my lips, but I admit I'm beginning to give credence to this "other world" thing. It's as logical as any other crazy explanation I can come up with.

Lindy cocks her head. "You said *us*. Are you saying you're like me?"

"If you mean as in we're both gingers, then yes, we are practically twins. However, I definitely don't have the ability to change into a wolf."

"Then what *did* you mean?"

"We are unique." I look to my left and then my right, feigning secrecy. Then, I lean forward and whisper in her ear, "I can talk to the dead."

Lindy gasps. "You can talk to the dead?!"

"In a manner of speaking, yes." I stand back up and offer Lindy a hand. It takes little effort to pull her to her feet. She can't possibly weigh more than a hundred pounds. "It's much more complicated than that, but essentially, yes."

"What's it like?"

"To be honest, I don't even know how to describe the feeling. It kinda burns and feels good at the same time. But that still doesn't really describe it well."

"How does it work?"

"I just touch a dead body and connect with it on some deep level. My father calls it *mind probing*."

"Sounds really cool. Much better than turning into a blood-lusting werewolf."

My cellphone rings. It's Seth. "I've got to answer this call, or they'll storm in here—" Lindy nods. "—and I have to tell them about Luca."

"I know, and it's okay. They'll never catch him on their own, anyway."

I answer the call. "Hey, Seth. I'm still alive, but Lindy's not the one we're looking for."

"She's playing you, Alice."

"No she's not," I argue.

"We got the lab results back from the evidence I collected yesterday in the interview room. Partial matches on the blood and saliva with the evidence collected from Garin's murder."

"No, you have inconclusive evidence at best, but it doesn't matter. I can prove that she couldn't have been there when Garin was killed."

"Really? How?"

"Check hers and Kenny Parker's phone records. They were talking to each other at the time of his death."

"We'll crosscheck the phone records again, but that still wouldn't prove she wasn't there."

"If she had been, Kenny would've heard screaming or something."

"Maybe so, but how do you explain the video footage Kenny showed us?"

"You and I both know it's irrelevant. As intriguing as it is, there's no shot of the face, person or otherwise, in that video. No evidence linking it to Lindy in any way."

Seth grunts. "So you're essentially saying we're back at square one?"

"No, what I'm saying is that we have a suspect, and *he* is dangerous."

"He who?"

"Lindy's brother, Luca."

"Didn't know she had a brother. Does she know where we can find him?"

"No. He's nomadic and could be anywhere."

Seth curses. "What now?"

"You said you thought you shot him at the flower shop. If you did, he could've left a trail of blood."

"I shot an animal, not a man. Besides, we didn't find one."

Sometimes, I want to slap some sense into Seth, but then I remember he can't see the things I've seen. Would I believe me if I were him?

Not a chance.

What I need is to give them something to chase after. "The trail could've been missed. Anyway, if the wound is severe enough, Luca might seek medical attention for the animal, so you might check local veterinary clinics. It's a long shot, but it's the only thing we have to go on right now."

"Do you think Lindy could draw her brother out?"

"He's too smart for that. Look how well he avoids cameras and other things. If not for Lindy, we wouldn't even know he existed."

"If not for you, we wouldn't even know we *needed* to be looking for a person."

"I know Lieut. Frost is listening to this conversation. I'll let you explain everything to him."

"I'll try my best." He hesitates, then, "You're sure about this, Alice?"

"Positive."

"Alright. I'll send the troops in for Lindy, and then we'll start a city-wide search for Luca."

"She's innocent."

"Maybe so, but you agreed to Lieut. Frost's conditions. Lindy must be brought in. You know that."

"Give me ten more minutes."

"Alice—"

"You owe me at least that much."

"Fine. Ten minutes, and then we're coming in." Seth terminates the call.

I dial Seth back using Lindy's phone. He answers on the first ring. "This is Detective Ryan."

"You need to listen to me, Seth. If we bring Lindy in again, I'm certain her brother will retaliate. Not only that, but the only chance we have of capturing him is with her help. That can't be done if we're holding her at the station."

"I don't like where this is leading," he says. "What are you asking of me?"

"To trust me. I've held nothing back this time, even when I knew you'd find it crazy. I trust you with my life. I trust you with my heart. Find a way to back the troops off."

The line is silent for several seconds, then Seth says, "I do trust you. Perhaps more than I should." He sighs. "I'll figure something out."

"Good. Oh, and there's one more thing."

"What's that?"

My pulse spikes. Palms dampen with perspiration. "Yes."

"I can't read your mind, Alice. Yes, what?"

"That's my answer to your question. Yes."

"Brex!" yells Seth.

Bang!

The gunshot echoes through the phone but gets cutoff.

Bang! Bang!

Lindy dives to the floor, her eyes wild with fear. "What's happening?"

"Seth!"

The line is dead.

CHAPTER TWENTY-TWO

I DIAL SETH AGAIN, and it goes straight to voicemail. I curse.

"Stay down," I say to Lindy.

Drawing my weapon, I ease over to the kitchen window and peer outside. There's no movement in the backyard. I move into the living room and pull back the curtains just enough to see the front drive. It's deserted as well.

The Shortest Straw blares from my pocket. Nearly sends me into cardiac arrest.

I answer it, not bothering to see who's calling. "Seth?"

"Brex narrowly escaped its attack. I clipped its shoulder with the first shot. Sent it running. We're in pursuit now."

"Be careful. Luca's more dangerous than any killer we've ever faced."

"Trust me, this isn't a man we're chasing."

"Fine," I concede. "Don't try to be a hero."

"Gotta go. Do whatever it takes." He hangs up.

"I'm a liability," says Lindy, spiking my pulse. Didn't hear her enter the room. "Luca will kill you to get to me."

Taking a deep breath calms my nerves. "It won't come to that. Promise."

"You don't know that."

"You're right, but I've got a plan." I select Rico from my phone contacts and punch the number into Lindy's phone.

Rico answers on the second ring. "Rico's Cane Shoppe. How can I best serve you?"

"Hey, Rico, it's Alice. I need your help, no questions asked."

"I'm glad you called, hijita. You've been on my mind, and I was worried about you. What can I do for you on this exceptional day of the Lord?"

"I'll be at your shop in twenty minutes."

"This is about your case, isn't it? The maulings."

"Yeah."

"Good. Dakota and Jake will be here as well."

"No, Rico. It must only be you."

"You can trust them. Dealing with this kind of situation is what they do for a living."

"We'll discuss it when I get there, but they're not welcome for now. Am I understood?"

He sighs. "Okay, but you're making this far more difficult than necessary."

"Perhaps, but I must be the judge of that. We'll see you in a few." I hang up, grab my keys, and give Lindy a nod. "Let's go."

Lindy follows me out the front door. "Where we headed?"

"Rico's Cane Shoppe."

"Never heard of it."

"You would've if you were blind."

"Are you saying *you* were blind?"

The car's door locks disengage when I press the button on my key fob. "Get in. I'll tell you all about it on the way over."

Lindy smiles. It only lasts a fraction of a moment, but it's the first time I've ever seen her do so. A few freckles spot her cheeks. She has a subtle beauty about her, all tied to her striking eyes.

Maybe that's what Rufin sees.

* * * * *

Rico's standing just outside the back door of his shop when Lindy and I arrive. His smile fades when he sees I'm not alone, and his expression turns grim when Lindy exits the car.

"You never said you had company, hijita." His tone sets me on edge.

"She's one of us," I say.

"No, she's one of *them*."

"It doesn't matter what she is. She needs our help."

"Sometimes, I can see and feel things others cannot." He stares intently at Lindy. "The girl's heart is dark and full of rage."

"So what. Mine is too. Furthermore, we have bigger problems to deal with."

"I can leave," says Lindy.

"No, Lindy." I grab her arm before she has the chance to bolt. "We need you."

Rico scowls. "You're compromising us by having her here."

"We can discuss this later, Rico. It's not safe standing out here in the open."

He groans and shakes his head. "Very well." He points a finger at Lindy. "Say nothing until we're in the basement. There are eyes and ears everywhere." She nods.

Once inside, Rico closes and secures the door, and then he presses the button hidden inside the cabinet. Lindy gasps as the entire row of shelves slide away from the wall and reveal the hidden stairway. Then, once we reach the basement, her eyes glow with wonder. I imagine my face looked much the same as hers the first time Rico showed me the basement.

With Rico's permission, Lindy tours the expansive basement, albeit quickly, and then she returns to the couches where Rico and I sit.

"How is this possible?" asks Lindy. "It's like we've been transported to another world."

"Some things are better left unknown," says Rico. He turns to me. "So what's this big problem we're facing?"

"I saw another Shadow Priest. He was tracking the Night Mauler—that's what I'm calling our killer—and tried to take him out."

Rico leans forward on the couch, his elbows resting on his knees. "Don't take this the wrong way, but wouldn't that have saved you the trouble if he'd succeeded?"

Lindy growls. "Luca's my brother."

The room is ripe with tension. Burrows deep within my bones. It's unsettling.

"What aren't you telling us, Rico? Why are you being so hostile?"

"He's a bigot," says Lindy. She springs up from the couch. "I'm ready to leave."

"Sit down, Lindy. We're not going anywhere." I sound just like Mother. It's a little frightening, to be honest. Turning back to Rico, I say, "Explain yourself."

Rico rubs his knuckles as he broods over something. Finally, he says, "Suffice it to say that I've never had a pleasant encounter with a gnoll."

"That's not good enough. I've never had a pleasant encounter with a lawyer, but that doesn't make them all sleaze balls."

"Fair enough. I won't go into details, but several of my family members were hunted and killed by gnolls, including two of my grandparents, my father, and my older sister."

The weight of his words fills the room with impenetrable silence. A deafening force that continues to build as the minutes pass. My skin begins to crawl on my bones, and it takes everything I have to keep my legs from twitching. But I don't want to be the one to end it.

Thankfully, Lindy breaks the silent spell. "I'm sorry for your losses, Mr. Rico, but not all of us are that way. At least I'm not. Luca didn't used to be, either."

"Thank you, and it's just Rico, or Mr. Blackburn if you really prefer to be formal, but I prefer the former. I didn't mean to offend you, but it's hard not to be bitter. Please forgive me."

"I know bitterness all too well. I was the same way with my mother." Lindy smiles at Rico. "There's nothing to forgive."

"Now that we've got that settled, can we discuss the current issues?" I ask.

"Sure," says Rico. "We have the issues of Luca and the Shadow Priest, correct?"

"Yes. I think with your help we can capture Luca."

Rico frowns. "And do what with him?"

"I don't know. Lindy says he refuses to return to his human form, so walking him into the police station isn't really an option. On top of that, we think he's become addicted to bloodshed."

"That's part of their nature," confirms Rico. "They're bred to kill."

Lindy shoots a glare at Rico but keeps silent.

"Regardless, Luca is a threat in his current state of mind," I say. "He's already killed three men, and he tried to kill me and Lindy's friend Rufin too."

"Yet you want to save him," says Rico. "Why?"

"He's had a rough life. I know there's no excuse for what he's done, but aren't we all worth saving?" Lindy looks down at Rico's knuckles. "You're obviously a man of God. Would Jesus reject Luca in his greatest hour of need?"

Rico smiles. "He would reject no one."

"Exactly." Her gaze meets Rico's. "Please be like Jesus and help me save my brother."

Rico stares at the rug for several moments, his brow furrowed. "It's certainly quite the predicament, but I think I might have a solution."

I lean forward. "Lay it on us."

"As I said before, Dakota and Jake can help."

"You won't even tell me what they do. How can we trust them?"

"I'm not at liberty to discuss the nature of what they do but suffice it to say they are well equipped to handle these kinds of situations. With their help, we can capture Luca and keep him safe."

"I don't like it," says Lindy. "There's already too many people involved. Not only that, but Luca won't meet a large group of people."

"What if he thinks it's just me?" I ask.

Lindy looks at me, her head cocked to the side. "What do you mean?"

"What if we lure him into the open and capture him," I say.

"I used to be a long-range sniper in a past life," says Rico. "If we can get him somewhere where I have the range to take a shot with a tranquilizer gun, we'd be good."

How many lives has Rico led?

"You'll have to get within at least fifty yards." I don't like it.

"With a regular CO2 gun, that'd be true—" Rico smiles wryly. "—but I've been working on a new type of weapon for some time. Uses nanite tech. It'll easily shoot tranquilizer bullets a good two hundred and fifty yards with precision accuracy."

"Regardless of how it's done, we'll need to meet Luca somewhere in the mountains," says Lindy. "It's the only way this plan will work. He won't go anywhere else."

My mind races back to the mountainous area behind the old Puge place. "We'll find a good location that's fairly remote, and you can have him meet me there."

"I'll have to be there, too." Lindy sits back down next to me. "Otherwise, he'll either not show himself, or he'll kill you before you even have a chance to talk to him."

"We still need Dakota," says Rico. "Without her, we'll have no place to keep him."

"How about your cube?" I ask.

Rico looks over at the massive transparent cube sitting in the middle of the basement. "It's a tough material, but I'm not sure how it would fare against his strength."

"Wouldn't it be worth trying?"

"And if it fails? What then? We'll have a gnoll on the loose in my basement."

"Good point. But it's still better than him running loose out in the open where he can kill at will."

Rico nods. "I'm inclined to agree, but Dakota is still our best option."

"No," says Lindy. "I don't even know or trust you. I certainly won't trust anyone else."

"Would you trust your great grandmother?" I ask.

Lindy frowns. "Of course, but what does she have to do with this?"

"Show Rico the picture you have of her."

"Why?"

I nudge her. "Just show him."

She pulls the picture out of her jacket pocket and hands it to Rico with reluctance. "I want it back."

"Of course." Rico looks at the picture and gasps. "Dakota…"

"See, Lindy. Dakota was friends with your great grandma. If your great grandma trusted Dakota, I think we can as well."

She crosses her arms and broods. "I want to meet her before I make any decisions."

Rico smiles. "That can be arranged. In fact, she and Jake are here now."

"I thought I smelled someone else when we came into the shop," growls Lindy.

I shoot Rico a dirty look, and he raises his hands in defense. "Look, they were already here when you called. After all, you're the one who insisted you meet in person."

I had totally forgotten about the meeting I'd scheduled for later.

"I told them to stay at the front of the shop until we were done." He walks over to the stairs. "I'll go get them. Hold on a minute."

Three minutes later, Dakota and Jake stand opposite us in the basement.

Lindy looks between her picture and Dakota several times. "How is it possible?"

"How is what possible?" asks Dakota.

"How can you still look the same age?" Lindy eyes the photo again. "This photo was taken almost fifty years ago."

"Plastic surgery," quips Dakota. "And lots of makeup."

"Seriously, what are you?" asks Lindy.

I'd like to know the same thing.

"Let's just say that time doesn't affect me the same way it affects everyone else. Think of it as a mutation of my ability when I entered this world." Dakota sweeps her hair away from her face with her left hand.

That's when I see it. A grayish-red birthmark on the inside of her wrist. But it's different from mine. A lightning bolt with numbers surrounding it. Reminds me of a clock face.

What does it mean?

"What do you mean by that?" presses Lindy. "When you were born?"

Dakota looks at Rico. "She doesn't know?"

Lindy curls her hands into fists and stomps the floor. "Ugh! Know what?"

"Why do you think you're different from everyone else?" asks Dakota.

"I don't know," admits Lindy. "Bad genes?"

Jake's been stoic this entire time, but he cracks a smile with the "bad genes" comment. Even though I can see his left arm from where I'm standing, he wears a wide leather band around his wrist. There's no way in hell it's a coincidence.

How many others have I missed in the past?

Lindy continues, "Maybe one of my relatives worked with materials or chemicals that changed our biology somehow, or maybe we're just science experiments gone wrong."

"No, Lindy," says Rico. "We're from another world."

Lindy slashes the air. "That's preposterous!"

"Why? Because you've been taught that other worlds don't exist?" asks Dakota. "You don't believe in aliens I take it?"

Lindy rolls her eyes and shakes her head. "Why would anyone?"

"Because it's true," Rico interjects. "Obviously not in the *little green men from Mars* kind of way, but we're aliens to *this* world."

Lindy sits down on the couch. "If what you're saying is true, how did we get here? Why did we come here?" Her eyes widen, and she looks up at Dakota. "How do we get back?"

Rico crosses his arms. "Unfortunately, it's not that simple."

Jake speaks up, his Texas accent even more prominent than over the phone. "If we *could* go back, I'm not sure what we'd find left of our world."

Lindy hugs herself. "My entire life, I've never felt like I belonged here. Now I understand why."

I can't believe how quickly Lindy takes the news as truth. I'm still not convinced, but those like Lindy make me question everything. Next, Rico will tell me that vampires are from this alternate world as well.

Maybe they are…

I shake the thought from my head and turn to Dakota. Her gaze always seems to be on me. It's a bit unsettling. "Did Rico brief you on the situation?"

Dakota smiles at Lindy. "He has, and we're available to do everything we can to help Luca."

Lindy sighs. "He won't come willingly. I don't think he wants help."

"Trust me," says Dakota. "Jake and I dealt with a gnoll just like Luca once before."

Lindy looks at Dakota, her eyes full of hope again. "You did?"

"Yes. It was actually your grandfather, Rufus. He was a bear to handle for almost a year, but we finally tamed the beast. Luca will be no different."

"Then I say we move forward with capturing him," says Lindy.

Jake winks at Lindy. "And I say you're a smart girl."

Finally, it's time for action. "Okay, here's the plan. Lindy, Rico, and I will meet Luca. Rico will shoot him with a tranquilizer dart, and then we will take him to you, Dakota. From there, you can get him somewhere safe. A place where he can be rehabilitated."

"Wherever that is, I'm going with him." Lindy stands back up. "Otherwise, we have no deal."

"You're more than welcome to stay with him," says Dakota. "I think it will help him recover more quickly if he has a familiar face to look upon when he comes to."

Lindy chews her lower lip. "He's going to be royally pissed at me though."

I touch Lindy's shoulder and squeeze it. "I know, but given time, he'll see why you had to do it. He knows you love him."

"I know, but still…" She stares at the floor. "He'll think I betrayed him."

"What's the alternative, Lindy?" asks Rico.

"I'm not saying there is one." She looks at me.

"There isn't," I confirm. "If we do nothing, he will keep killing and will eventually get caught or get himself killed. Would you rather that be the case than him being mad at you for a while?"

"No." Lindy sighs. "I just worry about him. He's always been a bit wild."

"How soon can you get in touch with your brother?" I ask Lindy.

"He'll find me in the morning," she says. "He always does."

"Good. Tell him whatever is necessary in order to get him to meet us in the mountains north of town at three in the afternoon. There's this sort of box canyon type area a few miles out. We'll wait for him at the bottom of it. Rico will be able to perch himself anywhere along the upper ridge. There are trees and large boulders good for cover."

"I can do that." Lindy looks at Rico. "Take a shower before you go, and *do not* wear any type of cologne or deodorant. And make sure that wherever you're located is downwind of our position. We have an extraordinary sense of smell. Oh, and be as quiet as possible. Sound travels easily, and we have excellent hearing as well."

Rico nods. "Noted." He looks at me. "We will be ready."

"We'll be a few miles away with transportation," says Jake.

"Tomorrow, then," I say.

Dakota grabs my arm as I'm about to head for the stairwell. "You said you have information about the Shadow Mirror."

I glance at her hand on my arm and then stare at her. "I had to say something to get you on the phone."

She releases my arm. "Perhaps, but you do know something. What is it?"

"We survive tomorrow, and I'll tell you."

"Fair enough," she says.

Outside, Lindy tells me that she'll meet me back at my house tomorrow and takes off into the night before I can stop her. In my car, I brood over whether or not I should tell Seth about tomorrow's meet up. Finally, I call him and tell him that we need to talk.

* * * * *

The lights are low when I enter Seth's condo. He has the TV tuned to some news channel, but he's not in the room. A quick check of his bedroom and bathroom confirms he's not there either. Then I see him through the living room curtains. He's leaning on the balcony rail, a beer clutched in his fist.

I open the fridge and reach for a beer, but then remember the reason I'm here. As much as I'd like a few swigs to ease my nerves, keeping a clear head is far more important. I close the fridge and head out onto the balcony.

"It's been awhile since I've seen you out here," I say.

"Just needed some fresh air to clear my head."

I stare at the bottle in his hand but say nothing about it. "I'm sorry I was so vague on the phone earlier, but we need to talk."

He continues to gaze into the distance. "I already know."

"You do?"

He turns to me, his eyes glassy with tears. "I knew this day was coming the night you refused to give me an answer."

"But I said yes—"

"In the heat of the moment, but I knew better even then. I should've known I could never compete with your obsession."

"My obsession? I admit that it's what kept me from saying yes when you asked, but you said you understood."

"I'll put in for a transfer as soon as we wrap up the cases."

A lump the size of Texas rises in my throat. "A transfer?" I squeak out.

"Looking to go to Albuquerque. It'll be a good change of pace for me."

I touch his arm as tears streak down my face. "You don't need to run away, Seth."

"I'm not running away, Alice. I'm trying to move on."

I can't feel my lips. My face. My hands. Every part of me numbs with sorrow. "I don't want you to go. I need you." My lower lip quivers. Heart aching. Breaking.

But you asked for this.

"I can't be around you and not be with you," he says.

I tug on his arm. "I'm not asking you to. My answer is yes. Why aren't you listening?"

He reaches into his pocket and pulls out a small felt box with a hinge. Hunter-green.

My eyes are transfixed by it, and a strange hope rises from my gut. Burns in my heart.

Is he going to ask me one last time?

It's absurd, the box is different from the one with the ring, but what else could it be?

Seth places the box in my hand, closes my fingers around it, and then he kisses my cheek. "I wish you all the best, Alice, and I hope you find what you're looking for." He turns and walks back inside, leaving me stunned and clutching a box I'm too afraid to open.

When I finally work up the courage to go back inside, Seth's gone. Tears stream from my eyes, and I cry without control, sobbing until snot hangs from my nose.

God, what have I let happen?

On my knees, I crawl to the coffee table and grab several tissues, shoving them in my face and wiping away the snot and tears. My eyes burn with fire, and I'm certain I look like hell, but no one's there to see me.

I dial Seth's number over and over, but he doesn't answer. Pulling myself up off the floor, I head into Seth's room and sit on the edge of his bed. A discarded shirt lies on the floor at my feet. I pick it up and bury my face in it, his scent so strong I can almost taste it.

Finally, I work up the courage to open the box. A folded piece of paper slides out and falls to the floor before I get it all the way open, so I set the box aside and retrieve the piece of paper. Unfolded, I recognize the handwriting as Seth's. The words rip a hole right through my chest and rend my very soul as I read them aloud. "You were always my only one. —Seth."

The entire world crashes down upon me. A weight I cannot bear. It suffocates me. Devastates me. Leaves me gasping for air. I cry into his shirt until I run out of tears. My eyes burn with fire. Swollen.

How can I move on without you?

After some time, I lie back and stare at the hunter-green box. No matter its contents, my heart will remain shattered.

But he gave it to me. It must mean something.

I sit up and take the box into my trembling hands. Stare at it until my eyes cross. With a deep breath, I pull the lid up until it snaps open.

The last thing I ever expected lies within the box. A piece of me I never thought I'd get back. I didn't know I still needed it until my gaze fell upon it.

Heart knocking against my ribcage and hands trembling, I remove the necklace and cross pendant from the box, place it around my neck, and hold on to it like I had a million times before.

Shame befalls me.

With tears in my eyes again, I look toward the ceiling and imagine the heavens above. "God, was I wrong about you, too?"

✶ ✶ ✶ ✶ ✶

Three in the morning. I still lie on Seth's bed clutching my cross pendant when the front door opens. I wipe my face with Seth's shirt and toss it on the floor.

"You're still here," says Seth. The doorjamb seems to be the only thing keeping him upright. His eyes are bloodshot, and he reeks of alcohol.

I slide off the side of the bed and walk over to him. My fingers push back wild strands of hair from his forehead. "I won't let you leave me."

He stumbles backward, nearly crashes to the floor. "You don't want me."

"You're wrong." The distance between us, a mere three feet, is more than I can handle. I close it and wrap my arms around his waist. Settle my head against his muscular chest. "I'm flawed. Broken. Obsessed. Those are my traits. Nothing a man needs in his life."

"You're right."

It's a gut punch, but what had I expected?

Then, his arms wrap around me. Pull me close. Tight. Squeezes the breath from my lungs.

Don't let me go!

"But I'm no man without you," he finishes with a whisper.

His grip loosens, and he quivers in my arms. Sobs. I hold him until he settles and the room falls silent. In this moment of silence, clarity befalls me.

I pull back and drop to my knees. Seth stares down at me, confusion in his eyes and on his face. Taking his hands in mine, I draw a deep breath and let it out slowly.

"Seth Allyn Ryan—" I can hardly get the words past the lump in my throat. "—will you take me as I am, warts and all, and marry me?"

Every passing moment of silence tortures me. There's too many of them to count.

"One condition," he finally says.

At first, I hesitate, fearful that he'll force me to choose between him and my obsessions, but then I remember that I'm nothing without him. A wretched, black soul. My obsessions can go to hell.

"Anything," I say. "I swear it."

"Allow me to share your obsessions."

No words could make me happier. "Done." I rise, grab his shirt, and pull him toward the bedroom. "You're one of them."

After a quick shower, we turn out the lights and obsess over each other.

CHAPTER TWENTY-THREE

A CUP OF COFFEE sits on the table in front of me, plumes of steam rising from its golden-brown surface. The aroma conjures memories from a distant past. A dark world brimming with love and warmth. Mother's love of coffee, Jesus, and me. It leaves me feeling euphoric and distills the bitterness within, much like the cream and sugar do my coffee.

The sizzle of bacon and sausage on the cooktop, clinking and scraping silverware on cheap china, and the buzz of conversation fills Wired Coffee like a satisfying symphony. Seth sits across the table from me, his gaze lost in a cup of black coffee. A smile sits crooked on his face.

"What is it?" I ask, stirring my coffee with a spoon.

"Just thinking about last night." His grayish-blue eyes are heaven when they turn up toward me. "Thought I'd lost you. Crushed my world. But seeing you on your knees…" His voice trails off. Light glistens off his glassy eyes.

I reach across the table and cover his hand with mine. "You are everything, Seth." Now I'm the one tearing up. A deep breath quells the storm of emotions raging within. "That's why I need to tell you something and beg you to understand."

Concern pulls on his brow. Weighs it down. "Now you've got me worried."

The trouble with the truth—with any words, to be honest—is getting it out without creating division and chaos. One misstep, and entire worlds spontaneously combust and burn out of existence. It's a minefield for someone like me, a woman with more secrets than entire intelligence communities.

"Do you trust me?" My confidence falters, sending my gaze plummeting into the depths of Seth's black coffee.

"You have my heart. My love. If those don't speak to the trust I have in you, what could?"

A crash-landing is imminent, but there's no turning back. The aftermath will be far worse if I bail out now. "Today, the Night Mauler will be brought to justice."

Seth leans forward, his brow furrowed. "What the hell does that mean?"

Bracing for impact, I say, "I and a few others have a plan. With Lindy's help, we'll draw him out and capture him."

Red crawls up the sides of Seth's neck and into his cheeks. A time bomb, tick-tick-ticking away. Any moment, and he'll explode.

Instead, he takes a sip of his coffee and broods over it. Seconds. A full minute. Then, he says, "I can't believe you're springing this on me."

"That's unfair. I told you yesterday that we needed to talk. *This* is what it was supposed to be about, but you wouldn't listen."

Seth closes his eyes and exhales loudly. When he opens them again, his stare is direct and intense. "You tell me every last detail. Who. When. Where. How. And, if you think there's any way in hell I'm not going to be involved in this plan of yours, you're mistaken."

"I know." No more steam rises from my cup. "But no one else can be involved."

"Agreed."

I take the coffee cup and down its contents like a shot. After tossing a twenty on the table, I say, "Let's go. I'll tell you everything on the way."

* * * * *

Lindy and I stand back-to-back in the middle of a clearing nestled at the bottom of a small canyon northwest of town. An easterly breeze sends wisps of hair into my eyes. The wind direction isn't ideal, but there's no way to control it.

Trees, shrubs, and gigantic boulders make for good cover all along the canyon ridge on its three sides, but it also makes spotting Luca when he arrives a difficult task. Once we make contact, Rico will move into position.

One ridge over from the canyon to the east is where we made our descent into the ravine and past the service road where we found Priscilla several months ago. The connection sends my mind reeling back to the strange experience with the Shadow Mirror in Unit 109 at Dunharrow Storage. I've relived that moment so many times and wished I'd done something different, but it's not something I should be dwelling on right now. I give my head a good shake to try to get my mind back into the present.

Focus, Alice. We're here to save Luca.

Without an ounce of sleep last night, my nerves are fried. White knuckles and an aching hand prove it, my grip on Esther ironclad. To compound matters, it's ten past three, and Luca still hasn't shown up.

"Are you sure he's coming?" I ask.

"He'll be here," Lindy assures me. "I'm sure he's watching us right now and making sure this isn't some kind of trap."

But it is a trap.

"What did you tell him to get him to agree to come?"

"Mostly the truth." Her fingers touch mine. Rest against them for a handful of moments. The calming effect is unmatched. "You're a homicide detective, and you want to charge him for the murders of Ernesto and Slavik."

My chest quakes, the calm short-lived. "You said he can't be reasoned with or controlled. Why would you tell him that?"

"It was the only way." Only the breeze keeps the silence between us at bay.

Static sounds in my ear, followed by Rico's voice. "We still on?"

Lindy grabs my hand. "He's here."

She lets go, and I touch my ear. "Time to move in, Rico," I whisper.

"Be careful," says Seth. "Anything goes wrong, you cry wolf."

Or werewolf.

Turning around, I stand shoulder to shoulder with Lindy and face Luca as he approaches. The vision through Slavik's eyes in the alley and the encounter in the dark hallway above the flower shop did little justice portraying the beast that stands on its hind legs ten paces away from us.

Thick, matted fur in hues of orange and red cover the young man from head to splayed toes. Elongated arms hang at his sides, capped with long, bony fingers and two-inch claws. Pointed ears rise from the sides of his elongated head, and sharp, yellowed teeth line his long snout and glisten with saliva.

His yellow-eyed gaze locks on me, and he growls deep in his throat. I can't help but meet his gaze, and from what I see, little humanity remains. It scares the hell out of me, and my grip on Esther tightens further.

Lindy steps forward and positions herself between Luca and me. "Thank you for coming, Luca."

"Step aside," he snarls. "I'm not here for you." Saliva drips from his jowls.

"She's my friend, Luca."

"You're delusional. We have no friends," he snaps. "We're alone in this world. All we have is each other."

"That's not true." Lindy stays between us as Luca circles.

Luca puffs out his chest and roars, "Get out of the way before you get hurt!"

"You won't hurt me," says Lindy with defiance, "and I won't let you hurt her."

"Don't be naïve. You can't stop me," he growls.

Luca lunges forward.

I stagger backward several steps, Esther glowing with blue energy in my raised hand, but Lindy moves to intercept Luca. Only she isn't herself anymore. My brain can't process what my eyes just witnessed, the shift complete in less than a moment.

The two beasts collide mid-air and tumble to the ground in a heap. Growls, yelps, roars, and gnashing teeth fill the afternoon air as the two of them fight for dominance. Dust rises from the dry ground, distorting my view of the action.

I slam Esther into the ground, sending out a concussive circle of blue energy that expands to the limits of my vision. The energy maps the surrounding terrain with a blue mesh, creating a picture within my mind. Aided by Esther's unique vision, the battle becomes clear through the cloud of dust. But the assisted vision comes with a cost, sapping a significant portion of my energy.

Lindy fights to subdue, landing blows with her elbows and the heels of her mutated feet, but Luca fights for blood, his claws ripping into Lindy's flesh without restraint.

I vie for position to strike, but the action is far too intense. One misaligned attack could cost me and Lindy our lives. Without warning, my assisted vision fades, leaving me staring at a wall of dust once again.

Retreating to a safe distance, I raise Esther above my head again, ready to strike the ground once more, but then the sounds of battle fall away.

A mournful groan resonates through the canyon as the dust begins to settle.

Only one beast rises above it, and it's not Lindy.

Chills skitter on my skin.

Luca's chest heaves, drawing ragged breaths. Blood drips from his snout and mats the fur across his torso, but none of it looks to be his own. He rises up on his hind legs and roars with a ferociousness I've never witnessed. The sound shakes me to the core.

My hand trembles as I fight to turn the top of Esther counterclockwise ninety degrees.

What the hell's taking you so long, Rico?

Luca stalks forward as I retreat farther. "You're gonna pay for what you made me do to Lindy."

Finally, Esther's top turns, and she sparks to life, glowing and crackling with blue energy. The change draws Luca's attention, but only for a second. When his hate-filled gaze meets mine again, no humanity remains.

Button depressed, Esther morphs from a cane into a whip.

A single heartbeat is all it takes for Luca to halve the distance between us.

But it's all the time I need.

Pouring energy into Esther, I lunge forward and strike with all I have, emitting a battle cry so fierce it shreds my vocal cords.

Crack!

Esther's split ends catch Luca right in the center of his chest, producing a flash of blue light that splits the air and rumbles like thunder. The concussive blow throws Luca backward half a dozen feet and onto his back. The energy drain takes me to my knees.

My chest heaves as I labor for each breath, but I'm not laid out on my back. Smoke rises from Luca's chest where Esther's three tips struck him.

Stay down.

Dread and fear ignite a fire in my bones when Luca sits up and shakes his head. A strike like that would've sent a normal human into cardiac arrest, but this beast rises. With a swipe of his hand, the hair from the three spots falls away, revealing flushed skin quickly darkening with bruises.

Stay down.

Rising back up on unsteady legs to meet his fierce gaze, I take a slow, deep breath and glare daggers at the beast in hopes that he won't see my weakness. Another strike from Esther as brutal as the first will render me unconscious at best and would likely be my last.

A voice whispers in my ear. "I'm almost in position. Another minute."

I won't last another minute!

Luca balls his fists and roars at the sky but doesn't make an advance. His hesitation gives me a chance to locate Lindy. When I do, my heart breaks. Relegated to her human form, she lies on her back, her head turned to the side in an awkward position. Blood covers the side of her face. From where I stand, I can't tell if she's still alive.

This isn't what's supposed to happen.

Anger rises in my gut and gives new life to my voice. "Give up, Luca. There's no escape."

His eyes narrow. Focus on Esther. He spits blood on the ground. "You're not like the others."

"He's just out of range. Move him toward Lindy, and I'll take him down," says Rico in my ear.

The wind swirls around us, kicking up dust as it begins shifting direction. I move to the right, away from Lindy, hoping to get Luca to circle back toward her. He follows me with his gaze but doesn't move, so I stalk closer, Esther raised and poised for another strike.

Just take a step back.

Luca raises his snout and sniffs the air. Wildness returns to his eyes. "We're not alone," he roars.

Damn!

I press on my earpiece, "Take the shot, Rico!"

"Get out of there, Alice!" yells Seth through my earpiece.

From that moment, everything goes sideways.

Abandoning caution, I charge forward with a loud cry, hoping to drive him back far enough for Rico to take the shot.

But it doesn't work.

And I'm not quick enough this time.

Luca twists away from my attack and manages to backhand me as I stumble past. The blow to the back of my head rattles my teeth and fills my mouth with blood, but I keep my feet underneath me.

I swing back around and he's on top of me. Knocking me to the ground.

A clawed hand arcs at my face.

There's nothing I can do but take the blow and pray it doesn't kill me.

Pop!

Bright-yellow liquid peppers the air at Luca's back.

Luca jerks back, the tips of his claws missing my nose by a millimeter.

Crack!

The delayed sound of a gunshot echoes across the canyon.

It takes a moment for my mind to catch up with what happened. To comprehend the cause of the yellow liquid spray.

Rico's shot didn't penetrate Luca's skin!

Luca abandons his attack against me and takes off across the canyon floor. At first, I think he's running away, but then I spot Rico, standing right in Luca's path.

Luca runs right through a spray of yellow liquid, not missing a step.

Crack!

The sound of Rico's second gunshot fills the canyon.

My pulse races. Heart thunders. Chest aches. I'm up on my feet.

Another burst of yellow liquid.

This time, Luca stumbles, falls, and rolls, but then he's back on his feet in a flash.

Crack!

Three shots, and Luca's still on his feet.

It's not working!

Everything happens so quickly, it's a blur.

Lindy groans and sits up. I head for her, my gaze still locked on Luca.

Luca's nearly upon Rico. Leaps in the air. My heart lurches in my chest.

"Rico!" I scream, staggering forward.

Luca's body contorts and twists mid-air, and he goes down hard on his back.

Crack!

The gunshot echoes.

Several moments tick by before realization of what just happened registers in my mind. Rico didn't take that last shot. He couldn't have. The way Luca's body contorted means one thing: someone shot him from behind.

Esther falls from my hand as I twist around, frantically searching for the source of the fourth shot. Then I see the shooter atop the ridge to the southeast. A hundred yards away. The bald man crouches among several large boulders, the sun glinting off the top of his head.

At such a distance, I can't make out his features, but one thing's clear: his rifle barrel points in my direction. In the open space of the canyon floor, there's nowhere for me to hide. I'm vulnerable. The only thing I can do is stare at the man with defiance, so I do. But then realization strikes me. My heart knows the man behind that scope.

"Reagan!" I scream, fists balled at my sides.

Why is he aiming for me?

It makes no sense. He thinks I can't be killed. Then it hits me.

He's aiming for Lindy!

I turn and dive toward the girl.

Crack!

A fifth shot rings in the air.

For the second time in as many minutes, my life flashes before me. What have I accomplished? What will I be remembered for? I can think of nothing, and it scares the hell out of me, but what scares me more is what I might find beyond this life. Will there be anything else, or will I cease to exist?

How long has it been since the shot rang out? A second? Maybe two? I take a deep breath and brace for impact. But it never comes. Then I remember the bullet would've found its mark before I ever heard the shot.

My memory rewinds and plays back everything that just happened.

Reagan jerks around to his left just as I dive toward Lindy. Then the last shot rings out. A cannon in comparison. Like its source is much closer. I lie over the top of Lindy, stunned.

What the hell just happened?

Looking back toward the southeastern ridge, I see Reagan recover, scoop up his rifle off the ground, and dash through the boulders and out of site before I take another breath.

Without thought, I'm on my feet and racing across the canyon after Reagan. My legs, still weak from using Esther's power, pump beneath me with pure adrenaline, but then a mournful wail echoes through the canyon and stops me in my tracks.

The sound carries deep into my soul. Takes me to my knees. Brings tears to my eyes.

I know that cry. I've been there. Felt it many times before deep within, and it sickens me just thinking about it. As much as I want to give chase to Reagan, my heart knows I need to be there to comfort Lindy. I'm all she has left right now.

Rising to my feet, I turn and head back toward the western slope of the canyon. From the northeast comes Dakota, a rifle slung over her shoulder. Jake isn't with her.

I smash the button on my earpiece. "Seth, Reagan's here. Southeast ridge."

"Jake and I are in pursuit," Seth's voice comes back.

Dakota and I arrive atop the ridge together and stop short of Rico and Lindy. He kneels next to Lindy, a hand on her back, and she lies over the top of Luca.

Dakota urges me forward, her hand against my back. But I'm not ready to accept what happened. Lindy trusted me, and I let her down. Got her brother killed. As with the rest of them, his blood is on my hands.

But she needs me. Now more than ever.

Finally, I step forward and take Rico's place. I pull Lindy into my arms, hold her tight against my breast, and stroke her matted, blood-soaked hair.

My gaze focuses on Luca and his naked body, and my eyes are drawn to his wound.

A single shot.

Right through the left shoulder blade.

Punctured his heart.

At least he didn't suffer.

CHAPTER TWENTY-FOUR

The next morning…

DAKOTA BARNES LEANS AGAINST the back wall of Rico's Cane Shoppe in the alley. A cigarette hangs from her lips, a tendril of smoke rising straight up from its lit end. Not even a hint of a breeze disturbs the unusually warm day. Makes me rethink my heavy jacket.

A blue-tail lizard captures my attention as it scurries across the asphalt and climbs up on a large volcanic rock beyond the curb. What I wouldn't give for a few hours of sunshine and sunbathing. For some strange reason, the lizard lounging on that rock reminds me of Ernesto's body lying on the gravel trail in the preserve.

"It was you, wasn't it?" I say, refocusing on Dakota.

Dakota turns and stares at me. "Sorry?" Her cigarette wobbles when she speaks but doesn't fall from her mouth.

"You're the one who stole Ernesto Vasquez's body from the morgue."

She yanks the cigarette from her mouth and frowns. "And why would I do something like that?"

"You did it to protect Luca."

"That's absurd," she scoffs. "I didn't know Luca."

"Maybe not, but we've already established that you knew his great grandmother."

Dakota's eyebrows rise. "True, but that doesn't make me a body thief."

"We both know things about each other that must be kept secret, so why don't you trust me with the truth?"

She retrieves a small device from her pocket and clicks a button on its end. A high-pitched noise buzzes in my ear briefly. When I stare at it, she offers an explanation. "Blocks others from listening in on our conversation."

I need one of those.

When I nod, she continues, "And what is it you think you know about me?"

"I know you're far older than humanly possible. That must be a burden to change identities every few decades. Plus, I saw the mark on your wrist. What does it mean?"

Dakota turns her left wrist up and pulls back her jacket sleeve. We both gaze upon the lightning bolt surrounded by numbers burned into her skin like a brand. "In this world, you could think of it as premonition."

Our eyes meet. "You see the future?" I ask.

"Sometimes, but often only moments before the event happens." She slides her sleeve back down. "A week at most on occasion."

It all makes sense. "That's how you knew Reagan was there."

"Who is Reagan?"

"The man at the canyon. A Shadow Priest."

Dakota nods. "I saw Lindy die. A single bullet right between her eyes. Brain matter exploding out the back of her head and splattering across the ground." She shivers. "I've never run so fast in my life."

"I'm glad you made it in time."

Dakota takes a long drag from her cigarette and then tosses it on the ground. "Me, too. She's a sweet girl, especially given her nature."

Her remark irks me, but I let it pass. "We all carry a darkness inside."

"Certainly." She snuffs the cigarette out with her shoe. "So what's yours?"

"My darkness?"

"No, your gift."

"I thought you knew."

She cocks her head. "And how would I?"

"I assumed Rico told you."

"You should never assume anything, especially where Rico's concerned. The man holds onto secrets like a dragon protecting its treasure."

"But he said I was the one he'd told you about that day we met at his shop."

"He did, but that was only in reference to Aaron's Staff."

"Esther." Dakota stares at me blankly, so I explain the name change. "Esther is the name I gave the weapon after he gave it to me. Aaron's Staff just didn't sound right."

"Ah, I see. Esther is a good Biblical name as well, although there's no mention of her having a staff."

"Does it matter if she had a staff or not?"

"I suppose it doesn't." She proffers her hand. "May I see your mark?"

I pull my sleeve back but offer no explanation when she nods.

"This is why you pursued Luca," she says.

"Not at first, but it helped lead me to him in the end."

Her gaze penetrates deep. Mesmerizes and leaves me uneasy simultaneously. "The body had to be taken to keep the Shadow Priests from finding out about Luca. Unfortunately, the data was in the system too long. That's why we didn't bother taking the second body and evidence as well. It no longer mattered at that point."

"How do you have the resources to pull off something like that? Better yet, how would the Shadow Priests have known? How would they have access?"

"As Rico says, they have eyes and ears everywhere. In this war, you can trust no one."

"You're telling me that they're not all cold-blooded killers?"

"And why would they be?" She pops a stick of gum in her mouth and offers me one, but I decline. "Think of them like any organized group. Take the FBI, for example. The FBI has people for every type of job imaginable, and so do the Shadow Priests."

From the moment I saw the monastery in Russell's memories, I imagined the Shadow Priests to be a tight-knit cult waging war from just a few locations. The thought of them being neighbors and coworkers leaves me cold to the bone. "How do we fight a war against an army of ghosts?"

"One day at a time." Dakota retrieves a business card from a concealed pocket in the lining of her jacket and hands it to me.

The card is perplexing. One side of it is solid black with a white rook on it, and the other side is solid white with a black rook on it. Both sides are portrait oriented, and neither side has writing of any kind.

"What is this?"

"My personal business card." Dakota smirks. "Consider it a lifeline if you ever find yourself in hot water."

I flip the card over again. "I don't understand. How will this help me?"

"Every government agency across the globe will recognize the symbol."

"Rook?"

She chuckles. "Good guess, but no. We are Mirador."

Mirador…

The word reminds me of the mirror and the promise I made. "Look, I owe you information about what I know of the Shadow Mirror."

"Yes, you do." She crosses her arms. "Please, enlighten me."

"While I was mind tethered to a Shadow Priest, I asked to be shown where I could find the Shadow Mirror. What I received was a collage of mountains and a monastery." The images flash in my mind once again. "Nothing else. I don't know where it could be. I scoured the internet for two months trying to find pictures that matched what I saw, but nothing ever came of it."

"Can you show me?" she asks.

"Show you?" Her request makes no sense. "And how would I do that?"

"Take my hands." Dakota proffers them. I do, with reluctance. Her soft, warm skin reminds me of summer. "Now, close your eyes and think about what you saw, and imagine those images traveling from your mind down through your arms and out through your palms."

We stand, hands locked together, for a solid minute, but nothing happens. No tingle. No sensation of any kind.

"This isn't working," I say, opening my eyes.

Dakota sighs and nods, releasing my hands. "In our world, it would have."

"I'm sorry."

"Would you be willing to work with a sketch artist?" she asks.

"I thought about asking one of the guys at the station, but he's only good with faces."

"No need." She pushes her hair back over her shoulders. "I'll have someone contact you."

My chest vibrates as Jake pulls up in his blue Maserati and revs the engine. Dakota rounds the car and climbs into the passenger seat. "Take care of yourself, Alice, and be careful of what you glean from the dead. Not all of them tell the truth."

Jake hands me a manila envelope through the window and then guns it, leaving me standing there by myself with my mind reeling.

The dead can lie?

* * * * *

A few hours later…

Seth, Kenny, Detective Roland, Lieut. Frost, and several others sit around the war room table when I arrive. Each looks at me as I head to the far end of the table and sit down, a manila folder clamped underneath my arm. Seth knows everything that's about to be revealed. The others are still in the dark.

Lieut. Frost sits to my left, his hulking mass looming over me. He eyes the manila folder when I set it on the table in front of me. "This last week has been hell on all of us," he says. "For the love of God, Bergman, tell me you have some good news."

I slide the folder in front of him. "You tell me."

He grabs the folder and unbinds it. Its contents spill out across the table surface. Six pictures. An evidence bag full of red fur. A vial full of a semi-transparent, yellowish-white, gelatinous liquid. Another vial containing blood. A single piece of folded white paper.

Each picture is gruesome, but to the point. The first one depicts a beast with red fur lying face-down in the dirt. Blood pooled around it. The second one is of the beast rolled over on its back. A massive hole through the left side of its chest, caked in blood and dirt.

The third picture is a closeup of the beast's elongated snout and razor-sharp teeth. Yellow eyes, devoid of life, fill the fourth image. A ruler lies next to one of the beast's massive paws in the fifth image. It measures six inches wide and almost eight inches long, not including the claws. Its three-inch claws look perfect for ripping apart flesh.

The sixth and final picture shows the beast lying at the bottom of a deep crevice. A flare lies next to the body, providing the only source of light between the two edges of sheer rock.

For several minutes, the room is devoid of sound beyond the occasional gasp and the handling of the pictures as they get passed around the table. The folded paper remains just so, the pictures stealing all the limelight.

Lieut. Frost removes his glasses and wipes his eyes with the back of his hand. Another thirty seconds pass before he finally breaks the silence. "So this is our Night Mauler…"

Just the name constricts my throat. Squeezes my lungs. "Without a doubt, sir."

He returns his glasses to his face. "Maybe so, but we'll have Dr. Dages run analysis against the samples to confirm it."

"Of course, sir."

Lieut. Frost stares at me, but without his normal edge. "And this is your doing?"

I glance over at Seth. "A team effort."

"And the girl?" asks Detective Roland.

"We have no proof that Lindy Baker had anything to do with the maulings, and as far as I'm concerned, I don't think she did."

"What about the phone call from outside the shelter to the first victim?" asks Lieut. Frost.

"Anyone could've made that call," says Seth. "Ernesto was a drug dealer, after all."

"You brought Lindy's name to us to begin with," says Detective Roland. "Why the change of heart?"

"She's a good girl. Even though some of the initial evidence pointed to her, I could never fully convince myself that she was involved. But I had to follow the evidence." I glare at Detective Roland. "Have you found anything to tie her to the cases?" Detective Roland scowls but says nothing.

Didn't think so.

"Any leads on Ernesto's body?" asks Lieut. Frost.

"Nothing," admits Seth. "But at least we don't have any family members breathing down our necks to produce it."

"No, but Mayor Daniels won't be thrilled." Lieut. Frost shakes his head and then addresses the room. "Where we at with identifying the woman from the psych ward?"

Spalding pipes up, "We're still going through all the case files from California, Utah, Nevada, Colorado, and Texas. So far, we've found nothing that links any of the victims together."

"We're basically at a dead end," confirms Seth.

My phone vibrates in my pocket. I slide it out and see that I have a new text message from Seth: *"Let it lie. Trust me."*

"And what about Mr. Mallard?" asks Lieut. Frost. "Has anyone interviewed him about the incident or how he knew this woman's sister?"

Seth clears his throat. "We did, but he swears he only recognized the perfume. He claims to have met the Dashna woman three decades ago in New York. Heard she'd died. Says he never knew her last name or if Dashna was an alias."

Lieut. Frost sighs heavily. "Not gonna lie, something smells rotten."

"Agreed," says Seth, "but I'm not sure how to proceed."

"What do you think, Bergman? See anything worth pursuing?"

My first impulse is to request the case be handed over to me, but then I remember Seth's text message. I trust him with everything. How can I not trust him with this as well?

Let it lie.

"If Detective Ryan says we've got nothing, then I'm inclined to agree with him," I say.

"Detective Roland? Your thoughts."

"The case certainly has more questions than answers," says Detective Roland, "but Mr. Mallard was clearly the victim in this. I'm not sure what we'll gain by pursuing it further. I say we zip it up and move on."

"My thoughts as well," says Lieut. Frost. "And what about protective custody detail for Mr. Mallard?"

"Seth and I will handle it," I say, perhaps a bit too eagerly.

"Fine, but only until his hearing." Lieut. Frost snatches the folded piece of paper off the table and opens it up. His eyes scan the page, and then his gaze bores a hole right into my soul. "You write this?"

"No, sir. Haven't seen it."

He hands me the paper. "So where did it come from?"

The letterhead sends my mind reeling and my heart pounding. Dunharrow Storage. My hands tremble as I read on. It's a month's lease for a refrigerated unit. Fifth floor. Unit 504. The lease date is October 15, 2018, and the lessee is listed as George Hallard.

A handwritten note is scrawled across the bottom corner of the paper. I read it aloud, "Double down: 5-2-8-6-1."

"That mean something to any of you?" asks Lieut. Frost.

"I think so," says Kenny. His fingers hammer his laptop keyboard with fury. "Yeah, just what I thought. That's the birthday of the first victim, Ernesto Vasquez. May 28, 1961."

"And likely the combination to the storage unit," I finish. "Double down."

"You're telling me that Ernesto Vasquez's body is in this storage unit?" questions Lieut. Frost.

I retrieve Dakota Barnes's business card with a rook on both sides from within my pocket and slide it over to Lieut. Frost. He studies it with an intense gaze, his brow furrowed over the top of his glasses, but makes no move to take it. After several seconds, he slides the business card back toward me.

"A team effort," he mutters.

I take the card and shove it back in my pocket.

"What the hell was that?" asks Detective Roland.

Lieut. Frost eyes Detective Roland. "A message for me. Now, get in touch with CSI. I'll get a warrant drawn up for the storage unit. Let's get that body back to the morgue." He looks at me. "Assuming it's there."

"Yes, sir." Detective Roland rises from the table and exits the war room.

Lieut. Frost scoops up the contents from the manila envelope and stuffs them back into it. "Looks like I might finally have some good news for Mayor Daniels." He rises from the table, says, "Good work, everyone," and exits the room.

Officer Spalding and the others follow Lieut. Frost out, leaving just me, Seth, and Kenny at the table.

I turn to Kenny. "You could've saved us a bit of time and trouble if you'd been upfront about talking to Lindy the night of Slavik's murder."

He grimaces. "I know, and I'm sorry. By the time I realized she was a suspect, it was too late. I was also afraid you might think I was in on it."

"Never crossed my mind," I say.

Seth says, "Next time, if there is one, be forthright about everything."

Kenny nods. "Will do."

"By the way, you were a tremendous help. Not sure we would've cracked the case without you. You should be proud of yourself."

Kenny's cheeks flush red. "That means a lot coming from you, Alice."

"It's true," Seth agrees. "Good work." Kenny grins.

I suddenly remember wanting to help Kenny. "So, how are you paying for college?"

"Got a scholarship that covers about eighty percent of the tuition. I'll have to work to pay the rest."

"Won't that take away from your time with Kellie though?"

He grimaces. "Yeah, but what choice do I have?"

"Let me help you," I say.

He frowns. "Help how?"

"I'll pay the difference."

Seth and Kenny both gasp. Kenny raises his arms. "Whoa, no can do."

"Why not? Once you get done and get that high-paying job, you can pay me back."

He scratches his head. "I'd never consider it… unless I also pay interest."

"Whatever you deem fair," I agree.

Tears glisten in Kenny's eyes. "Why would you do it, though?"

Goosebumps tingle across my arms. "So you can see Kellie smile again."

Kenny just nods, obviously too emotional for words.

Let it lie.

I turn and eye Seth. "Explain the text message."

He glances at Kenny. "Later."

I'm about to concede when I see it. Left wrist, inside. A birthmark that isn't one. But his is unlike any I've seen—a screw with a lightning bolt through it.

He's one of us… but what does it mean?

My gaze meets Kenny's, and he frowns. "What is it?"

A conversation for another time.

My lips curl into a smile. "Kenny's proven himself both loyal and resourceful. Spill it."

Seth reaches into his pocket, retrieves a small thumb drive, and slides it over to me. "Everything Spalding found is on there."

My pulse quickens. "You found something, didn't you?"

Seth smiles. Melts my heart. "I think it's time you start a new wall."

And I know just the place.

CHAPTER TWENTY-FIVE

Three weeks later…

"ALICE, IS EVERYTHING READY?" asks Mother, her voice carrying from the living room as though she stands at my side.

I fluff the pillows on the bed and give them a good chop in the middle with the side of my hand. Every last detail, from the bed to the furniture to the window treatments, looks professionally designed. The new grayish-white hardwood floors give the space a touch of warmth and hominess that the concrete floors could never achieve.

Stepping back, I take in the space I called home for the last twenty-six years. It's almost unrecognizable. "It's as ready as it's going to get."

"Okay. We're headed back," she says.

I can hear Father. "Gladys, none of this is necessary. I can find a place of my own."

"Perhaps you can," says Mother, "but not until *after* your hearing. Until then, you're staying here with me. No arguments."

In light of everything that happened to Father at St. Thomas Psychiatric Center, Judge Carmen Santos granted him a new hearing and a psychiatric evaluation. And, with a good recommendation from Mayor Daniels, Judge

Santos released him into Mother's care until his hearing. A good word from Lieut. Frost helped, too.

It all came about so suddenly that I'm still trying to wrap my head around the idea of my father and mother living under a single roof. I never imagined such a day. Mother's face glows when she wheels Father into the room.

I've not seen her happier since the day I first saw her face ten years ago. Then again, her happiness might also have something to do with the people gathered in the backyard.

And my white dress.

"Thank you, Alice," says Mother. "The room is beautiful, as are you."

My gaze meets Father's. He's a strong man but can't hold back his tears. Mother hands him a tissue, unfazed by his reaction.

She knows.

When I look at her, she smiles. "I'm no fool, Alice."

"You told her?"

He looks up at me, his eyes still glassy with tears. "Didn't have to. Your mother's extremely perceptive and smart as a whip."

"You'd better pull yourself together, Isaiah. Otherwise, everyone will know your secret."

"Everyone's eyes will be on our angel," he says. "No one will even notice me."

Kenny's head pops into the room. A grin stretches from ear to ear. "It's time. You ready?"

"Take my mother with you and fire up the music, DJ."

He escorts Mother out of the room, leaving me alone with Father. "You sure you're ready for this?"

He pulls up the footrests on the wheelchair with his feet and scoots forward in the chair. With a grunt, he hauls himself to his feet. "Nothing could keep me from walking you down the aisle."

"Can I ask you a question?"

"Anything. I'll answer it if I can."

"With mind probing, have you had different experiences?"

"Like what?" he asks.

"I've used this ability four times now and have had three different experiences. With the first two, I lived their experiences. I *was* them. Felt everything they went through. With Milton Russell Puge, the Braille Killer, it was different. I was aware of who I was while still being him in a strange way. This last time, it was different still. It felt like I was a bystander or voyeur. I saw through Slavik's eyes and read his thoughts as though they were my own, but I didn't experience the pain of the attack or of his death the way I did with Sarah and Cara."

He rubs his chin. "Three different types of people, right?"

Could it really be that simple? The more I think about it, the more I realize he's right. "Yeah. Two like us, one Shadow Priest, and some regular guy."

"Well, there you have it." He grimaces. "Alice, I hope you understand that this gift of ours is also a curse. The more you use it, the quicker the blindness will come back. Only use it as a last resort."

My mind races back to Sarah. It never occurred to me that mind tethering to her had been the cause of my blindness coming on so quickly. But it makes sense. "I will keep that in mind going forward. Thank you."

"You're welcome." He takes my arm. "You ready?"

My heart yearns for Seth. "Nothing could hold me back now."

Arm in arm, we exit the room and head toward the kitchen. Veronica awaits us in the doorway. Her cheeks are streaked with tears but take nothing away from her beauty. In fact, they might make her more radiant than she already is.

"Ally…" Her gaze sweeps me from head to toe. "You're the embodiment of perfection." She kisses my cheek and then wipes away the remnants of lipstick.

The music starts. "That's your cue, Vee."

Terry Roland comes through the back door. He winks at me, and then holds his arm out for Veronica to take. I'm still not sure what made Seth choose him as his best man, but at least our wedding pictures will be full of beautiful faces.

Two minutes later, the music changes. *Mendelssohn's Wedding March.* My cue.

Am I ready for this?

Father takes my arm. "Let's go give them something to remember."

As soon as we step outside, my gaze meets Seth's, and the entire world fades around us. This moment, and all the ones that follow, blur together and take us right to the point where Seth pulls me into his arms and presses his lips against mine.

Cheers erupt, but that too fades as we hold each other closer than I can ever remember. Together, hearts united, and souls intertwined. We will conqueror the world.

* * * * *

Three more weeks later…

"I still feel weird about all of this." Lindy stares at herself in the full-length mirror. "I've never worn a dress before. And I don't even know how to dance."

I squeeze her shoulders from behind as my gaze meets hers in the mirror's reflection. "Dance with your heart, and your feet will follow. Trust me."

Lindy sighs. "Maybe I should call the whole thing off."

"You and Rufin have been through a lot, and he's been looking forward to this evening for weeks. Besides, what girl doesn't like going to Winter Ball?"

"I know he has, and I don't want to disappoint him… but I'm not a *normal* girl."

I kiss her cheek. The sensation is strange yet satisfying. Makes me wonder if Mother gets the same feeling when she kisses my cheek. "You could never disappoint him, Lindy. He loves you with all his heart. And why do you say you're not normal like it's a bad thing? None of us are *normal*, and that's what makes us special. *Unique.*"

Lindy adjusts her dress straps and fluffs her hair. "I know you're right, but I still don't understand why you're so nice to me. I nearly got you killed."

I turn her around and hold her by the arms. "I've never looked at it that way, and you shouldn't either. As I said before, we're sisters, born of different blood, and we will always look out for each other."

She smiles softly and looks to the floor. "I know, and I feel the same way, but you didn't have to pay six months' rent on this apartment for me."

I grab her chin and lift her head until our eyes meet. "You're exactly right. I didn't have to do it. I *chose* to. Besides, it's only a studio apartment."

Lindy pushes my hand from her chin, her eyes glassy. "You say that, but it's more than I've ever had. How will I ever repay you?"

"You won't. One day, when you're in a position to do so, pay it forward."

She smiles. "I can do that—no, I *will* do that."

"Good." I step back, eye my handiwork, and smile. Lindy's come a long way from the reclusive loner I met two months ago. Her beauty will outshine all the other girls, especially that which comes from her heart.

The doorbell rings, sending flashes of terror through Lindy's eyes. "I'm not ready!"

"You've never looked better." I cross the room and open the door. "Hello, Rufin. You're just in time."

Rufin stands at the threshold, a yellow corsage in his left hand and his mouth agape. A statue of both terror and utter joy.

"She's all yours," I say, stepping aside.

He swallows hard. "Mine?"

"Hello, Rufin." Lindy's dress sways as she walks toward the door. Its deep yellow fabric beautifully offsets her fiery-red hair and matches the corsage perfectly. Takes my mind back to the *Spider-Man and His Amazing Friends* cartoon.

Now she's the true Firestar.

CHAPTER TWENTY-SIX

Fourteen months later…

SKILLET'S *MONSTER* BLARES FROM my phone on the nightstand just as I walk out of the bathroom. Water drips from my hair and runs right into my eyes, the tightly wrapped towel around my head failing to do its job.

I answer the phone half-blind. "Detective Bergman."

"Good morning, Detective. This is Pierre." The man's French accent is nearly undetectable. "How soon can you get to Paris?"

Paris?

I wipe my eyes and check the caller ID on my phone. An international number. "I'm sorry. Who is this?"

"Special Agent Pierre Lamont. Were you not informed I'd be calling you?"

"Informed by who?"

"Ah, yes. Sorry for the confusion. Please, let me begin again." He clears his throat. "Your name was given to me by a mutual friend with the assurance that your *specialized skill set* would remain a secret. Given your talent, I believe you're the single person in the world that can help me crack a case I've been working for the last ten months."

"First off, I'm not sure who you've been talking to, but my *skill set* is nothing more than instinct and intuition. Second, I can't just drop everything and jet across the world. I'm not independently wealthy, and I have a demanding job."

"Really? From what I understand, it's been quiet in your Desert Springs for some time now." Pierre chuckles. "Do you enjoy working cold cases?"

Who the hell is this guy?

"How would you know what I'm working on?" I ask.

My phone beeps in my ear. The display says I've got a second call coming in from an anonymous number. "Look, Pierre. I've got another call to answer."

"By all means, go right ahead," he says. "I'll wait."

Switching lines, I answer the incoming call. "This is Detective Bergman."

"Hello, darlin'."

I never forget voices. "Jake Barnes."

"The one and only," he says.

It's funny how a person's smile can be detected by the smallest inflections in their voice. From what I recall, Jake has a nice one.

"It's been a long time. What can I do for you?"

"Don't think about it. Just say yes."

I frown. "Yes to what?"

"Pierre. He's a good guy. Tries to make a difference in the world. Same as us."

"You're the one that gave him my number?"

"Not technically." He's doing that smile thing again. "Mom—Dakota did."

"I see." I remove the towel from my head and start patting myself down with it. "Tell her I'm flattered, but I already have a job."

"The world is much bigger than Desert Springs, darlin'."

"Everything I need is right here."

"You and I both know that's not true. You'll never take down the Shadow Priests if you never leave your little town." Jake pauses for several moments and then continues, "Is that not what you still want?"

My cheeks flash with heat. "Of course it is… but it's complicated."

"Doesn't have to be. Take a few weeks of vacation in Paris and help Pierre with his case."

"If you saw my paychecks, you'd know I can't afford to do that."

Jake laughs. "Pierre will foot the bill, right down to your morning cups of sugar milk with a hint of coffee. The only expense you'll incur is your time, and you'll be compensated well—a thousand dollars per day. How could you say no to a deal like that?"

It's a good question. I toss the towel on the foot of my bed and cover myself with my arm even though I'm the only one in the room. "And what does this case in Paris have to do with the Shadow Priests?"

"Take it, and I'm certain you'll find a connection," says Jake.

There's got to be more to it.

"What's in it for you?" I step into a fresh pair of panties and pull them on.

He chuckles. "Let's just say this is a test run."

Hopping around and yanking with one hand only gets my jeans up so far. "Test run for what?" I say with a grunt.

"You joining Mirador." The line clicks, and Jake is gone.

Mirador…

I lower the phone from my ear and take a seat on the edge of my bed. My pulse races as excitement tightens my throat. This could be the one thing I've been longing for. A reason to get out of bed each morning. Reagan's beady, hunter-green eyes and plump cheeks rise in my mind.

I will find you, you little rat.

"Hello? Detective Bergman? Are you still there?" The Frenchman's voice is distant.

Pierre!

I totally spaced him being on the other line. "Yes, sorry. I'm intrigued, but I won't go anywhere without my husband."

"I had a feeling you'd say that," says Pierre. "Detective Ryan is more than welcome to come along. In fact, I insist."

Excitement tingles down to my toes. "Very well, but we'll have to request the time off."

"No need, Detective. I made all the arrangements with Lieut. Frost earlier this morning."

"You what?" My phone vibrates against my ear.

"I just texted you a link to your boarding passes," says Pierre. "Your plane leaves in four hours."

Four hours? I look around my bedroom. It's a total disaster and can't be left in its current state.

"Pack lightly," he says. "Everything you and Detective Ryan will need will be provided, clothing included."

"What about our service weapons?" I ask.

"I don't think you'll need weapons, but they will be provided if the situation requires it."

"Very well." My gaze focuses on the black cane in the corner. *Time for a trip, Esther.*

"I'll personally meet the two of you at the airport here in Paris tomorrow night," says Pierre.

"See you then." I end the call and see that I have two new text messages from the same number. Boarding passes for Seth and me.

My chest tightens with excitement. "Seth!"

"Yeah, babe?" He walks into the bedroom, ogles my bare chest, and grins. "Thank you."

I roll my eyes even though I'm thrilled he still finds me attractive. "Stop messing around and help me get this place in order."

"We having company over?" he asks.

"Not even close. You'll need to grab your toiletries. Oh, and your passport. We've got a plane to catch in a few hours."

"Plane? Passport?" He frowns. "Where we headed?"

I slip my bra on and then kiss his cheek before heading back into the bathroom. "Don't make me spoil the surprise."

Seth leans against the door post and raps on it with his knuckles. "Can't afford much else after purchasing this palace."

"Twenty-six hundred square feet doesn't qualify as a palace."

"Compared to my old condo?"

I concede. "Maybe so, compared to it. But at least we paid cash for this place."

"True. Feels good to own something." He cocks his head. Stares at me through the mirror's reflection. "It's Mexico, isn't it?"

After spritzing a bit of detangler in my hair, I brush it out. "Your guess isn't even on the right continent. That's all you're getting. Now hurry up, and don't worry about packing clothes. It's literally all-inclusive."

Seth groans. "All-inclusive? I can hear the death of our savings account now."

Eying Seth through the bathroom mirror, I say, "Don't be so dramatic. We're not paying for any of it. In fact, we're getting paid to go."

He steps into the bathroom, his gaze locked with mine through the mirror's reflection. "Now you've got me worried. What have you gotten us into?"

I kiss his cheek. "Nothing we can't handle, lover. Trust me, it's all taken care of, Lieut. Frost included."

He raises his arms and walks out of the bathroom. "Fine, but don't come crying to me when you're attacked by a kangaroo or dingo in the Outback."

"You can keep guessing, but I'll never tell."

In my mind, I picture the two of us standing at the top of the Eiffel Tower, peering down at the city far below and watching the sun set in the west. It's a sight I can't wait to experience.

Here we come, Paris.

TO BE CONTINUED…

Alice's story continues in *The Chrono Slasher*. Visit **danielkuhnley.com** for more information.

PLEASE TELL OTHERS WHAT YOU THOUGHT

Thank you for taking this journey with me. If you'd like to show your support for my work, please leave a review wherever you purchased this book. It's free to do so, and it'll only take you a minute to write a quick sentence expressing your thoughts about the book.

Your review is especially important to independent, self-published authors like me. Internet and online bookstore algorithms favor books with reviews. They display in search results and at the top of search results more often than books without reviews.

Did you know that there's a minimum number of reviews needed to purchase certain advertising? It's true. Help me reach that threshold by leaving a review. Doing so will help more people find this book and will in turn help me sell more books, which means I can keep authoring more books for you.

Go to danielkuhnley.com/reviews if you need a link to where you can leave a review.

Thank you!!

READ *BIRTH OF A KILLER* FOR FREE

Curious how Alice gained her sight as a teen?
Want to read about the attack that started it all?

danielkuhnley.com/become-a-conqueror

Sign up and read *Birth Of A Killer*, An Alice Bergman Novella. Be the **FIRST** to get sneak peaks at my upcoming novels and the chance to win **FREE** stuff, like signed books.

A paranormal serial killer thriller that'll keep you turning the pages.

Be careful what you dream when murder is on your mind.

My name is Alice, and I'm a sixteen-year-old ghost. No, I'm not actually dead, but I was born blind. The sad thing is the world's more blind to me than I am to it.

That is, until the day he noticed me. A bully. He ruined my life and turned my dreams into nightmares, so what could I do? The same thing any girl my age would do—I wished he'd die.

Then… he turns up dead. Naturally, I freaked out. Am I to blame? Did my nightmare kill him? Would anyone believe me if I confessed?

It's absurd. I know it. Nightmares don't come true… do they?

Birth of a Killer is the suspenseful prequel novella to *The Braille Killer*. If you like unique sleuths, origin stories, and a hint of the supernatural, you'll love Daniel Kuhnley's nail-biting tale.

Buy *Birth of a Killer* today to see how Alice's story began!

EXPLORE CENTAURIA

Curious about the world Rico spoke of? You can explore that world, Centauria, in Daniel Kuhnley's epic dragon fantasy series, *The Dark Heart Chronicles*.

Read *The Dragon's Stone*, book one in the series.

Available on Amazon and other retailers. Visit danielkuhnley.com for more details.

ABOUT THE AUTHOR

Daniel Kuhnley is an American author of Epic Dragon Fantasy, Supernatural Serial Killer, and Christian YA Sci-Fi/Fantasy stories. Some of his novels include *Reborn*, *The Braille Killer*, and *Kiara Kole And The Key Of Truth*. He enjoys watching movies, reading novels, and programming. He lives in Albuquerque, NM with his wife who also writes.

CONNECT WITH DANIEL

danielkuhnley.com/connect

ACKNOWLEDGMENTS

First and foremost, thank you to Jesus Christ, my Lord and Savior. I am nothing without your saving grace.

Second, every single book I write is a team effort, from the cover design to editing and proofreading to beta reading. I couldn't do it without the relentless love and support of my wife, Marsha. You carry me through from beginning to end every single time and help me make sense of my scribblings. I love you more than infinite words could ever describe or express.

Third, to my beta and ARC readers, thank you for your feedback and your early reviews of *The Night Mauler*.

Last, but not least, to my fans—thank you so much for your support and for reading through to the very end.

Warm regards,

Daniel